DIAGNOSIS: DEATH

"Don't you wonder where they get all these girls?" the anesthesiologist asked. "I've never seen this many cancers in all my life."

"We're a referral center, Ed," Carlsie answered.

"Don't be naïve! Aren't you a little curious about how they got to be so famous? What made this place, out of all the hundreds of hospitals in the country, start getting so many patients and finding so many malignancies?" His voice had a bitter edge. "And have you noticed how rich these guys are? They're making more money than any surgeons I know."

"I'm just trying to learn their techniques, Ed. I don't pay any attention to the money."

"Well, you'd better start paying attention, honey pie. Because that's what it's all about."

He started away, but she grabbed his arm. "You can't say things like that and just walk away. Tell me what's going on."

"I don't know much. I just know there's too much surgery, too many cancers . . . and too many secrets. And you'd better wake up, Carlsie. Before you learn a lot more about doctors than you ever wanted to know. . . ."

FATAL ANALYSIS

Cliff Patton and Leah Temple

ZEBRA BOOKS
KENSINGTON PUBLISHING CORP.

ZEBRA BOOKS

are published by

Kensington Publishing Corp.
475 Park Avenue South
New York, NY 10016

First printing: May, 1988

Printed in the United States of America

Dedicated with love to our lost mother.
JANICE LOUISE GRAHAM TEMPLE WOODS
1938–1982
"Sam," we hardly knew ye.

We appreciate the technical assistance and encouragement of David Temple, James Butler, and Scott Storm.

We also thank Audrey Wolf and our editor, Carin Cohen, for keeping us focused.

Cliff Patton, M.D.
Leah Temple, R.N.

Other Zebra Books by the Authors

THE OMNI STRAIN
GHOST RIG

Chapter One

The young woman lay nude on her back. The paleness of her small breasts rose in marked contrast to her suntanned upper body. She was asleep, lightly anesthetized. In the coolness of the operating room, her pink nipples and areola, which had not yet been darkened by the pigment changes of pregnancy, had contracted and hardened. Bright lights hung over her, brilliantly illuminating her anterior chest and upper abdomen.

A nurse covered the patient's slender legs and pelvis with a green sheet, and splashed orange antiseptic scrub solution onto her right breast to begin the surgical prep. The excess liquid ran in rivulets down the side of her chest and across her flat belly, accumulating in small pools of bubbling foam.

The silence was broken only by the slow rhythm of the respirator expanding the pretty young woman's lungs with oxygen, nitrous oxide, and the anesthetic vapor of Forane.

The chief resident, Dr. Gordon Keene, entered the room holding his dripping wet arms in front of him. Tall and lean, with curly blond hair and a boyishly charming face, he was the nurses' favorite resident at the small but renowned Palm Beach hospital which specialized in surgery of the breast.

"Another young one," he said, glancing at the anesthesiologist. "The chief must be running a special this month."

Before the conversation could continue, the senior surgeon, Dr. Ritter, arrived. All discussion not directly related to the surgery at hand abruptly stopped. The anesthesiologist rechecked the blood pressure, the scrub nurse continued arranging her instruments, and the circulating nurse finished the prep of the breast. Everyone remained silent while Ritter was gowned and gloved, and the patient was draped almost completely by Dr. Keene and the nurses. Only one vulnerable breast remained exposed within the sterile operative field.

Ritter carefully examined the breast in question, sliding his experienced fingers gently across the small nodule in the upper outer quadrant of the organ. He spoke to the circulating nurse, "Let pathology know we have a biopsy coming. We'll need a frozen section."

His deep masculine voice carried a Texas accent which matched his ruggedly handsome appearance and obvious physical strength. It was typical of him to forego pleasantries when he was about to operate. In surgery, he was more intent than any doctor the others on the team had ever observed.

At forty, Ritter had earned a reputation envied by his colleagues. His skill and innovative ability in

10

plastic and reconstructive surgery of the breast was of such magnitude that he was already being hailed as one of the greats' by the other members of a specialty traditionally critical of a particularly successful peer.

Satisfied that all was in order, Ritter received the scalpel from the scrub nurse and swiftly plunged it into the delicate flesh. Minutes later, the offending tissue had been grasped with a Babcock forceps, pulled through the one-inch incision, excised from the woman, and placed upon a towel draped across her abdomen. While Ritter packed a cotton sponge into the oozing wound, Gordon Keene cut halfway into the harmless-appearing mass, opened it, and said, "Feels benign. Must be an adenoma."

The senior man did not look up, nor did he speculate on the results of the biopsy. Nothing counted except the microscopic examination, so he never guessed.

Satisfied that the bleeding was controlled, Ritter picked up the specimen and turned to give it to the nurse who was to, immediately, deliver it to the department of pathology. The particular person he was looking for was not in the room. "Where the hell is Val?" he grumbled.

"She's coming right now," the circulating nurse answered, referring to the operating-room supervisor, Val Ryan. "Would you like me to take it?"

Irritated, Ritter declined. "Just tell her to get in here, would you? The policy regarding who transports specimens was set for a good reason. She should have been ready."

At that moment Val Ryan — middle-aged, a little overweight, but still pretty in a wholesome sort of way — rushed in, grabbed the specimen, and quickly disappeared. Her harried and exasperated expression brought a smile to the anesthesiologist, Dr. Edward Grossman. He was new to the hospital, having joined the staff only a few weeks earlier. "Have you ever seen an O.R. supervisor who wasn't in a hurry?" he asked the two surgeons.

Keene nodded in agreement. Ritter busied himself closing the small wound, then applied a dressing and removed his gloves. Stepping back from the table, he spoke to the anesthesiologist. "And now we wait, Ed." He was already displaying his frustration at the inevitable delay of the pathologist's interpretation. "That's why I want Val here and ready to go the minute we get the thing out."

"Well, this one shouldn't take long," Grossman replied. "She's pretty young, and it certainly looked okay."

Ritter gazed at Grossman in a manner that suggested he was contemplating the naïveté of the man he had helped recruit, the new chief of anesthesia. "I guess where you come from they don't see cancer the way we do here."

Grossman smiled. "That's the understatement of the year."

"You boys in Detroit are more used to gunshot wounds and car wrecks the way I hear it," Ritter added.

The comment got a chuckle from the ex-medical-school professor of anesthesiology. "Yeah, but the

12

good thing about those kinds of cases is you don't need a pathologist to tell you whether you can operate or not."

"Good point, Ed. Damned good point." Nobody hated waiting for pathologists more than Ritter did. "Gordo, listen to what this man has to say. He may have something to teach us."

There was a lull in the conversation as Grossman turned back to the job of monitoring his patient. "Our new resident should be here in the next day or so," Gordon Keene interjected, anxious to keep Ritter in a good mood. The staffman was a perfectionist, and he didn't want to irritate him, make him even more demanding.

"I thought the new guy was due in today," Ritter replied, aware of the effort to distract him.

"He was, but there was some sort of mix-up. He had to come all the way from New Orleans."

"Sloppy. The old man won't like it."

"The chief will never know. I figure it's the least I can do."

Ritter nodded. Gordo was a good man. Many residents would be happy to see a new fellow stew in his own juice for a while.

"There's one more thing," Keene added. "The new resident is a woman. She's supposed to be some sort of hotshot from Tulane." The surgical mask did not hide Keene's grin.

"I don't believe it," the senior surgeon said, shaking his head. Gordo knew why. Walker Barret, M.D., the founder and chief of surgery at the institute, one of the last of the old-time surgeons, was convinced that practicing surgery was too rigorous for women, given their frailties and hormonal inconsistencies. For years he had resisted the intrusion of females into his unique and quite popular surgical fellowships. The chief was not likely to have changed his opinion this suddenly.

Gordon Keene shrugged. "I'm telling you, Hank, it's just what I heard. The word is she's a real whiz kid . . . a future rising star and all that."

Ritter seemed unconvinced.

"You know I don't make up the rumors around here," Gordo continued. "I just repeat them."

"I wouldn't bet on this one, Gordo — not while Walker Barret is in charge."

"I make it a policy never to argue with staffmen," Keene responded quickly. "If you and the old man say this resident is male, damned if I'll dispute it. I don't care what her pelvis looks like."

Ritter smiled, humoring his young associate. "No doubt you'll be the first to check out that part of her if there's any truth to the story." He enjoyed, vicariously, the romantic exuberance of his young friend.

Keene chuckled. "Lady doctors are not my type. I prefer the expertise of a well-trained nurse."

"Preferably trained by yourself, right?" Ritter commented, then gazed toward the large clock on the wall. Exhaling a long exasperated sigh, he addressed the nurses again. "Call the damn lab and get that report. We have other cases to do. Can't that jackass down there understand that?" That was the way he was, a pleasure to be around when he was relaxed but quickly annoyed when it came to patient care.

The two surgeons presented a striking contrast, though they were equally popular with the female nursing staff for different reasons. Keene, friendly and easygoing, had the good looks of a California beach bum. Several of the younger nurses had imagined him surfing in on a killer wave, hanging ten, and then jogging up the sand to a bevy of admiring beach bunnies. He possessed no surfing skills, but he knew of, and enjoyed, his reputation as a womanizer. Ritter's appeal was different.

He represented male maturity, was intense and, at times, reserved. He wore a full mustache that matched the blackness of his unruly hair, perpetually in need of a cut. Women desired him because of the masculine power he seemed to represent. They also perceived something else in Ritter, something that wasn't in the other surgeons. Emotional sensitivity. That made him extra special. He understood the agony of mutilated women: he cared more — not just in the manner of the concerned physician but in a deeper way. The nurses sensed his compassion when he treated patients who came to him in desperation, and they felt his sadness when he had to perform the surgery required to rid a woman's body of life-threatening carcinoma of the breast.

To the nurses at the institute there were many excellent surgeons but only one Hank Ritter.

Occasionally, competitors criticized him in petty ways. He was called neurotic, compulsive, a man

15

obsessed — accused of being a showman — but through it all he remained unchanged. He was practicing surgery the only way he could — going all out.

Going all out was the way he lived life, period. His high-school football coach had once warned him not to hit so hard during practice scrimmages. "Hank, you're the most aggressive kid I've ever coached," he'd been told. "Lay back a little when it's not important."

That was the hard part for Ritter: deciding when it was "not important." Through it all — undergraduate work, medical school, internship, and surgical training — he had never found the part that was not important. So he had never let up, and now he didn't really give a damn if a few less successful surgeons took potshots at him because of the way he was. It was the only way he knew how to be, and it had brought him a long way from that football coach in Fort Worth, Texas.

Knowing all this, Gordon Keene and the others hoped the Path report would come back soon. Familiar with Ritter's reaction to delay, they knew it would be to their advantage to move things along, get this fashion model off the table, and push on with the day's more serious work. There was a lot of it. This was going to be another busy day in the institute's O.R.

For three years Val Ryan had been making the trip from the O.R. to the pathology lab to deliver the specimens. It was ironic that this was her assignment. Not long ago a piece of her own breast had been taken to a Path lab while she'd awaited her fate on an operating table in Atlanta. Then, less than a year after her mastectomy, her husband of two decades, a physician, had left her for a younger woman. Humiliated, she had resigned her position as director of the surgical suite at a large Atlanta hospital, and had retreated to the anonymity of this lesser job in Florida.

She had originally thought that she could make a special contribution here, but bitterness continued to get in her way. She was still angry about the unfairness of her lot, thought about it almost every day as she came down these stairs. Her husband had been a pathologist. That made this job hard for her. She didn't know which part of it she hated more: dealing with the egomania of doctors — that reminded her of her husband — or putting up with the rich-bitch females who came to have their pampered bodies treated.

On this day, two floors below surgery, just as she had so often, she exited the stairwell, crossed through the main lab and arrived at the frozen-section room where she encountered the sweet aroma of cherry tobacco and the waiting pathologist. Without comment, Val delivered to Dr. Oscar Mendel the specimen and the accompanying paperwork. Her task accomplished, she returned quickly to the O.R. She disliked the Path lab and all it stood for.

Dr. Mendel watched with interest as she departed. He found her a curious woman: uncommonly quiet, efficient, and devoid of apple-polishing pleasant-

ness. He liked that. She also seemed to take an unusually personal interest in the specimens she was
responsible for delivering, occasionally even asking
him questions about the various types of carcinomas of the breast. And she knew a lot about pathology, she'd picked up this knowledge from the
ex-husband she so obviously disliked. He wondered
why the man had divorced her. She wasn't bad
looking. Her short, brown hair gave her sort of a
French look, and he liked the curves of her slightly
heavy figure.

As usual, Mendel was smoking one of the many
hand-carved pipes he had accumulated over the
years. Although he had attempted to use a more
foul-smelling tobacco to enhance his image as a
stern and fearsome taskmaster, he had never grown
accustomed to its bad taste and he'd finally settled
for the rather benign scent of aromatic cherries. It
was a small point, he figured. No real harm done if
the lab girls liked the smell. He could project authority in other ways.

Mendel was a husky man, short, heavily muscled,
and athletic. His deeply tanned face had strong features and a dominant chin. He appeared younger
than his fifty-four years, despite the graying hair he
wore closely cropped, as he had since his army stint
in Korea. Beneath thick, ragged eyebrows, his slate
gray eyes, usually narrowed into thin stern slits,
were widely set, creating the illusion of an unusually broad nose. To the hospital staff he was an
intimidating figure, almost military in demeanor,
unquestionably a man not to be trifled with. He

18

was trusted, nevertheless, by most of his staff, more than they would publicly admit, and many of them viewed him as a paternalistic boss who would take care of them if the need arose.

Still puffing his pipe, Mendel scrutinized the small piece of yellowish red tissue, then cut a thin wedge from it. This he placed in the freeze compartment of the waiting cryotron. Leaning back in his chair, he scraped his pipe clean, and refilled it. When it was lit once more, he sat reflecting upon the present situation, savoring it, enjoying it. Upstairs they were waiting for his decision. They could do nothing without him. He was king now. The nurses, the anesthesiologists, that bastard Ritter and the other surgeons were all at a standstill, marking time until he rendered his opinion.

Upon his word, and his word alone, the decision would be made regarding this woman whom he had never seen and never would. Only by the tissue in front of him did he know her, although he had already read her chart. He always did in cases such as this.

She was a model. A woman bought and sold for her body. She was married—now for the second time—and had no children. Her medical record indicated she used an I.U.D. for contraception and frequently took amphetamines for diet control. He shook his head in disgust. Obviously, she was a woman obsessed with her body, but it was in his hands that her destiny now lay.

To Oscar Mendel it was one of the great ironies of life that surgeons received the glory and the reverence when he was the one who really called the shots, the one who knew the difference between salvation and doom. To him, surgeons were carpenters—skilled mechanics with inflated egos. And every one of them had a superiority complex. Occasionally, he fantasized about the day he would put them in their place, along with the foolish patients who had created these sham heroes. He owed it to his specialty to do so, but there would be time enough for that later. Right now he had to concentrate on the task at hand. It was certainly going to be satisfying, though, when the time came to melt the ice castles built by those tunnel-visioned, overpaid technicians.

Delicately, he shaved several ultrathin slices of the frozen specimen onto glass slides, and prepared them for microscopic examination. While he carefully inspected each section, using one lens and then another, his expression remained unchanged.

He flipped on the intercom and depressed the numbers for operating room three. After identifying himself, he called out the name of the young patient and her surgeon, and then said, "The biopsy is malignant. It's an adenocarcinoma . . . intraductal type."

The response from the surgeon came swiftly. "Are you sure? It certainly looked benign, up here."

Mendel, pleased to note the evident displeasure in Ritter's tone, replied sarcastically. "If you had already made the diagnosis, why did you send it to me?" He hated the way surgeons invariably asked if he was sure. Did they think a pathologist was foolish enough to give them an answer one minute and then change it the next?

Only silence came from the O.R.

Mendel turned off the intercom. He was sorry Ritter had not spewed more invective; it would have provided a good opportunity to give the man a little of his own medicine. The arrogant bastard needed it. As far as Oscar was concerned the Texas hick was nothing but a publicity hound, and should have been chased out long ago. There was no need for more prima donnas, and this particular holier-than-thou asshole irritated him more than the other surgical hacks he was forced to work with.

He glanced back at the original specimen, examining it under the light once more before wrapping it with paper towels and placing it alongside the slides he had just made.

Then Mendel paused and massaged his temples. The tension of his task had stirred up the headache again. He pulled from his coat pocket the codeine he always carried, and downed two of the pills, hoping they would go to work before the pain became too great.

Wearily he locked his desk, pulled on his suit coat, and double-locked the office. It had been a stressful morning and he was ready for an early lunch. Perhaps a small steak and a baked potato would make him feel better. Silently, under the watchful gaze of the wary lab techs, he crossed the large room and went out into the corridor. After leaving the hospital through a side entrance adjacent to the old morgue, he stood in the open air,

21

enjoying the midday sunshine, and relit his pipe.

It had taken ten extra minutes to re-prep and drape the breast for the mastectomy. Finally, impatiently and without enthusiasm, the steel blade was thrust once more into the young woman. A wide, elliptical incision was made, from the center of her lower chest around each side of the breast almost to the armpit. Because of the extraordinary skill of the surgeon, within forty-five minutes the mammary gland and the attached lymph nodes were removed. A modified radical mastectomy procedure was performed, leaving the muscles of the chest wall intact. A few minutes more and a bulky dressing was being placed where once a sensual organ had rested. The light-hearted mood of those in the O.R. had long since vanished.

"Doctor, she's only twenty-eight," the stunned husband said some minutes later.

"I'm very sorry, but I'm sure we got all of the tumor. She can have a normal life." Ritter hated these moments—these desperate moments when people learned that their lives have been irrevocably changed for the worse. Trying to explain what had happened, he used all the usual words, the hollow phrases that supposedly made the bitter pill go down a little easier. They didn't help much.

Tears streamed down the husband's cheeks. He turned away and walked slowly, aimlessly, down the hall. His wife's surgeon watched him go, knowing there was nothing he could say to alleviate the pain now. After the shock had passed he could help them both, but the first and inevitable reaction was grief. Much later came calm and unhappy acceptance. Life for this young woman had taken a terrible turn. Both she and her husband had many days of emotional agony ahead.

It was no one's fault; there was no one to blame. He had done the best he could for her. Hopefully, she had been saved from the premature death nature had had in store, yet he felt no sense of victory. Disfiguring fine young women was not a source of joy for him, no matter how dangerous the disease or how successful his surgery. He would reconstruct her breast later, although what he could do wouldn't compare with the supple splendor of nature. No matter how hard he worked, her loss was irreplaceable.

For the unlucky ones, life can be a bitch, he thought. Why this one? What genetic or environmental quirk had done in this unfortunate girl? Out of millions, why had she drawn the short straw? Why did anyone have to?

Saddened, he went back into the O.R., but the young girl never left his mind. He wanted to get her through the first few days with as little pain and emotional turmoil as possible. He saw that as his duty as her physician.

In the postanesthesia recovery room, the anesthesiologist gave his report to the nurses, then stayed to observe his patient a few minutes more. He was deeply troubled by this unexpected tragedy. Never in his career had he witnessed such an incidence of cancer in young women as he'd seen since his arrival at the institute.

Val Ryan came in to tell him the next patient had arrived and they were ready for him back in the O.R. "I'll be there in a minute," he replied. "I'm just so surprised at this one."

Ryan shrugged. "Cancer doesn't play favorites. The richest and the prettiest get it just like the rest of us." To Dr. E. J. Grossman, it seemed a heartless thing to say. His questioning eyes met Val Ryan's, and she quickly turned away.

Leaving the bedside he walked to the desk, limping awkwardly, as he had since infancy due to a malformed hip joint. He felt deep sympathy for this young patient and wondered what the mastectomy would do to her marriage. It was not a topic on which he was expert. He wasn't married, and having reached age forty-eight, he probably never would be. When asked why, as he frequently was, he never knew what to say. He guessed it was because he'd never found anyone to love. It wasn't the leg that had stopped him from knowing romance, like some people thought. It was something else, maybe just bad luck. He liked women, though, and struggled hard to understand them. Never having lived with a woman, he felt it was harder for him to appreciate their nuances than it was for most men. But he tried hard, and he had a good idea of the emotional price of a mastectomy—for both patient and husband.

As he finished his charting, the young woman moaned softly and stirred for the first time. She pushed the oral airway from her mouth, then lay quietly for several minutes. Moaning again, she continued to emerge from the anesthetic. She grimaced in pain and partially opened her eyes. Under the sheets her left hand moved slowly upward to rest upon the mound of bandages across her chest. Bewilderment and fear came to her face. "Oh no," she whispered, focusing groggily on the nurse taking her blood pressure. "My breast? Did they take my breast?"

The recovery-room nurse, who was about the same age as her patient, placed a gentle hand upon the young woman's shoulder. "Yes. They had to. You'll be all right. We're going to take good care of you."

"No!" she cried in despair. "It's not true! Please help me. Please! Tell me it's not true." She began to sob, desperately clutching the nurse's hand, then winced with pain as she tried to move her right arm.

"Lie still and take some deep breaths now," she was told. "Your husband will be in to see you soon. Everything is going to be all right. Trust me."

"Oh God," the patient murmured, crying hopelessly. "What am I to do? What's Jeff going to think?"

"He loves you. He'll be with you soon."

After a while the nurse went away to check on her other patients, and Grossman limped back to the O.R. The woman closed her eyes once more. She didn't stop crying, though . . . not that afternoon and not that night. Whenever she was awake she was crying, and nothing her husband or the nurses or her doctor said lessened her pain. She had been mutilated, and was no longer what she once was.

Instinct told her she was unlovable now. She was afraid.

Three blocks away, his headache much improved, Oscar Mendel had finished his steak and was starting on his Key lime pie. Ritter and Keene were finishing their coffee in the surgeons' lounge before scrubbing for their next operation, and Val Ryan was in her office, working on next month's call schedule. Downstairs in the administrative offices, paperwork was being done on afternoon admissions, patients on the following day's surgical schedule. It seemed to be an ordinary, busy day at the institute.

In O.R. two, Ed Grossman eased back on the anesthetic concentration his patient was inhaling because her blood pressure was falling a little more than he liked. But his thoughts remained on the girl in the recovery room. He was still amazed that she had actually had cancer.

26

Chapter Two

Dr. Carlsie Camden sat alone on the restaurant terrace. She signaled the waiter, and gazed once more out over the ocean which was still, its smooth surface glistening in the glare of the morning sun. There was not even the slightest puff of a breeze, and the humidity was surely one hundred percent. Warm and rapidly becoming hotter, this was one of the those steamy midsummer days in Palm Beach she'd been warned about. Already she was uncomfortably damp with perspiration. She thought of the bayous of musty sweet air, heavy with water in the stillness of trees and marsh.

Carlsie smiled at the comparison. This place was so different, but the bayous of southern Louisiana had been on her mind all morning. Years had passed since she had last returned to the swamps that had been her momma's home, but never really hers. Carlsie had only childhood memories of the place where she'd been born.

Her reverie was interrupted by the young waiter who returned to the terrace. He watched as she signed for her breakfast. "Are you with the institute?" He glanced across the boulevard to the beautiful old hospital set well back from the street and almost hidden by lush tropical vegetation.

"I start this morning. I'm already a day late, maybe two."

"What's in a day?" He shrugged, smiling.

She flicked her shoulder-length, curly black hair away from her face. "In a hospital? Twenty-four hours of work, that's what's in a day, particularly when you're on the bottom of the totem pole like I will be. I'm merely a surgical resident. Gump would probably be a better word for it."

He nodded, concealing his lack of understanding, and gazed for a long moment at her softly aristocratic face which revealed only a hint of her French and Indian heritage. He was especially taken with her deep green eyes and mysteriously expressive features. He would later describe her as sultry . . . almost exotic. She certainly wasn't like the girls from Florida or New York.

"May I bring you something else, more coffee perhaps?" He enjoyed her presence.

"I don't think so. I'd best be going."

"I can't place your accent. It's Southern, I know that." He smiled again, hoping to engage her in more conversation.

She nodded. "Louisiana."

He laughed. "Cajun country. I should have known. I visited my brother there last year. Good-looking women those Louisiana girls."

She bade him farewell.

From a distance he watched her as she walked. She carried her body elegantly. At the moment, he would have paid a week's tips for just ten minutes with her. That night his wife would unknowingly benefit from the haunting sexuality of the lovely stranger.

On the street, Carlsie paused to admire the structural elegance of her destination. The spacious, well-landscaped grounds and buildings of the Palm Beach Institute for the Breast were as impressive as its reputation. Built in the grand style of Mizner, Florida's most famous architect in earlier days, its design included parapets, towers, and intriguing odd angles here and there. Intricate decorative sculpture highlighted the front façade. The newer wings, at the sides and behind the building were of a more conservative style, but the whole came together rather beautifully Carlsie decided. The place looked exactly as she had guessed it would.

Surveying the famous institute in all it's grandeur, she wondered how many hopeful women, each knowing she was fortunate to have gained admission, passed through those heavy bronze doors each week. Certainly many less lucky ones tried in vain to be treated at this outrageously expensive, very discreet, private clinic.

The institute was a mecca for surgeons interested in breast disease and Carlsie had looked forward to her arrival for many months. Although her final year of general surgical residency had been rewarding, it had been tough, and she was glad the time had come for her to leave the Charity Hospital world of cholecystectomies, hernias, colon resections, and Saturday night knife and gun wounds. Now, she would be taking up the great passion of her fledgling medical career: esthetic and reconstructive surgery of the breast.

This promised to be the most exciting period of her education. And it would be less depressing, she thought. Having seen so much of the vulgar aspects of life and disease in past years, she looked forward to not taking care of people with bleeding ulcers, ruptured appendices, bowel obstructions, and every other god-awful thing that can go wrong with the human body. If she never saw another gangrenous leg or perirectal abscess it would be fine with her. At last she was to be a part of the elegant side of surgery. She would learn about beauty and creativity and develop a new way of thinking. She would study the artistry of those graceful masters of plastic surgery, skilled professionals who transformed the unsightly into the pretty or, at least, into the tolerable.

The journey from New Orleans to the glamour of Palm Beach was a big step for her, and she was eager to move into this new phase of her life. She passed through the massive doorway of the institute, and stood alone in an expensively furnished hospital lobby. After inhaling deeply, she smiled. She was here . . . finally here.

The middle-aged, rather dour secretary outside

the administrator's office was noticeably surprised when Carlsie identified herself as the new resident. She quickly summoned the chief resident.

Carlsie always enjoyed the startled reactions of those who assumed she would be male. She met them quite frequently, particularly in the clinics. Pediatricians could be female, internists maybe, and sometimes gynecologists, but never, not even in their wildest imaginings; did most people expect a surgeon to be anything other than a symbol of machismo. If it were not so amusing, it would be irritating.

Seated on a couch across the office from the administrator, Carlsie waited for the chief resident, experiencing great joy at the prospect of being part of this stimulating environment. The institute was the one place in the medical establishment where diseases and surgery of the breast did not suffer from neglect. Not cardiac surgery, neurosurgery, or any other glamour specialty siphoned off the money and attention in this special hospital. Here, for once, the problems of women were number one.

The institute had been famous for years because of the beautiful cosmetic results of the augmentation mammoplasties done there. And more recently its reputation had broadened to include cancer surgery and reconstructions after mastectomy. Its clientele was international, its quality of medicine academically perfect, and its professional staff well respected for their extraordinary talents and technical innovations. Indeed, the institute had earned recognition as one of the safest and best places

places for the woman with a need for mammary surgery of any type.

Dr. Keene did not take long to arrive. He glanced quickly around the room, his gaze resting on Carlsie long enough to inform her she was being admired. It was not an unusual sensation for her, and sensed it was not unusual for this young man to send such a messages.

"So where's my man?" He spoke to the secretary in a friendly relaxed tone, while continuing to watch Carlsie.

"What man?"

He turned his eyes to the secretary. "Come on Edith, Dr. Camden . . . Dr. C. L. Camden. You just called me about him. He's a day late and a dollar short already. I have work for him to catch up on."

"I never told you there was a man down here."

Gordon Keene feigned incredulousness. "What is this? I spoke to you three minutes ago. Are you having a stroke, or what?" He frowned suspiciously but benevolently. "How many Valium have you had today, Edith?"

"I never said there was a man here. I told you Dr. Camden had arrived."

"Right, right. So much for semantics. So where is this yokel? I've got to get moving." He glanced at Carlsie again, smiled and winked. "They don't want me to get any work done around here," he said to her. "I have to spend all my time chasing down junior residents."

Carlsie grinned back, despite the teasing game

32

he'd been playing. The blond surgeon seemed satisfied for the moment to continue gazing pleasantly toward her while he waited for his new gump to suddenly appear.

Since the secretary did not seem about to introduce her, Carlsie did it herself. "I'm Carlsie Camden. Back at Tulane some of the profs called me. C.L. They thought it sounded more professional or something. I thought it was simply chauvinism."

Keene stared intently at her while she stepped forward with right hand extended. He seemed to be considering and then reconsidering this situation.

"What do you think?" she asked. "Is a name like Carlsie too casual for a surgeon? My mother liked it."

His expression revealed his disbelief. Carlsie couldn't decide whether he was going to have a petit mal seizure or faint. "Tell me this isn't true, Edith." he said.

"It's true." The secretary was taking great delight in the situation.

"Ritter swore this was only a silly rumor."

"Yes, but now it's the silly truth."

"Does the old man know?"

"I haven't the foggiest."

Gordon Keene's suntanned face slowly worked its way into the most amused grin Carlsie had seen in a long time. "Dr. Camden, you are going to be the biggest shock that's hit this place since a male transsexual checked in last year screaming 'Equal rights!' and demanding an augmentation."

"Sounds reasonable," Carlsie replied. "Did he

33

get his surgery?"

Keene chuckled. "Dr. Barret ran him out on a rail. Nearly killed the man . . . or woman . . . or whichever he was."

He turned to the secretary. "Don't tell anyone about this. Give me time to prepare Dr. Barret, just in case he doesn't know. No sense in risking her life merely because she doesn't wear pants."

"Wait a minute," Carlsie interrupted. "I am wearing pants!"

"So you are," Keene replied, surveying her body thoroughly. "And you look quite nice in them I might add. That's part of the problem though. Perhaps we should get you into something that doesn't show so many curves." He stared teasingly at her chest. "I don't know what we can do about that."

Carlsie smiled again. Dr. Keene was certainly pumping this for all it was worth, but she already liked him. She enjoyed his animated overreactions. Every time he smiled, two adorable dimples appeared, making him look boyishly mischievous. "It can't be all that bad," she said. "You make this sound like a hotbed of die-hard chauvinism."

The secretary opened her eyes wide, nodding vigorously.

Keene glanced at her and then back to Carlsie. "Not quite that bad, but close." His voice unexpectedly took on a humorous oriental accent. "Not to worry, little one. Gordo find solution to problem. You in good hands now."

"Oh brother!" the secretary responded. "That's what I was afraid of. You'd better watch him close,

34

Dr. Camden, particularly those infamous hands. You know how surgeons are with their hands."

"Ignore her, sweetheart," he advised. "She's only jealous. Stick with me, and I'll take care of you. Nobody pushes Gordo's girls around."

As Carlsie laughed at the perfectly ridiculous scene, he led her from the office and they started across the lobby.

"Where are you taking me?" she asked.

"Guess." He grinned slyly.

"Are you sure you're the chief resident?"

"Are you sure you're C. L. Camden?"

"How do I know I'm supposed to come with you?"

"How do I know you're a lady doctor?" He raised his eyebrows, feigning suspicion.

She was determined not to lose this contest. "Are you sure you know what you're doing?"

"Is the pope Polish?"

"How do I know you're who you say you are?"

He gazed at her without blinking. She thought she could detect a small glint of impending victory in his eyes.

"Didn't your mother teach you to trust men dressed in white?" he asked soberly.

"Only if I knew for sure they were doctors."

"Fair enough. I'll prove I'm one by checking your lungs." He smiled confidently, and pulled a stethoscope from his coat pocket. He clearly thought he had her.

She started to speak, but nothing came. She had no rebuttal. She waited, hoping her brain would send her a message soon, something cocky and terribly clever with which to put away this overconfident man. It had never let her down her before. "Brain, don't fail me now," she said plaintively, a hopeless grin coming to her face.

He laughed hard, happily victorious, then smiled his famous smile, the one that had probably won a lot of ladies' hearts, she decided. "Carlsie, I think you're going to fit in here. I'll make sure of it."

She felt great. The institute was going to be a wonderful place to learn. "One more thing," she said.

"What's that?"

"Where are you really taking me?"

He laughed again. "To the conference room. Ritter is lecturing the medical students on cancer."

"Dr. H. T. Ritter?"

"That's right. The one and only Hank Ritter: courageous defender of woman's rights, famous rebuilder of their bodies, and experienced connoisseur of the pleasures of feminine flesh."

"Hank?" she said, surprised. "The eminent H.T. is a Hank? Where did he get a down-home name like that."

"The usual place, my young friend . . . his mother." He winked and took her by the arm. "Now let me tell you a few things about him. For your own good, of course."

"I'm sure it is."

Keene chuckled. "It's very easy to come under Ritter's spell, you see. Particularly for a young pretty thing like yourself. I know he's quite famous and all that, because of the celebrities he has operated on, but—"

The comment about Ritter's fame was the first thing he had said that she totally believed. She interrupted. "How did that get started? He seems to have come out of the woodwork so suddenly in the last few years. How did he get so well known so quickly?"

Keene smiled knowingly. "In a word—Rona Randy. When a Hollywood sex queen has a much publicized mastectomy, then flies across the country for reconstructive surgery, the word gets out. When she starts wearing see-through blouses again, that's all it takes. They've been beating a path to his door ever since. The fact that she's been on every TV talk show in the world, telling them he's a miracle worker hasn't hurt his reputation one bit."

"I've seen her. She does lay it on a bit thick."

He nodded. "There've been lots of others that you didn't hear about; it's all kept quiet. No matter who it is, if the patients themselves don't tell, the media gets no information. There are no press releases, no news conferences; and no names are released. The work done here is absolutely confidential. The gals worship him, though, and some of them are anxious to tell the world about it. It's his patients who've made Hank a famous man."

They paused outside a large lecture hall. "Now don't say I didn't warn you. He's a real ladies' man, so watch out. If he makes any moves, just let me know and I'll take care of it. He's got an eye for a thigh, so to speak."

She eyed him suspiciously. "Don't all surgeons?"

"Are you including female surgeons in that sweeping generalization?" Keene raised one eyebrow lasciviously.

"I'm told it's a testosterone-mediated effect," she said.

"That's an old wives' tale." He was shaking his head confidently. "You shouldn't believe everything you hear, Carlsie. For example, I'm much more of the platonic type myself. I'm interested in a lady's brains and personality more than her body."

"I gotcha. You like the real intellectual type."

"You said it. Give me a good book or even some science journals and I can happily while away the evening, rather than waste it with some good-looking, oversexed female." His voice held a tone of prudent righteousness.

"An admirable attitude. I'm sure your mother is very proud."

Gordo grinned. "Yes, but don't misunderstand me. I don't mind doing a physical favor for a nice girl like yourself when called upon. I have an ethical duty, you know. Far be it from me to turn down an opportunity to help a lady in need, particularly someone like you, a fellow doctor and all."

"I'll try to remember that," she replied. "It'll be comforting just knowing you're here."

"By all means." He nodded sympathetically. "I'd certainly hate to see you fall into the hands of the likes of Ritter."

"Certainly not. I have my reputation to protect." She was enjoying the repartee. A physician with a quick wit was rare. Generally Carlsie was the recipient of suggestive remarks that contained little real humor.

He led her into a small auditorium half-filled with medical students in white jackets. The lights were dimmed, and a screen displayed the huge image of a mammogram. Quietly they took seats in the top row at the back of the room. She noticed immediately, even in the darkness, that only about a tenth of the students were women, a ratio somewhat below the national average.

She was at home in this academic setting. It was here that she thrived. In this environment where male-female competition was minimized she was more than equal. While still an ambitious young girl, Carlsie had recognized that education was her way out of the poverty and sexual bias she so resented.

It had been difficult being smarter, understanding more than the strong-willed, domineering, Southern men she'd grown up around. She had learned to be a gracious listener, quietly disregarding their rampant ignorance on many subjects. Even though she had known from an early age that she was brighter than most of those around her, her strict Catholic father had made sure she was humble. He'd demanded that she be respectful, almost submissive, but he'd understood her. She'd disliked the label Cajun, but he'd always reminded her she was one. "How else could you be such a fighter and still be a woman?" he used to say. Carlsie's evolution into the person she had become would have been difficult, if

39

not impossible, without him. She would probably be in the bayou still. Few people ever left it — particularly women. They were too soon pregnant and almost always uneducated.

For Carlsie, medical school had been a new life. She had at last entered an environment in which she could speak her mind and be appreciated for it. Recognition had come quickly from her male colleagues. She enjoyed working with men, and was in no danger of acting like one, as she felt some females in medicine were doing. Papa's insistent training had made sure of that. No Cajun girl could ever move so far away from her bloodline that she could lose her inbred femininity. Intuitively she knew how to stroke the masculine personality in a way that did not diminish her own importance. She never purposefully tried to put a man down, unless of course, she was angered or backed into a corner by some unthinking egomaniac. And there were plenty of those in surgery.

On the other hand, she never minded the playful flirtatiousness of an associate such as Gordo. He was only recognizing the innate differences in men and women. It was downgrading treatment, by those who believed females couldn't hack it, that irritated her. She hoped that Gordo's joking references to his chief's attitude about female surgeons were just that: jokes.

Waiting for her eyes to accommodate to the subdued light of the lecture hall, she listened as the speaker discussed the unreliability of mammograms in ruling out cancer. His deep voice carried a Western drawl. She imagined he could have been a rodeo announcer.

The lecturer paused as the lights came on and the screen dimmed. He was tall with broad muscular shoulders, quite handsome in a rugged sort of way. His black, somewhat shaggy hair hung down over his ears. A bushy mustache and an intense, sun-darkened face combined with his accent to create, in her judgment, an attractive version of a South-western bandido or maybe a Marlboro advertisement. She especially liked the appealing brown eyes that gazed expectantly at his audience. When he stepped from behind the podium, she was surprised: he was wearing Western boots!

She realized immediately that Gordo was playing a little joke. There wasn't one chance in a thousand that this intriguing man was the talented surgeon and eloquent medical writer whose publications she had studied in detail.

"That's not him," she whispered. "That's not Ritter."

Keene stared at her curiously. "Are you kidding? Of course that's him, straight out of 'Dallas.' He could have been J.R.'s brother."

Gordo was so serious Carlsie was almost willing to believe him. She turned to study the speaker once more. It might be possible, she thought. "I expected an Ivy League type. He looks more like a cowboy."

"A cowboy? Are you crazy? Of course he's a cowboy!"

"That's what I said."

"He walks like a cowboy, talks like one, acts like

41

one, even raises a few horses around here some-where. There's only one thing he doesn't do like a cowboy."

"What's that?"

He looked straight into her eyes, his expression more serious than before. "Operate." He paused, waiting for his meaning to sink in. "That man's the smoothest surgical technician I've ever seen, and I've seen plenty, believe me."

"There're a lot of good technicians around, Gordo, but it takes more than fancy blade work to make a great surgeon."

He nodded thoughtfully. "For breast work there's no one that can touch him. I'm sure of it. He molds tissue like a sculptor. I'll swear he has hands computer-designed for plastic surgery. I've never seen him misplace a stitch or make even the slight-est mistake. He's so perfect it's incredible. You'll see." Keene smiled again. "He's a cowboy all right, but put a scalpel in his hand and he turns into a goddamn ballerina."

Carlsie was amused by the analogy. "That good, huh?"

"Probably better. I think he'll even impress a Tu-lane girl." He winked and continued gazing steadily, almost fondly, into her eyes.

"He's done that already. I always fall for guys who wear boots."

"Yeah, you and every other starstruck female around here." Keene chuckled just loud enough to attract the speaker's attention.

"I'm glad at least someone is enjoying this lec-

42

ture," Ritter said dryly, peering upward at them, and noticing Carlsie for the first time. "Dr. Keene, I've told you not to try impressing these lady medical students with your bloody suit and stories of bold surgery." He glanced at Carlsie. "Honey, you'd better stay away from that man. He's still a poverty-stricken resident, and besides, he has a bad reputation around here. He's a dyed-in-the-wool heartbreaker. Ask any of the nurses."

The students laughed.

"Oh, lord," Gordo whispered. "He thinks you're a medical student."

Carlsie smiled.

Ritter turned back to his audience and asked for a volunteer to interpret the next mammogram. He scanned the room, looking for a hand. There was none. Finally, his eyes returned to her. "Would you give it a try?" he asked. "Surely sitting with Dr. Keene is worth something. He's so full of knowledge, I'm sure some of it has rubbed off."

His question caught her off guard. He was serious. He actually wanted her to perform. Gordo was right. Ritter had no idea who she was. "In all fairness, sir, I should tell you —"

He interrupted. "No excuses. If you weren't listening we'll know it soon enough."

"But —"

He held up his hand to stop her. "If you'll just come down here, we can get this over with and I can torment someone else."

His command irritated her; he should have let her identify herself. She rose and walked down to the

43

front of the room. The medical students were watching her with curiosity and anticipation, wondering who in the world she was. Keene's face was buried in his hands in a show of mock horror. He looked so miserable she couldn't resist smiling at him.

"Now there. That's not so bad is it?" Dr. Ritter consoled her. "I'm sure you'll do just fine. If not, we'll know who to blame, right?" He shot a quick look at Gordo, who nodded glumly.

The new mammogram appeared on the screen, and Ritter began the presentation. It was a routine problem involving the evaluation of a new lump in a thirty-five-year-old with a history of fibrocystic disease. The patient had already undergone three previous biopsies and did not want another.

Carlsie enjoyed his voice, and found him even more handsome than she had from the back of the auditorium. His somewhat folksy presentation was quite charming, and fit beautifully into his established image of unpretentious supersurgeon. He was smiling, waiting for her to answer, his warm eyes watching her closely, very closely. This man seemed to be amused by what he thought was a good joke on Gordon Keene.

She confidently explained how the case should be managed, with needle aspiration and immediate biopsy if aspiration did not eliminate the tumor. She then interpreted the mammogram as benign, and expressed the opinion that it was an unnecessary x-ray in this particular case because the mass had to be surgically evaluated regardless.

Predictably, he was surprised by the completeness of her analysis. He gazed suspiciously at her, then described an infinitely more complicated case. One which the smartest medical student in the country would have had a hard time discussing.

A nervous murmur swept through the students when she quickly described how the problem should be handled. By the time she finished interpreting the accompanying mammogram, the class was chattering noisily about this brilliant new student.

Carlsie's attention was momentarily attracted to the back of the auditorium, where an older physician in a white lab coat had stepped from the shadows to stare silently toward her. She felt a twinge of uneasiness.

Gordo was no longer watching the proceedings. His head hung down, a helpless grin curling his lips.

Ritter appeared good-naturedly chagrined, and Carlsie stood, arms crossed, smiling victoriously, almost daring him to try again. After a long appraising look at her, he glanced toward the supremely tickled Keene. Carlsie loved it. The famous surgeon had refused to allow her to reveal herself, probably assuming he was going to have a little fun with a young female medical student, and now she was the one having the fun. She couldn't have asked for a more delightful situation.

"My dear Dr. Keene," Ritter said, "is there anything you want to tell me about this friend of yours?"

The chief resident couldn't answer. He was struggling too hard to keep from laughing.

"Gordo. We can't hear you. Speak up." Ritter was smiling.

The chief resident finally found his tongue. "She's no friend of mine. I thought she was with you."

Hank Ritter turned back to Carlsie, and asked the question to which he presumably knew the answer. "Are you the new resident?"

"Yes sir. I tried to explain."

"That you did. It's just that I didn't believe the rumor. I never expected you to be . . . well . . . I guess I never expected you to be female."

The class laughed as a wise guy in the back whistled suggestively. Then someone yelled out, "She's female for sure. We can see that from here."

Medical students can be such jerks, Carlsie thought, blushing slightly as the clown at the back repeated his whistling act. She tried to pinpoint the whistler, hoping to have him assigned to her on the wards where she could make him pay for his humor.

"And what sort of research are you interested in?" Ritter asked, squelching any additional loss of academic decorum.

"I want to expand a study I've begun on breast cancer in the very young. I'll be working with Dr. Farber in the department of pathology, as well as doing my surgical work."

A sudden hush came over the group. She had said something wrong. Ritter's expression revealed his discomfort. All eyes were on Carlsie, but she had no idea why the mood of the group suddenly changed so dramatically. No one appeared anxious to explain the awkwardness.

From the back, from the lone figure she had noticed earlier came the first explanation. The speaker was an austere, older man in a long white, perfectly starched, unwrinkled lab coat. His expression was severe, his blondish gray hair short; and his eyes were narrowed into a suspicious glare. He spoke with an accusing harshness. "I don't think you are going to do any work with Bernie Farber."

Slowly, he descended the stairs, while the silence remained unbroken, except by him. "Dr. Farber is dead. He died two weeks ago." He glanced toward Ritter, and then intently surveyed the class. It was the most amazing thing she had ever seen. This doctor, whoever he was, had taken total command of the gathering. The relaxed interest of the students was gone. The friendly attitude of everyone present had evaporated. She wondered who could so effectively dampen the spirits of so many people.

Ritter's voice broke the silence that had come over the room. His tone conveyed a certain coolness to the new arrival. "As everyone can see, Dr. Mendel is here to give the pathology half of this lecture. I'll see you next week and we'll talk about reconstructive surgery." He gathered his notes and left without another word.

As Carlsie returned to her seat she glanced back to the pathologist, the unpleasant Dr. Mendel. He was staring disapprovingly at her.

She attempted to smile at him, but found it quite impossible. His stony expression was intimidating and embarrassing. She could sense his critical appraisal as his eyes traveled up and down her body. Unconsciously she fingered her Joan of Arc medallion, her only remaining inheritance from her mother, still filled with wonder at what this stranger had done. He had said little, yet had communicated much.

Nervously, she whispered to Gordon Keene, "Who is this guy? Darth Vader?"

He grinned. "Almost. Oscar Mendel is chief of pathology. Looks like you'll be working with him. Some people have all the luck." The sarcasm was not lost on her.

"What happened to Dr. Farber?"

"Here one day, gone the next. Poor bastard. Mendel fired him. He fell asleep in bed two days later, with a lit cigarette. Did you know him well?"

"Not at all. He called after I'd been accepted into the program, said he'd seen what my research interests were, and seemed anxious for me to help him. He wanted me to work with him on some slide and chart reviews of young mastectomy patients. It sounded great."

"He was a nice guy. Now you'll be stuck with Mendel. There's a real bad one for you."

Carlsie was dismayed at the news.

Gordo, observing her reaction, seemed sympathetically concerned. He spoke softly. "I'll tell you something about Mendel. He's not the most pleasant person in the world, and he's way too powerful. He's been here from the beginning of time, on the board of directors and all that. But there's one thing you have to give him credit for: he's brilliant. Absolutely brilliant. You'll learn from him."

In response to her doubtful expression, Keene raised his eyebrows, nodded, and made the face people make when they are letting someone in on the real unadulterated truth. "No kidding. Just wait until you hear his lecture. He knows more about breast cancer than three ordinary pathologists put together. It's his specialty. He's published hundreds of papers, written textbooks, the whole nine yards. You've probably read some of his stuff."

"He doesn't seem very friendly."

Gordo nodded in agreement. "That he is not. He doesn't care for professional women either. It's common knowledge. He doesn't think they should be doctors . . . they should be nurses, according to him."

She frowned. That was the last thing she wanted to hear. She wasn't interested in fighting the battle of the sexes with some antifemale old jackass. "Doesn't he know this is the twentieth century?"

"Just wait. There're a lot of things about him you're gonna love. He's loaded with all sorts of theories about cancer causes and effects. Religious stuff. You know, disease as a form of punishment . . . or a result of guilt . . . really weird concepts like that."

"You're joking!"

"Nope. It's like . . . well, I don't know." He looked pensively into her eyes. He seemed to have more to say, but wasn't quite sure he should. "Unusual," he said, shrugging. "The man is very unu-

49

sual."

"Just what I need."

He smiled and patted her on the leg. "Don't worry. You'll win him over. I'll bet he never met a surgeon like you."

"How does he survive, with attitudes like that?"

"Politics, my dear. He's entrenched, even more than some of the surgeons. Besides being a real prick, though, he's an excellent pathologist . . . maybe even a genius. You'll see." He gazed at her somberly. "You just have to be careful around him, that's all. Never cross him, no matter what. You'll be sorry if you do. That I can promise you. He's very vindictive."

Gordo stood up to leave. The pathologist was at the podium waiting while his slides were readied. There was nothing pleasant about him that she could see. "Looks like he's in a better mood than usual," Gordo joked, and then excused himself so he might go to assist Ritter in the O.R. "I guess I never officially welcomed you aboard, Carlsie. I'm glad you're here. I really am," he added, smiling warmly.

"Thanks," she replied, nodding acceptance of his friendship. "I think this is going to be great."

Keene asked her to meet him in the surgical lounge after the lecture, to begin orientation to the department and her new duties, and then he was gone.

Mendel did not glance her way again, as if he were purposely avoiding her. His lecture was as Gordo had said it would be: nothing short of phenomenal. The man gave a virtuoso performance, discussing the etiology and pathological characteristics of mammary carcinoma. His slide presentation of the various cell types of the terrible disease was the best she had ever seen.

There was something that didn't feel right, though. The lecture had been an intensely sterile presentation of scientific fact. Almost too scientific. Not once, even as he showed pictures of terribly advanced cases of the disease, did he reveal a trace of emotion or refer to any aspect of the human tragedy involved. He appeared totally insulated from the horrors the disease wreaked on its unfortunate victims.

Mendel concluded with a blistering denunciation of the growing tendency of surgeons to do operations less extensive than the classical Halsted radical mastectomy, the procedure of choice for decades past which had fallen into disrepute. Afterward, he gathered his papers and departed without allowing questions, leaving the impressed students to chatter enthusiastically about what they had seen and heard.

Carlsie, awed by the profound knowledge of the man but shocked by his attitude toward his subject, remained in the auditorium after the others had gone. She felt estranged from this environment. Her first hours in the institute had been so different from her expectations. She was moved by the greatness of the place, yet unnerved by it. A disquieting anxiety had taken the pleasure from her first encounters with the people from whom she hoped to learn so much.

51

Someone in the projection room dimmed the lights, and she was suddenly aware that she was alone. Silently she climbed the stairs in the semi-darkness, trying to recall where Gordo had said to meet him.

A door opened far below just as she reached the top. It was Mendel. He was standing at the side of the podium, retrieving a forgotten folder of notes. A large unusual pipe was clenched tightly in his mouth, and a mild cherry aroma reached her. He was peering at her with intense curiosity. His deep voice penetrated the silence. "Where are you from?"

"New Orleans."

He ran a hand through his hair. Somehow he looked more tired now, less intimidating. "So, you must be Catholic."

"Yes, I was raised that way. Why do you ask?"

"I was Catholic once, many years ago," he said softly.

"I take it you've left the church now."

He nodded. "It's a long story. What was your connection with Farber?"

"He invited me to review some young cancer cases with him. I guess he found out it was one of my interests."

"He told you we have a lot of young ones here, did he?"

"He didn't say. Is that what he thought?"

Mendel glared at her. "It makes no difference. Farber's gone now." He shook his head and abruptly left the room. Carlsie felt responsible for the sudden ending of the conversation. It was not a good way to begin a relationship with someone she was going to be working under. Her curiosity was rising, though, about Farber. His phone call had been unusual. Why had he needed her to help him with a research project carried on in his own department? She hoped Gordo could tell her a little more about the man.

Chapter Three

By late morning Carlsie had toured the hospital, checked in with the various departments, and met her fellow residents. It was evident that her personal workload was going to be very heavy. As a final formality, she was taken to pay homage to a man who, for years, had been the driving force behind modern breast surgery: the very famous and very wealthy Dr. Walker Barret. Having practically built the institute, and being almost single-handedly responsible for its early success and growing reputation, he was a man whose authority was unchallenged. According to Keene, in addition to being chief of surgery, he was the major stockholder, president of the board, and executive administrator of the operation.

She expected him to be tough, irascible, demanding, dogmatic, extremely talented, a workaholic, and to ooze charm when he chose. He turned out to be all that and more. Her appreciation of his power and prestige began to rise when she was shown into his office suite.

The rooms were startling in their elegance.

Setting off very expensive antique furnishings were numerous pieces of art, all emphasizing the breast. The beautiful pantings and sculptures were everywhere. It was readily apparent that Barret equated the work done at the institute with these stylized interpretations of the feminine figure.

The inner office into which Carlsie was eventually led by the secretary was even more elaborately decorated with objects of art, the central theme of which was the physical beauty of woman and predominantly of youthful woman. Nowhere to be seen was any reference to feminine strength, endurance, or accomplishment. There were no paintings of pioneer women, plow in one hand and baby in the other. No statues of female coal workers. No photos of Sally Ride roaring into space. No oils of Joan of Arc leading armies into battle. Everywhere Carlsie looked there were only artistic renditions of soft, pretty, feminine flesh. The kind any male would find instinctively appealing.

Carlsie was surprised and disappointed. She had hoped for a less sexist orientation, at least some reference to the beauty of well-kept mature women or a picture of a successful older woman, Eleanor Roosevelt perhaps.

In the center of the impressive chamber, behind a Chippendale desk flanked by a mahogany bookcase, sat the famous surgeon. He obviously considered himself more than merely a chief of staff and a plastic surgeon. Everything about the environment this man had created for himself reeked of pompous self-esteem. Carlsie had been in plenty of wealthy physician's offices, but this was the nicest she had ever seen—or the worst, depending upon one's viewpoint. It resembled something the president of A.T.& T. might want . . . or better yet, the king of Siam.

Without a word the secretary retreated from the room, gently closing the door.

Barret was studying a letter and did not glance up for an uncomfortably long while. He was a tall slender man with attractively styled silver hair and a handsome, although aging, face. His remarkably powerful eyes radiated arrogant self-confidence. He was older than she had expected, but otherwise looked the perfect image of the successful surgeon and businessman. In fact, with his pin-striped suit and manicured nails, she imagined he could have come straight from the corporate boardrooms of Wall Street.

"I was told that you arrived somewhat later than we expected," he said finally. His stern voice carried a trace of the English accent he had brought to his country decades ago when he'd come here to study the new techniques of the young American geniuses working at the rapidly developing art of reconstructive surgery.

"Yes, sir. It's just that it took longer—"

His expression remained unchanged as he interrupted her. "I do not know what you have been allowed to get away with at other hospitals, young lady," he was saying. "Here at the institute we expect our staff to be punctual and reliable. As a

57

matter of fact we demand it."

"It won't happen again, sir."

"I'm sure you're right."

After another uncomfortable silence during which he gazed at her intently, he went on. "There are a few matters I wish to emphasize from the start. Number one: this is not the charity hospital you are used to. Our orientation is to quality, and we serve many rich and famous patients. They come to us because they want, and can afford, the very best. And that is what we deliver. I also wish to remind you that we treat individuals, not cases. Conduct yourself accordingly."

As he lectured her, he sounded more and more British, more and more protocol and procedure oriented. She was not offended by his brusque manner because it was, after all, his game and he had the right to expect it to be played by his rules.

The harsh edge to his voice diminished, however, as he went on to tell her to disregard whatever she had heard about his opposition to women in surgery. He respected intelligent women, he said, and was pleased to give her an opportunity in his program, although he admitted he still had reservations about the ability of a female to keep up the pace a surgeon must maintain. All she had to do was prove to him that she could carry her own weight and she would have no greater supporter, he stated, but she'd better not use her sex as an excuse to get a reduced work load. He frowned as he emphasized the point. "I will not tolerate a slacker. No doctor working for me will be allowed to stay home due to menstrual cramps, if you get my meaning."

He leaned back in his chair smirking slightly.

It was not the first time Carlsie had faced snide remarks of that type, but this time the barb went deeper. Perhaps because it came from a physician whose career was built upon a reputation for helping women, it carried more sting. She had thought he would be more sensitive, less crass somehow. Anticipating his toughness and demanding nature had not prepared her for such chauvinistic pettiness, almost meanness.

"I hear you," she replied, not trying to hide her disdain for the remark.

"Yes, I hope you do." Barret gazed steadily at her until she turned away her eyes. He had a powerful personality, and she found it difficult not to be totally intimidated. Her throat was dry as sandpaper. He was turning out to be more of a demigod than she had guessed he would be. But she should have expected it. No surgeon gets to the top of the pyramid without being, or at least becoming, somewhat brutal, almost cutthroat. The harshness was inbred in the system. Barret was the natural result of the long route to the top.

If even the most ordinary of surgeons could be counted upon to be arrogant, competitive, and chauvinistic, what else should she have expected from a spectacularly successful one. Every trait that went into the making of his breed was exaggerated in him. Of course he didn't think women had stamina enough to be surgeons. Who would have expected him to, considering his background? And of course he would think any woman in surgery would be in need of much help from her colleagues. Why wouldn't he think that? He had climbed to the very top of the pyramid by being as masculine as he could be. The implication was that it took balls rather than brains to cut some poor bastard open and save his life, Carlsie knew she should be used to that by now.

Passing out medicine or writing prescriptions or delivering babies was fine for women. But don't pick up a scalpel. Using it right takes the guts found only in a man.

All of this Carlsie understood because of her years in competition with these rather melodramatic men. She didn't deny that the same qualities that made them what they were also made them more attractive to her than other doctors. She understood surgeons, and was similar to them in many ways. After all, she was one of them.

When Walker Barret spoke again, his voice had softened. "Now about this research project of yours. You know by now about Dr. Farber. Mendel has been working quite diligently to make up for Bernie's absence. Naturally he has been under a strain, doing two men's work, so he's a bit more difficult to get along with than usual."

"I can understand that."

"I'm sure you can. Bernie always seemed to take delight in annoying Oscar, so I wouldn't be surprised if Dr. Mendel wants nothing to do with any research dreamed up, as it were, by you and Farber."

"Dr. Farber was so enthusiastic about the study he wanted me to help with," Carlsie said, "I was shocked to hear that he'd left the institute . . . and then, of course, about what happened."

Barret eyed her thoughtfully, bringing his eyebrows almost together across the bridge of his nose as he pondered her comment. "The police say it was a cigarette fire. Bernie had taken to drinking alot lately, and I suppose that had something to do with it. The quality of his work here had slipped, quite frankly. I think he was having some personal troubles. He was a nice fellow, though, and we're all sorry it happened. In any event, I suggest you postpone your little project. Don't bother the staff with it right now, particularly Mendel. Like a child at dinner, new residents should be seen and not heard. Keep that in mind."

The office intercom interrupted him at that moment causing one of the most amazing personality transformations she had ever witnessed. He had a long-distance call from an important patient in Los Angeles. She could feel his immediate pleasure, his delight in being renowned. He changed instantly from uncaring tyrant into an apparently gracious, compassionate physician filled with love for humanity and grateful for his opportunity to serve.

Carlsie was dismissed quickly, and by the time she reached the door Barret was happily leaning back in his chair, smiling and conversing warmly with the Hollywood caller.

He is quite a character, she thought, one of those rare doctors who has evolved into much more than a physician. Firmly in control of his life and environment, he has become almost an institution. She admired and envied him as she had known she would — as any surgeon would. Already though, she knew she didn't like him, and never would. He reeked too much of those things she wished some doctors would not pursue so vigorously — money, power, and fame.

Chapter Four

It didn't take long for Carlsie to discover that the pace for a resident at the institute was busier than any she had experienced. She had no complaints, however, at least none she was willing to express and thereby risk accusations of estrogen-induced weakness. She pushed harder than ever. She was the first to arrive, the last to leave, and was always willing to accept more work. She vowed not to be worn down, no matter what. If they needed her until midnight, she worked till two A.M. If they wanted her to arrive at seven, she was there by six. She planned to carry the battle straight to them. She would give no quarter and ask no relief.

For a while she was working longer hours than the rest of the medical staff combined. She was almost invariably the last one to leave. The only physician who ever stayed as late as she did was Oscar Mendel. Several days in a row she saw him in the parking lot. It was so unusual for a pathologist to work such late hours she became curious about it and began to watch for him. That was when she noticed how interested he seemed to be in her.

On one occasion she came out of the building well after midnight and happened to spot him sitting in his car, staring at her. When she realized she had seen him, he departed immediately.

It seemed like such a weird thing for him to be doing that she finally decided she had been mistaken or had misinterpreted coincidental circumstance. But the suspicion that she was being watched persisted. It was bothersome, and began to make her nervous. Living in New Orleans had taught her there were more than a few strange people in the world, and she had no interest in being surreptitiously studied by one of them. Vague anxiety which struck her, particularly at night, made her feel silly when she realized she was looking around to see if anyone else was there even when she knew she was alone.

In the early morning, though, she never saw Mendel. It was a different person she usually met — and under more pleasant circumstances. She never seemed to arrive at the hospital earlier than Dr. Ed Grossman, the chief of anesthesia. Tall and skinny, with an almost bald head and a big nose, he was not particularly handsome, and he was partially crippled. However, he was a charming and clever fellow who showed an interest in her and her efforts to get settled down in her new job. On a number of occasions they sat together in the nearly empty cafeteria having coffee and doughnuts before he went up to the O.R. and she went to make pre-op rounds on the surgical patients.

Carlsie was surprised to discover that Grossman was not entirely happy with his new position. To take it, he had left the teaching staff of a medical school after a fifteen-year academic career.

"Why did you come here?" she asked.

"I'm not sure, now. I needed a change, I guess. Organizing the department offered a nice challenge. They never had an anesthesiologist before I came."

"You're kidding!"

"No. It was a nurse-anesthetist department. Just like the old days."

"I didn't think that was legal, not anymore."

He grinned. "How naïve you are, young one. The law has nothing to do with it. If a surgeon is willing to take medical responsibility for the anesthetic, he can have anybody he wants administer it—as long as the hospital says its okay."

"What surgeon would do that? Most of us aren't knowledgeable about giving anesthesia."

Grossman found her amazement amusing. "A lot of old-time surgeons knew how to do it. Besides, when you let an anesthesiologist into the O.R., you have a new M.D. in there watching what goes on. Some surgeons don't like another doctor, who presumably knows how things should be done, looking over their shoulders."

She arched one eyebrow in a humorous way. "Certainly an understandable attitude for second-rate surgeons. Surely no one here has that problem."

"Says who?" Grossman replied. "Barret was one of the old guard who thought anesthesiologists were

65

an unnecessary evil he could do without it."

"What changed his mind? Did a patient die?"

"Naw. It was the liability issue."

"I would have thought the patients would have demanded anesthesiologists."

"Carlsie, get serious. The average patient doesn't have the remotest concern about who's giving the anesthetic, and sure as hell isn't worried about an anesthetist's credentials."

She frowned. "That's not true, Ed. Educated people care. I know they do. I've been asked about anesthesia. Patients are scared of it. They've heard too many horror stories. Don't you remember that book *Coma?*"

Grossman grinned. "Well, in any event, I think the other surgeons pressured Barret to enter the twentieth century. So, Ritter recruited me. He wants me to get a couple more M.D.s for the department when I can."

"Sounds like a great opportunity. Why don't you like it?"

"It just hasn't turned out the way I thought it would."

"Too busy? Does being the only doctor in the department keep you from having enough free time?"

"Nope, that's not my problem. I've always been willing to work hard. Somehow the work here isn't as satisfying as doing anesthesia in the real world."

His description was puzzling. "What do you mean 'real world'?" she asked.

He put down his coffee and gazed at her more

seriously. "I think you know, Carlsie. This place isn't like a normal hospital. We don't have normal patients. We don't have normal surgeons. There's nothing normal around here. I'm not used to working with doctors as famous as these guys — or as rich." He paused, as if thinking. "Hell, I'm not used to working with guys that have this much power. These surgeons are untouchable. In the eyes of this hospital they can do no wrong. The patients think that, too."

"It's true, Ed. But these men really are the best at what they do," she said.

He shrugged. "Yeah, that's what they tell us. One thing is sure: they don't appreciate the work anyone else does. The only doctors that count in this hospital are the surgeons. As for me, it's pretty clear I'm here just to take legal responsibility. They don't really see me as part of the team — particularly Barret. He doesn't even include me in surgical staff meetings."

"Be seen and not heard, right?" Carlsie said.

He nodded. "Exactly."

"He told me that, too," she added.

"He's an ass, Carlsie. I know that now. Of course, a lot of surgeons are."

She was surprised by his blatant expression of hostility, but such feelings weren't unusual in an anesthesiologist. "Why do you stay?" she asked.

He took another bite of his doughnut, then seemed to want to drop the topic. "I didn't mean to unload my problems on you. Pardon me."

She smiled. "I would hardly say you're unloading

on me."

He looked into her eyes for a moment, as if he were considering his next words carefully. "You know, they've never been sued here. Not even once . . . ever."

She was surprised, but wasn't sure what point he was making.

"Don't you think that's a bit strange in this day and age?" he asked. "I mean this is south Florida, the litigation capital of the world."

"Maybe they just do good work."

"Too good, if you ask me."

"How can surgeons do work that is too good?"

"Just look around for a while, Carlsie. See what you think."

It was obvious he was driving at something. "You're confusing me, Ed. What in the world are you talking about?"

He sighed and pushed back his chair. "I've said too much already." He rose. "I've gotta go. We have a lot of cases today . . . and you know how surgeons react when an anesthesiologist slows them down."

She stood with him. "It's not fair to hint around like that and not tell me the story."

He grinned and his mood suddenly seemed to improve. "There's no story, Carlsie, I'm just a grumpy middle-aged anesthesiologist who doesn't like taking orders from surgeons. Forget what I said. Treat it as the ramblings of a madman. These guys are perfect, they never make a mistake, and this is the best place in the world for a woman to bring her breasts. If you have any doubt, look at the stats. Everybody's getting cured."

He limped to the doorway, turned back to her, and smiled. "See you tomorrow? I'm getting used to having breakfast with a smart attractive lady. I enjoy it."

"You know what, Ed? You're a mess. I think you're having a mid-life crisis."

He chuckled. "I'm not having one, I *am* one."

She sat for a while finishing her coffee, wondering what was really bothering him. It probably had to do with exactly what he had referred to—having to take orders from surgeons. She didn't blame him. She would never put up with the treatment anesthesiologists received. They did stressful work and weren't appreciated by the people they had to please: the surgeons. And Grossman was right about surgeons' attitudes toward the slightest delay in anesthesia. One would think it was the end of the world, judging from their reactions to even a ten-minute postponement, and the most vitriolic complaints usually came from the slowest surgeons, the ones who could hold up the O.R. for hours on end because of their lethargic techniques.

She remained puzzled, though, by Grossman's persistent references to how perfect the surgeons of the institute were. She would have guessed an anesthesiologist would love working with surgeons as fast and efficient as these men.

Despite long hours and much effort, learning the

ropes around the hospital was harder than Carlsie had anticipated. For one thing, the setup at the institute was different. The emphasis was not the same as in a teaching hospital. The big push was to handle cases quickly, and without any hint of complications. There were infrequent conferences, no daily teaching rounds, and only occasional lectures aimed at the medical students periodically rotated through the hospital. All instruction was done in the O.R. or at bedside during rounds. Even that was minimal.

Most of what she was learning came from Gordo, who was clearly interested in becoming more than a friend. He'd even chided her on several occasions for working too hard. Evidently, she was making it difficult for him to show her the sights of Palm Beach. He wanted her to spend some time with him, away from the rigors of duty.

The only other teaching of significance was offered by the seductively moody Hank Ritter, who regarded her as an interesting but puzzling curiosity. One afternoon, he invited her to accompany him when he did the first dressing change on a middle-aged lady who had had a mastectomy. In contrast to most surgeons, he insisted the woman's husband remain while the bandages were removed. In this way, he later explained to Carlsie, the ice between the spouses was broken early. The man was forced to cope with what had happened and to see what his wife must deal with. Any misconceptions about the results of the surgery could be corrected, and the husband was encouraged to be a supportive participant instead of an outside observer.

It appeared to Carlsie that Ritter was right. In this case, the husband relaxed visibly as he helped tape the new dressing across his wife's chest, and the amount of eye contact between patient and spouse increased dramatically. This was one of a number of occasions on which Ritter's unusual sensitivity and compassion impressed Carlsie.

In contrast, Walker Barret never volunteered any useful information. He seemed to deliberately ignore her until the day they came into unexpected conflict. That dispute helped Carlsie discover why she had been chosen for the coveted fellowship at the institute despite the competition of scores of equally talented young surgeons. The first hint of the truth was revealed when she survived a major altercation with the chief only a few weeks after her arrival.

Carlsie had done the admission history and physical exam on Mrs. Ann Jacobs. Ann was forty-six, a little on the heavy side, mildly pretty, with a gentle personality. When Carlsie first saw her, the patient's eyes were red and puffy from prolonged crying. Mrs. Jacobs was scheduled for a breast biopsy, and was as frightened as she could be. Tears welled up in her eyes as she listened to Carlsie's explanation of the next day's procedure, and she clenched her teeth to keep from crying again. "Do anything," she said, covering her face with both hands. "Just don't let them cut my breast off. Please don't let them do it." She broke down into uncontrollable sobbing.

Carlsie learned that Ann Jacob's sister, only two

years older, had recently undergone a mastectomy and was presently dying from metastatic cancer of the breast after having gone the whole therapeutic route from radiation to chemotherapy. Ann, being aware of the inherited factor of the disease, was in a state of near hysteria at the prospect of a similar fate. At the moment, her biggest concern was being anesthetized and not knowing what would happen to her.

Carlsie suggested that only a biopsy be performed the next morning and that any further surgery be postponed until the following day, after Ann had had time to learn the results. Based upon her examination, Carlsie was almost certain additional surgery would be necessary. The mass was large, and the overlying skin was dimpled and firmly attached to the tumor which had been growing for three months while the patient had fearfully procrastinated.

Ann Jacobs grasped at the idea as if it were a final reprieve, and profusely thanked the young lady doctor who had given her an extra day's salvation.

This was the way Carlsie believed the problem should be approached anyway. There was no medical data to support immediately following a biopsy by a mastectomy. The procedure could just as easily be done in two stages, and was probably slightly safer that way. There were even a few cases reported of pathologists, under the pressure of making immediate decisions from the frozen-section slides only, misinterpreting the tissue and unnecessarily removing breasts. It was easier to make such an error using rapidly prepared frozen sections than it was when working with permanent slides carefully preserved and treated with helpful diagnostic stains.

But she hadn't anticipated Dr. Barret's reaction, even though the morning she'd first begun seeing patients, Gordo had warned her to do nothing that would impede the rapid flow of surgical cases through the O.R. "Order anything you want, lab work, x-rays, consultations—anything. But never delay surgery. We're an assembly line and anyone who monkeys with the machinery will pay the piper."

It was advice she should have remembered—and didn't. As a consequence she was totally shocked to be paged—"stat"—to the fourth floor. Assuming some sort of emergency was at hand, she rushed up the fire stairs, burst onto the floor, and all but crashed into the back of Walker Barret, chief of staff, as he waited impatiently in front of the nurses' station.

Gordo, in surgical greens, appeared frustrated and thoroughly miserable. He was shaking his head back and forth, his expression quite somber. On the other side of the counter was Ritter, studying a chart, and several unhappy floor nurses, all staring at her in the manner of those about to watch the condemned die. She did not doubt that she had fouled up, but she had no idea how.

Walker Barret proceeded to read her the riot act for interfering with his surgical plans for Ann Jacobs, who was apparently insisting that her surgery be done in accordance with Carlsie's advice instead of as he'd planned.

"Sir, the woman is very frightened." Carlsie didn't intend to argue. She felt he at least needed to know why she had recommended the biopsy be performed separately. His expression immediately told her it was the wrong thing to say.

"What patient facing cancer isn't frightened?" Barret roared. "How could you do such a thing?" He was becoming even more infuriated.

"A lot of surgeons delay the definitive surgery until the day after biopsy," she answered.

Gordo, who was out of Barret's line of sight, grimaced and shook his head while putting a finger to his lips. Ritter, who had been ignoring the scene, now looked up expectantly. The nurses winced.

"Goddamn it!" Barret bellowed. "It is of no concern to me what other surgeons do. We do what is best for our patients, not what is popular in the *Ladies' Home Journal*. I won't put a patient through anesthesia twice. It's an unnecessary risk, and I'm not about to have my decision contested by a damned resident. Do you get my meaning?"

She certainly did. The more he ranted and raved, the more she understood. His earlier warning that junior residents should be seen and not heard was now perfectly clear. The only thing he cared about was his own narrow-minded opinion.

She stood, red-faced with humiliation and anger, as he continued to berate her for meddling with his patients. Finally, he instructed her to inform Mrs. Jacobs that her recommendation had been wrong and should be ignored.

Carlsie's problem now became one of self-control. She was very close to losing it. This pompous, self-righteous old bastard, who had verbally flogged her in public, now wanted her to deny what she knew to be the truth. He wasn't merely asking her to recognize that things were to be done his way and his way only, he actually expected her to concede that her viewpoint was without merit, and to deceive the patient into believing there was no reasonable way to get the job done except his.

She was not going to do it! She would not tell a patient a lie like that. As a matter of fact, she wanted to tell Barret exactly where to put his screwed-up hospital and—

Gordo's horrified expression suddenly came into focus. Even Hank Ritter appeared anxious as he and everyone else stared, in unbelieving amazement, at her. Walker Barret's face had turned white, and the others present sensed that she was about to explode, to lose her cool and spew out venom. Carlsie Camden was on the threshold of blowing it, in the way every surgical resident knows it can be blown.

Scream at the night nurses, if you must.

Become enraged at interns and junior residents, get irritated with younger staff men if you absolutely have to.

But never, never, never, even under the most stressful circumstances, display anything even resembling anger at the chief, not if you are a resident who values your future. To do so is the sweet kiss of death—a swift good-by. Men at the top, like Walker Barret, were known to can residents for clearing their throats in a disapproving way. It was completely unheard of to raise your voice at the chief unless you already had your bags packed and had a confirmed reservation on the next flight out.

Even then it was ill-advised.

Gordo was silently mouthing the word "no!" She knew he also meant *Shut up* and come back to your senses. The price of this rebuttal will be too high. *Do not do it!*

Carlsie struggled to win the battle for self-control. All she had to do was eat a little crow and everything would be fine. Relax and cooperate, she told herself.

It should have been easy.

But not for her.

"I won't do it," she said quietly but firmly. "I'll tell her what your routine is, but I won't deceive her. She has options, and we all know it." Carlsie stood silently before a ticking bomb. Her throat was so dry she couldn't swallow. Gordo was ready to faint. Several of the nurses put their hands to their mouths in shock.

Barret's expression was not easily describable. He had come across a situation for which he had no ready response. Never having faced such a dilemma, he had no plan for dealing with a foolishly resistant trainee. He glanced incredulously at Ritter, as if seeking advice on how to handle the suicidal insubordination of a still-wet-behind-the-ears junior resident.

Everyone assumed he was going to blow her away.

Instead, he simply laughed.

Then he looked at the others and shrugged as if to say I don't believe this is happening. Soon all were chuckling nervously, including Carlsie.

He addressed her in a gentle paternalistic tone. "They told me you had excellent hands, young lady, although no one mentioned your mouth. I wanted a female I could turn into a great surgeon, not a woman telling me how I should do every little thing. I already have a wife to do that. Thank God she doesn't come into the O.R."

Everyone laughed again. Gordo released a deep breath of relief, Ritter turned back to his chart, and the nurses busily exited the scene.

Only Barret remained immobile, curious about the impressive spunk of this young woman. He was glad he had let her off the hook, but he hoped she realized she would get no more such breaks. She had probed beyond the accepted limit. He had liked what he had seen during those fateful seconds. He now knew things about her it sometimes took months to learn about a new resident. He would give her a second chance, because if he was going to waste his time on a female, it might as well be one with guts. Perhaps she was the one in a million who was worthy of the opportunity. Maybe the recommendations from Tulane had been accurate. She might be the one female he had been looking for, the one he could turn into the first truly outstanding woman surgeon. If so, that would be another feather in his cap, another public relations coup to enhance the reputation of the institute.

It was the only challenge he had left. He wanted

his hospital to be more renowned than Mayo, and it took more than good surgery to do that. It took publicity. A beautiful, personable, and exceptionally talented lady surgeon would be good for a lot of publicity.

"Your bite better be as good as your bark," he said quietly to her after the others had drifted away. "If not, you're gone."

Carlsie, who now wished she hadn't been so stubborn, believed him. She knew she had been right, but she also understood she had been lucky. It wasn't until a week later that she really learned why she had gotten away with her insubordination, and what Barret's last comments had meant.

Gordo told her.

Apparently Barret, feeling a need to explain to his colleagues just why he had been so lenient with Carlsie, had hinted to Ritter about his plans for her, if she panned out. Hank had passed the explanation on to Keene who revealed the good news to her. It was a two-edged sword of classical proportions, however. If her technical skills were up to it, then great. If not trouble lay ahead. Everything depended upon the way she used her hands.

Behind the doors of the O.R. that was all that mattered. Surgeons either had good hands or they didn't. Those who didn't were wise to abandon the effort and take a detour into a subspecialty, like orthopedic surgery, urology, or gynecology, where elegance was not a necessity.

Yet there were klutzes who persisted, who blundered on in a general surgical residency, investing

78

year after year in a specialty for which they were poorly equipped. And since Board certification, the single objective criteria by which a surgeon could be judged by the public or by hospital credentials committees, was an intellectual examination process, the most clumsy surgeon in the world could hit the books hard and waltz through the certification process like a whiz kid.

The Board didn't even look at the hands!

But that made no difference in the inner circles. The surgeons knew who was who. It had little to do with Board certification, and they didn't hesitate to talk about it, either. As Carlsie had expected, at the Palm Beach Institute for the Breast, the surgeons were all of the highest level of technical ability, and, as she soon discovered, like all humans who'd reached the top of a pyramid based on skill or talent, they were obsessed with comparisons of their aptitudes. A klutz could last no longer than his first operation. A surgeon without good hands, though merely a resident, was enough to cause apoplexy among a staff driven to probe the outer limits of surgical skills. An unwritten policy of the institute was *no klutzes,* not ever. The recognized corollary of that went something like this: any resident who doesn't quickly demonstrate that he has very good hands must go, and swiftly.

Carlsie's original belief that her application for the training program had been accepted because she was bright, enthusiastic, and a hard worker with a good record turned out to be naíve. She soon realized that the professors who had recommended her to the institute were well aware of the short unhappy stays of less than talented residents, and wouldn't have encouraged her if she hadn't met the institute's unspoken neurosynaptic speed and eyehand coordination standards. When it came right down to it, she had been allowed to come to the institute because she had a reputation for possessing good hands.

Under ordinary circumstances Barret was the first staff surgeon to scrub with the new men — after they had cooled their heels for an appropriate period, of course. He felt it important to evaluate a resident's talents himself. After all, he had the most to lose if a klutz had somehow weaseled in. The clinic was his life, and he was not prepared to allow any erosion of the quality that had lifted it to professional preeminence. Accordingly, his judgments were harsh.

It was to avoid problems at this stage that he had taken over the admissions procedure for incoming residents. He felt it was better to refuse a position initially than to have to call a man's previous chief and explain why his all-star resident was being sent packing after only a few weeks in the institute. A medical school prof could become quite indignant when Barret explained, oh so gently, that Dr. Golden Boy's outstanding research into the micromolecular aspects of surgical wound healing in pregnant ewes didn't alter the fact that his surgical skills resembled those of a brain-damaged orangutan.

In Carlsie's case Barret decided to pass the buck to Ritter. In this way, if she had to go, no one would believe it was the chief's prejudice that had done her in. He was tired of hearing how chauvinistic his attitudes toward female surgeons were. Those accusations were ridiculous. After all, it had been his decision to invite Carlsie to the institute.

So, in due time he sent word down, through channels, that the time had come to get a real good look at this young doctor's ability to handle a blade. The nurses liked her, the patients took to her, her histories and physicals were adequate, and she talked a good line when questioned about her patients or surgery in general. So much for the bullshit. Now everyone was ready to find out whether she was a surgeon or not. It was as simple as that.

Thus, over dinner one night, about two weeks after Carlsie's blow-up with Barret, Gordo informed her that she would be "scrubbing in" the next morning to assist Dr. Ritter with a reduction mammoplasty.

She was ecstatic. The biggest thing she had done in the institute's O.R. so far was hold Ann Jacobs's hand during the induction of anesthesia. And now here was Gordo, adorably handsome Gordo, nonchalantly dropping the bomb between the entrée and dessert. She was actually going to be scrubbing with Ritter — the legendary surgeon of the decade, Dr. H. T. Ritter.

But Carlsie was puzzled as to why Gordo was behaving as if this news were nothing. Didn't he know how ambitious she was, how anxious? And how much this meant to her? Finally getting back into the O.R. would be great relief from the mundane tasks she had been assigned so far, mundane in the way surgeons view medicine; i.e., drudgery being anything not taking place in an operating room or not utilizing hemostats, scalpels, or sutures. To understand surgeons is to realize that the most fascinating medical problem in the world not requiring immediate invasive intervention is of little interest to them, and is usually positioned as far down the totem pole as possible.

At the institute, Carlsie was at the bottom — a position she had not occupied for several years, for she had worked her way up the residency ladder to the point where she'd done a great deal of independent surgery, particularly on late-night emergencies.

Now she was ready once again to start moving up. Before Gordo's casual announcement she had done more histories and physicals on pre-op patients than she had thought possible without getting to actually practice surgery. "I was beginning to doubt I'd ever see the inside of an O.R. again," she said smiling. "This calls for champagne. I'm buying."

Gordo nodded in approval, all the while wondering if she understood the real reason she was being brought to the O.R. She didn't seem nervous enough about it, but he certainly didn't want to enlighten her and dampen her enthusiasm, or perhaps shatter the excellent mood she was in on that particular evening. The night was young and all sorts of appealing possibilities lay ahead.

More than anyone at the hospital, he wanted her to do well—and not just because of professional concern. He didn't want her to leave Palm Beach prematurely. He was, in a word, infatuated with her.

Beauty, charm, intelligence—she had everything he desired in a woman. Not to mention her body: a graceful, elegant form which moved in a way that absolutely captivated him. She was feline, mysterious, cool, soft, yet seemingly charged with an energy aching to be unleashed. He daydreamed about her and nightdreamed, too. He desired her, and he wanted their coming together to be just right.

For the first time in years he found himself making cautious moves with a woman. He wasn't about to risk blowing it. For once, it mattered. This was not another cute nurse to be enjoyed at leisure. This was a special woman, a female whose image haunted him, whose smile brought him sensations of carefree joy; a sexual creature who caused stirrings in his groin and fire in his heart.

She was a new experience for him, a man usually very much in control. Until Carlsie had come along, it had always been the ladies who'd heated up first. He had been perpetually calm, enjoying and loving them, and never experiencing rejection anxiety. It had never mattered if occasionally a woman didn't want him; there were so many others available, so many luscious bodies, willing bodies. But now it was a particular body that he badly desired. No one else's would do, and it was more than just physical. He wanted her attention, her laughter, her inner

83

thoughts. He wanted all of her. It had crossed his mind that Carlsie might possibly be the perfect woman: the female for whom he had searched all his life.

The champagne arrived and he poured. "To you," he said, lifting his glass. "To your success."

She sipped the wine. "And to you," she toasted, then thought for a moment and added, "To us." She enjoyed Gordo. He was becoming a very good friend. They worked closely, dined together frequently, and enjoyed the night life of Palm Beach whenever possible. In addition, from his Mako outboard, he had introduced her to ocean fishing and snorkling. She loved it all, and was growing to trust him. Gordo was easy and entertaining, not an egotist like so many men in their profession. He told stories with college-boy bravado and eagerness, and enjoyed laughing at himself and the situations he had been swept into throughout the years. He spawned a sense of gaiety in her—that was refreshing—and she appreciated his adoring gaze and unhidden willingness to let feelings be known.

Later that evening, on the balcony of his apartment they watched the moon rise over the ocean. Carlsie's responsibilities seemed far away, and it felt good to be securely held in his arms. As a cool breeze blew in, she snuggled close to him. He brought her body into a full embrace and surprised her with a kiss.

Then, turning her so the moonlight illuminated her face, he gazed at her for a long while. "You're too gorgeous to be a doctor," he said softly.

"Why do you say that?"

"I've never wanted to make love to a surgeon before." He kissed her again, letting one hand slip down across her hips onto her thigh while the other came up beside her breast. She could feel his hardness against her.

She put a finger to his lips, blocking another kiss, and reached for her glass of wine, pulling slightly away from him in the process.

She wasn't ready for this yet, not ready to make love to him. Although he was handsome and appealing, and was a surfer girl's dream just like the nurses said, she still saw him as more of a friend.

Gordo, surprised at being turned down, accepted it gracefully. There was no need to rush. He was confident that he would eventually be her lover, and when the time came he was going to love her with style — romantically, and at just the perfect moment. The way a woman like Carlsie deserved to be loved.

He could be patient. Some things were worth waiting for, and this lady surgeon with the intriguing green eyes was definitely one of them. He prayed that tomorrow she would pass her test.

Chapter Five

Carlsie practically waltzed into the surgical suite the next morning, more than an hour early. At long last she was to be allowed to take the measure of one of these great surgeons. The talking was over. The façade was to be peeled away. Soon she would know whether they put on their pants one leg at a time or if the myths and reputations enveloping them had a basis.

While waiting for everyone else to arrive, she had a cup of coffee in the surgeon's lounge. It was the nicest of many such rooms she had seen over the years. A picture window overlooked the intracoastal waterway on which two large yachts were slowly moving away from a nearby marina.

Without warning the surgeon's dressing-room door opened and from it emerged one of the biggest, fattest doctors she had ever seen. Middle-aged, with curly red hair, he was clad only in jockey shorts, shoes, and socks. He fit Gordo's description of Dr. Fulton Greer, a staff surgeon who had been vacationing since her arrival.

Before she could speak, he had taken several steps toward the coffee pot. Suddenly catching a glimpse of her, he whirled his corpulent, quite hairy and almost nude body about and stared at her in startled disbelief before hightailing it back to the dressing room with all the grace of a bowl full of jelly.

"This lounge is for surgeons only!" he bellowed angrily as he disappeared.

"I am a surgeon!" Carlsie yelled, struggling not to laugh at the comic entrance and expedited exit of the funny-looking man.

"Like hell you are!" she heard him roar from somewhere beyond; then all became silent.

Shortly, Val Ryan; the chief nurse and supervisor of the surgical suite, appeared in the doorway. She was wearing a grin as broad as her face. "I hear you've met Dr. Greer," she said.

"Not for long. He left as quickly as he came. He was wearing some cute little B.V.D.s."

Val Ryan chuckled, then told her about Greer — a quite capable surgeon with a blustery sarcastic attitude that belied his benevolent warm-hearted nature. Predictably, he was also a much-respected gourmet cook whose dinner invitations were highly coveted. "He's out there raising Cain about this, claiming that surgeon or not, no woman is allowed in this lounge," Val said. "I told him he was full of bull. A surgeon is a surgeon. The way I see it you can even use their locker room if you want to."

Carlsie smiled. "I think I'll dress with the nurses. No point in pushing my luck."

Val agreed, but admitted she didn't hold the doctors in as much reverence as most of the institute's nurses did. "I've been through it with these guys, Carlsie. They're more hot air than everyone knows. I'm gonna be the first person to laugh when one of them falls on his ass." She paused for effect. "And believe me, one will fall . . . you can take my word on it. Egos that big aren't foolproof."

Carlsie liked Val, in a way. Although she found her too cynical about the institute's patients and the way surgery was practiced there — an attitude Carlsie attributed to the fact that Ryan had undergone a mastectomy herself a few years earlier — Val did a good job. She was one of those very efficient, strong-willed but flexible, boss-type nurses: pleasant yet tough enough to handle a truculent surgeon, and very perceptive about the psychosocial interactions that occurred in the operating room.

The biggest problems nurses like Val Ryan dealt with were usually not medical. More often than not they were social: temper tantrums of surgeons, angry hurt feelings of nurses, and the barely hidden sexual currents running between the same two groups.

It was all part of the unique junglelike O.R. subculture that fascinated Carlsie and made her love the surgical suite environment. Of course she was an anomaly in the system, being on the wrong side of the gender line, but surgery was where she was happiest. Now, after years of training and what seemed to be centuries of drudgery, she was about to work alongside the best of the breed. She was exactly where she had dreamed of being. Home at last.

Scrubbing with Ritter was her first real interaction with him, one on one. Prior to that they had only exchanged casual greetings and made contact on rounds, in a group. Actually not a word had passed between them that was not professional. He seemed to be an intent, dedicated man, and there was another aspect to him Carlsie found intriguing. He was not married, had never been; and there was no local girlfriend that anyone was aware of, although he was sometimes visited by a longtime female friend who flew in from Texas for the weekend. Carlsie wondered why a man so attractive and eligible had remained for so long a rolling stone.

On that early summer morning, as she waited for the first time across the operating table from Ritter while he marked the sites of his incisions, she thought of him not as an interesting male but as a surgeon. What she observed when he began to operate met her expectations and exceeded them. Everything Gordo and the others had said about Hank was absolutely true.

He had a grace of movement and a skill unmatched by anyone she had seen. He was not merely more talented than others, he was vastly superior. Only another surgeon could appreciate the fineness of his coordination, the elegance of his hand control. His speed was exceptional, his technique impeccable, his precision nearly perfect. He wasted no motion, stressed no tissues, and handled human flesh with a very delicate touch.

Hank Ritter had hands made for surgery. Surprisingly big and strong, they were nevertheless capable of supreme gentleness. If excellent surgeons have "good hands," his were "extraordinary."

Even more impressive than his technical skills was his judgment of space and shape. He was an artist in a surgical medium. His sense of proportion and symmetry was highly developed, and his intuitive understanding of spatial geometry guided his movements in wondrous ways. He began with two grotesquely huge pendulous breasts and painstakingly reduced them to perfectly balanced, still large, but now attractive organs.

Through it all he remained silent, his concentration unbroken until the final stitch was placed. Then, momentarily drained of energy, he glanced up from his patient for the first time and looked at Carlsie. She felt his exhaustion and also his pride. He resembled a great athlete after an outstanding performance. The accomplishment spoke for itself, so Carlsie said nothing. No praise could have communicated her admiration or her unbounded respect.

She met his gaze and nodded, in awe. He had without fanfare done what no doctor had ever done better. At that moment she understood the enormity of his talent. There was no one in the world who could touch him. In a universe of surgeons he stood alone, at the top. To her, he was beautiful . . . a shooting star.

He relaxed for a minute or so in the limelight of her appraisal before silently leaving the room. After he was gone, the quiet spell was broken as the others began to chatter and move about while preparing the patient for transport to the recovery room.

But Carlsie's attitude toward Ritter and his art had been forever changed. She had experienced for the first time in her life the inspiration of being near greatness.

Before the morning was over he had duplicated his achievement with two more cases. One was a reconstruction mammoplasty on a fifty-two-year-old victim of an old-fashioned radical mastectomy done several years earlier in Tennessee, and the other was a simple augmentation mammoplasty on a young Palm Beach woman. His style and abilities continued to overwhelm Carlsie, who complimented him only with her eyes. It seemed vulgar to attempt it in any other way. No words imparted enough meaning to express what she felt.

After a quick lunch they went back to work and he conversed with Carlsie while they both scrubbed outside the O.R. He was clearly warming up to her, but the discussion remained strictly medical.

"I'd like to hogtie the surgeon who did the radical on that first case," he said with obvious disdain. "There is no reason to do that operation. None at all. What do they say about that in New Orleans?"

She told him she had been taught to do modified radicals only, leaving the pectoralis major muscle to prepare for a reconstruction later. On this subject, Carlsie had strong convictions. To her, the modified procedure was the only reasonable operation. Statistics had proven that survival was not improved by doing the more mutilating surgery. Still, many surgeons persisted in doing the more extensive procedure—either from stupidity or stubborness. Maybe a little of both. Carlsie regarded this as a particularly cruel form of incompetence.

"Some surgeons don't care, Carlsie." Ritter started into the O.R. ahead of her. "Someone needs to kick their butts—tell them what life's about, make them understand what they're doing to these women and how much needless suffering they cause by refusing to change their ways." The strength of his statement pleased her, as did his willingness to allow her a glimpse of his feelings.

She assisted him in two more augmentations, during which no conversation took place, and then scrubbed to help him on a simple breast biopsy. The patient was Melissa Bates, age twenty-six, a lawyer from Mobile, Alabama, who had just passed her bar exam a week earlier. She almost certainly did not have cancer. The mass was small, freely movable, and mildly tender. Carlsie had examined the girl the night before and had enjoyed her happy personality. Bates was engaged to a malpractice attorney who had flown in that morning to be with her for the minor surgery.

After the usual prep and draping procedure, Ritter and Carlsie reexamined the lump. Then he offered her the scalpel. "Let's see if you learned anything today," he said. "Give me a one-inch periareolar incision at about nine o'clock. Don't go any deeper than the skin."

Caught off guard by the unexpected invitation, she hesitated momentarily, so he pulled back the blade and started to do it himself. "You'll never learn a thing by just watching, Carlsie."

Her mind raced along, putting this unexpected offer into context. So this is the test, she thought. Although she had known all along one would eventually come, it surprised her to encounter it on this first day in the O.R. She suddenly felt quite nervous, which was ridiculous. She had done dozens of breast biopsies. This was a nothing operation. She couldn't choke now. No guts, no glory. The room had grown very quiet, the others were paying close attention to the discussion. She glanced at Ed Grossman who was giving the anesthetic. He gave her a thumbs-up sign.

"Wait," she said softly, holding out her open hand. Without comment Ritter placed the handle of the scalpel gently into her palm.

"Sponge please," she said to her scrub nurse, who responded quickly. When Carlsie was ready, she plunged the blade carefully into the incision site and extended the cut one inch around the areola. Without hesitation, she deepened the wound and palpated the mass she was seeking.

"Pickups," she said, and was given the instrument with which she grasped the tumor.

"Scissors." She deftly cut the small lump away from the breast, and placed it on the instrument tray, where she incised it and inspected its interior. Ritter studied the tissue with her.

"Looks benign," she commented.

"I gave up trying to second-guess pathologists years ago, Carlsie," Ritter said quietly. "If you jump to conclusions before you hear the report, you're going to be disappointed more often than you think." He passed the specimen off to Val Ryan, who departed for the lab.

After using the cautery to coagulate a few small, bleeding vessels, she received sutures from the nurse and placed three stitches deep in the wound. Then she began to approximate the skin edges with a delicate subcuticular running stitch.

Ritter disagreed with her plan of wound closure. "I prefer interrupted stitches on the skin near the nipples. They have less tendency to distort the areola."

She modified what she had done to meet his request, and several minutes later was ready to place a dressing on the closed incision.

Without a word, Ritter removed his gown and gloves, and started out the door. He had given no indication as to whether she had pleased him or horrified him. He seemed bored with it all.

When he was gone, she glanced at the scrub nurse who shrugged. Carlsie figured he must not have cared for her work, then decided it couldn't have been too bad because he'd allowed her to complete it. She was disappointed, however, by his lack of interest.

A few moments later, Ritter stuck his head in the

doorway and reminded them to leave the patient on the table and anesthetized until the Path report on the frozen section came back. Glancing at Carlsie he added, "Not bad work. Not bad at all, for a girl." He winked at her and then disappeared.

She was elated.

Ed Grossman, at the head of the table repeated the words, knowing full well how much they meant to a young resident. " 'Not bad,' " the man said, " 'not bad at all.' "

The scrub nurse corrected him. " 'Not bad for a girl' were his exact words, I believe."

Everyone laughed, and was happy for Carlsie.

A couple of minutes later, a pleased Gordo strolled into the room. "Let's get a look at those hands, Carlsie. Ritter was just telling me about them." He studied her fingers for a moment while she continued to grin. "That's funny," he finally said, with an exaggeratedly puzzled expression. "They don't look like all thumbs to me." He laughed uproariously and quickly exited before she could throw anything at him.

It was a moment of satisfaction for her. One of those rare events in the life of a surgical trainee, being accepted by those above as worthy of attention. Having recognized talent. This was the kind of moment a surgical resident slaves years to experience. In a short burst of glory Carlsie knew, more than ever, that she could really make it if she tried. She still had to pay the price, but the opportunity was hers.

Before the Path report came back, Gordo returned and instructed her to go scrub with Dr. Barret, who needed some help on a particularly tough reduction mammoplasty. He winked at her as she left to make sure she realized the significance of the big man waiting to see her in action now that she had been judged worthy. It was a great personal triumph for her.

It was early evening before Carlsie had finished surgery with Barret and joined Gordo and several nurses making late rounds on the post-op patients of that day. As the group moved slowly from room to room examining dressings, checking vital signs, and assessing each patient's general condition, she felt really good about herself. It was a day of achievement and she was feeling satisfied, professionally proud. When they neared Melissa Bates's room, her euphoria ended.

A distraught young man, Melissa's fiancé, came out to meet them. "I can't get her to talk to me," he said pathetically. "She just lies there staring at the ceiling. She won't let me help."

Gordo nodded and stepped toward the door. "That's not unusual. Give her a little time. A terrible thing that has happened to her."

Carlsie's stomach knotted. It couldn't be true. She grabbed Gordo's arm to gain his attention. He understood from her bewildered expression what she was asking.

He grimaced and nodded. "We got the word after you left. I thought you had heard. Hank did a mastectomy."

Deep within Carlsie, a silent scream began. "No," she said softly. "I don't believe you." She experienced a strong compulsion to avoid going in to Bates's room. It reminded her of the desire to flee that had overcome her upon first viewing her brother's closed coffin the day it arrived from southeast Asia.

Gordo gave her a quick what-the-hell-do-you-think-you're-doing type glare that told her to get control of herself, she was facing someone associated with the patient's family.

The chief resident went into the room and Carlsie reluctantly followed. Melissa Bates lay on her bed, staring icily toward them. A huge dressing covered the right side of her chest.

This girl didn't have cancer, Carlsie thought, she couldn't have.

But the evidence was there. An angry, hostile young woman, a frightened, bewildered fiancé, and the physical reality of what had been done. It was the worst moment of Carlsie's career. She could do nothing other than look back into the eyes of that terrified and shattered girl.

Carlsie had a premonition that there were going to be many patients like this one.

Chapter Six

The next afternoon, between surgical cases, Carlsie slipped down to the pathology department. The tech in the histology section, although reluctant, was persuaded to let her examine the just-completed permanent slides of Melissa's tumor.

The tissue was unremarkable in its malignant characteristics. It was the sort of cancer specimen she had looked at many times during her rotations on pathology in early residency.

As she was replacing the slides in the little box in which they were stored, Oscar Mendel came into the room. He was obviously surprised to see her. "What are you doing?" he asked.

She told him.

He did not hide his irritation. "You should have checked with me first. A resident owes a staff physician at least that much courtesy."

She was surprised that he was offended. "I will next time. I didn't realize it was an issue here."

"I don't think there will be a next time," he declared. "I don't intend to work with rude, pushy residents."

Now she was offended. "Dr. Mendel, I hardly think looking at the slides of a patient I'm taking care of qualifies as being rude and pushy."

"I'm not concerned with what you think, Camden, and I'll appreciate it if you do not interfere with the duties of my personnel again. We are short-handed and too busy."

"In that case, how do I see the slides of my patients?"

"With an attitude like yours, you don't. Simple enough? You stay upstairs and help with surgery as you're supposed to do, and you leave the pathology to us, okay?"

Carlsie tried to be polite. "That doesn't seem fair. I'm here for the education. I would really like to see the slides of the tissue we are removing. I could do it at any time convenient for the lab."

Mendel's expression didn't change. "I'll take your opinion under advisement. In the meantime, the door is right over there."

Realizing the futility of pursuing the issue, Carlsie thanked the distraught tech for her help and departed as he had suggested. As she was leaving she could hear Mendel berating his employee for participating in the episode. It was clear the chief of pathology was not willing to assist in the study Carlsie had hoped to carry out. As a matter of fact he had confirmed her earlier opinion that he was callous. She found it hard to believe that he was entrusted with such important medical functions.

Oscar Mendel strode silently, angrily, through the large laboratory, glancing neither left nor right. None of the technicians looked up from their work or greeted him. As a matter of fact, they appeared more busy than usual, having no desire to be noticed by their chief. His attention was always unwelcome when he was irritated or in a bad mood. Sharp disciplinary action or even abrupt dismissal was not unheard of at such times.

Mendel understood this, and took pride in the busy, efficient atmosphere of his domain. It was a source of satisfaction to him that his lab produced more work with greater reliability, though using fewer personnel, than any other of which he was aware.

He knew why.

Discipline. It was all a matter of leadership and strict discipline. If he had his way the entire hospital would be administered in the same manner. He couldn't understand why the casual and sloppy workmanship he observed in the wards and in the other departments was allowed to continue. It was a disgrace.

He opened the double locks and entered his private office. After swallowing two codeine tablets to forestall the headache this kind of stress usually brought on, he methodically filled his pipe and lit it. Smoking was the one vice he allowed himself. The pipe was a habit he'd picked up in Korea during the long, cold nights of waiting for the Chinks to come rushing suicidally through the underbrush, charging like madmen despite the fierce firepower of his platoon, which mowed them down by the hundreds. He had bitter memories of those months. The yellow bastards had been drugged, he was sure of that. How else could they have come on so insanely, howling and screaming, wild-eyed with fear and rage. They were more like animals than men. He remembered being splattered by the blood of one he'd shot in the face as the man had leaped toward him bellowing some oriental curse.

On this day, though, Mendel didn't dwell on the war. He only pondered this woman, this Dr. Camden. What an irritating bitch she was. He could remember a time not long ago when something like this would have been unthinkable. Residents had known their place. They'd respected the senior men. In those days a trainee would have never dreamed of coming into his lab without first seeking permission—doing so was a well-established courtesy.

And as for women . . . they had also known their place. And it wasn't in the role of a physician. It was in more appropriate occupations, the ones God had intended them to pursue. The whole problem with females today was disgusting, but like every other problem of this so-called modern society no one wanted to do anything about it. But not him. He was doing everything he could to make his feelings on the issue clear. The problem was, no one else seemed to care. It was a pathetic situation.

At times it seemed to Mendel that he was the only person willing to do anything about it. Clearly, somebody had to.

That night Mendel awoke in the predawn darkness of his bedroom, as he always did after the dream. He felt frightened, yet exhilarated. It was as if he had actually been there again, living through the hell of his childhood, fighting for survival, struggling to be accepted as the talented boy he was.

Yet his efforts had been of little use. The nuns never recognized his genius. They were hateful, spiteful women. The deserved what had been done and even more. They were false servants, selfish and irreverent, using the holiness of the church for their own aggrandizement and financial support. They were not what they presumed to be. Wearing cloaks of innocence, they came slithering into the world, sucking up the protection and honor mistakenly accorded them by good and noble men.

The dream was always the same. It was as if he were outside himself, watching the events, hoping they would treat him differently, more fairly. They never did, and they always received their just reward—always. Just as they had on that night so many years ago. . . .

The solemn fourteen-year-old boy walked ever so slowly into the empty classroom.

"And what is your penance?" the stern-faced nun asked.

The boy did not answer.

"Answer me, Oscar! What is your penance?

Tell me or go back to confession for disrespect. And mind you, be honest."

Sister Elena stared piercingly at the boy who so often disrupted her classes. She was determined to force him to conform to the orderly conduct acceptable in the Catholic orphanage.

The boy answered belligerently, never making eye contact with her. "Father said twenty-five Hail Marys and . . ." His voice trailed off as it became difficult for him to speak.

"And what, Oscar? Speak up!"

"And that I must apologize to you," he said coldly.

"I see. Well, let's have it. What do you have to say about your meanness in class?" She planted her hands authoritatively upon her hips.

Silence . . . moments passed . . . still silence.

She would defeat this young troublemaker. She would wait until he complied.

More silence.

The boy remained obstinately quiet, stone faced. She grew impatient.

"All right, Oscar. If you are unable to speak, write out the apology and the Hail Marys." She pushed the lad into a chair and slapped paper and pencil in front of him. "Write! You have an hour."

Slowly, spitefully, he began. The hour passed with only eight lines completed. The sister had reached the end of her tolerance. She grabbed the paper and read the shocking words written by this incorrigibly irreverent child.

Hail Mary, full of grace,
The Lord is with thee.
Blessed art thou among women.
Hail Mary, Mother of God.

Hail Elena, full of hate,
The demons are with thee.
Evil art thou among women.
Hail evil Elena, whore of Satan.

Sister Elena screamed in horror. "You bad boy!" she shrieked, red with rage. Trembling, she pulled him, by the hair, to a standing position. "You'll go into seclusion for twenty-four hours or as long as it takes, without food and water. Do you hear me? . . . fasting and prayer. Pray for help, and when you are ready, you'll go to confession again." The nun closed her eyes briefly, crossed herself, and then led the silent, unremorseful boy to his room for solitary confinement.

"You had better be ready to make restitution when you are finished praying," she said loudly, and forcefully closed the door. "God help you, Oscar." She locked him in.

The boy lay awake until after 2:00 A.M., waiting for the last sister to make night rounds. "Meanness," he muttered as he went to his closet. "They will find out what God does

105

to punish meanness." He pulled out the liter canister of alcohol he'd taken from science class, retrieved the matches from their hiding place, and opened his bedroom window.

At first there was only the constant, pale blue-white flame of the burning alcohol. Then, in an explosive burst, rampant fire consumed the chapel bench that had served as its kindling. Oscar watched with delight long enough to see the drapes and altar come alive with dancing waves of fire that raced upward to engulf the giant crucifix hanging above.

Later, there were sirens and screaming and flames against the dark night sky. Amid the pain and destruction, Oscar felt more complete than ever before.

Justice had been done, and certain persons would never bother him again.

Mendel went downstairs and poured himself a glass of sherry. He needed to relax. The dream always left him unsettled. The fire at the orphanage had clearly been a turning point for him. In a way it had been a terrible thing he had done. But the system that allowed the abuse he'd suffered had clearly needed punishment. He was merely the instrument that had carried it out. The act had marked his emergence from childhood into being a man of courage — a man of action.

Chapter Seven

The fate of Melissa Bates affected Carlsie immensely. She couldn't get it out of her mind. Each afternoon she visited this patient, for more time than she should have taken from her other duties, and the two became friends. Initially she was quite impressed by the personal resilience the young lawyer displayed in adapting to her situation. Carlsie even commented to Ritter on how beautifully Melissa was doing. He saw it differently.

"She's not adapting, she's compartmentalizing," he said. "It's a modified form of denial. Melissa's acting like this is no big deal, and she can just bounce back and forget it ever happened." He shook his head slowly and his compelling brown eyes gazed into hers. "It doesn't work that way, Carlsie. She has to face the horror of this sometime. I always think it's better to do it immediately, get it over with. I don't like it when a patient acts too brave. That can lead to psychological trouble further down the road."

Carlsie wasn't so sure. "Maybe she's one of those

women who are mature enough to realize that she can lead a normal life, that this is really only a cosmetic problem."

Hank frowned slightly. "You don't really believe that, do you? Think about it. A young pretty girl, about to get married, shrugging this off like it was a minor thing? Don't kid yourself. This girl has got to be devastated. It's tearing her apart, I guarantee it."

She sipped her coffee and thought about what he was saying while he continued.

"Do you know why you want to believe she's adapting so nicely and this is all going to work out fine for her?"

"No. I guess not."

He smiled gently. "It's a defense mechanism. You don't want and to have to share her pain. You want to avoid the discomfort of watching her suffer because of what we've done. It's a hell of a lot easier for us to let ourselves believe she's doing great than it is to see her true agony . . . to have to experience it with her."

He let that sink in, then went on. "It's human nature to look away from things that are unpleasant. We don't want to be part of anything miserable. But that's our job now, Carlsie. We have to share her pain. If we don't, who will? Nobody, that's who. It's not right for us to turn our back on her now and allow her to deny all this. If we call ourselves doctors, then we have to be doctors. We have to help her whole being, not just whittle away the parts of her that are cancerous and let it go at that. The hardest part of being a good surgeon is taking care of the spirit. Any hack can learn to cut and sew. It takes a doctor to help the inner wounds heal."

Throughout her training, Carlsie had heard such statements, but always in philosophical or theoretical contexts. She had never seen this approach practiced.

But Ritter spent as much time with Melissa as he could, encouraging her to talk. He tried to bring out every fear she could express — loss of femininity, unattractiveness, what changes in sex would occur, and similar causes of anxiety. He and Carlsie worked together, along with the floor nurses, to give Melissa Bates an opportunity to work through the initial stages of her grief without resorting to denial.

As her façade of strength came down, Melissa's mood deteriorated. She cried and became depressed, but only temporarily. By the end of the week she had begun to accept what life was going to be like for her.

Only after Hank was sure that her adaptive processes were functioning well did he discuss breast reconstruction with her. He showed her before and after pictures of some of his other young patients and assured her that she could depend on a reasonable, though not perfect, replacement for what she had lost.

Melissa's wound healed rapidly, and soon she was ready to make the journey home. She seemed anxious to begin to practice law with the large firm she was joining, and had made a number of major decisions about the direction of her future.

"I've called off the wedding," she told Carlsie the day she departed. "I just don't think it's fair to Andy, now that all this has happened."

"Oh, no! I'm so sorry, Melissa."

"Don't be." The young woman's brave smile could not hide her misty eyes.

Carlsie understood her anguish. Melissa's fiancé had disappointed everyone by not remaining with her during the first few days of her convalescence. Hank had foreseen trouble when the man had departed so quickly. He had hoped to have more time to explain the surgery available to Melissa in the future. But her fiancé's rapid departure, though explained on the basis of business demands, had seemed prophetic.

"Don't you think he will eventually understand?" Carlsie asked. "This shouldn't stand in the way of real love. You two are such a good match."

Melissa shook her head. "I can't go through with it. I feel I would be cheating him. Like I'm damaged merchandise or something." She wiped away tears. "Maybe in a year, after I've had my breast reconstruction, if he's still around. I'll see. I just have to wait. I can't spend my life wondering if he married me out of obligation or if he loves me as I am — I mean the way I really am now.

Carlsie put her arms around her new friend, and hugged her hard. "Stay in touch with me, okay? The next time I'm driving to New Orleans I'll come see you, all right?"

"I want you to. We'll have a lot to talk about. I'm sure by then everything will have worked out."

Carlsie nodded.

"I really appreciate everything you've done. I hope you know that," Melissa declared.

"You deserve it."

Melissa hesitated, then said, "There is still something I need to tell you. I don't want you to think this is more denial, because it's not. And it's not because I don't trust the doctors or anything like that, because I do."

"What is it Melissa?" Carlsie became uneasy.

"Well, I think I've honestly faced this, and I'm getting it worked out. But you know, Carlsie, way down deep — I mean at the very center of my soul — I still have a hard time believing I had cancer." She gazed pensively at her friend. "I'm sorry. I just don't believe it."

Carlsie could think of nothing appropriate to say.

Melissa shrugged. "I'll get over it, though. I'm tough."

An awkwardness having come between them, they broke off eye contact and walked together out to the nurses' station, where Melissa busied herself thanking the nurses for the care they had given her.

Carlsie had been caught off-guard by the frankness of Melissa's statement, but she was not surprised by the meaning of it. She had not yet eradicated her own feeling that the surgery had been a mistake.

With this unpleasant thought on her mind, Carlsie struggled to keep smiling as Melissa's good-

111

bys were said. This courageous young lawyer is still quite an attractive girl, she thought. With her temporary prosthesis in place, she looked as pretty as she did the day they first met.

Having a few minutes to spare before she was needed in surgery, Carlsie accompanied Melissa to the car waiting at the side entrance of the hospital, and gave her a final good-by hug. Feeling a little sad, she watched the cab disappear around the corner, then turned back to reenter the building. As she did, she happened to glance upward and caught a glimpse of Oscar Mendel watching the the scene from a second-story window. It was an odd moment, and caused her to shudder involuntarily. He withdrew immediately, leaving her with thoughts of what a weird man he was. His persistent spying on her was irritating. She never knew when he'd be watching. She wondered how often she had been observed by this creep and been unaware of it.

That evening, after a late dinner of Thai food, she told Gordo all about Melissa. He couldn't understand Carlsie's continued reluctance to believe what the biopsy had shown, and became annoyed with her for raising such a troublesome issue.

"Look," he said finally, "why don't you examine the slides yourself? Maybe that'll convince you. You can't go on like this. It's irrational."

"I have look at them Gordo. I did that the next day. I even had Mendel on my back about it."

"Nothing Mendel does surprises me. So what did

112

you see?"

"Aberrant cells, abnormal nuclei, strange cellular structures. Everything you are supposed to see in malignant tissue."

"Well?" he said expectantly.

"Well what?"

"Well, what the hell did you think about that?"

She sighed. "I think it shows she has cancer. That's not the point, though. If you would listen to me, you would understand that intellectually I'm not denying she had it. My problem is that something inside me keeps saying she didn't. My guts disagree, Gordo, not my brain."

He frowned unsympathetically. "So why don't you tell your guts to talk a walk? You can't practice medicine that way."

His lack of understanding hurt her feelings, but she tried not to overreact because it was the only rational position he could take. Did she expect him to jump to the conclusion that a mistake had been made because she didn't feel right about the operation?

She finally broke the silence. "Gordo, do you think it's possible something is wrong? We hang a diagnosis of cancer on an awful lot of young girls." She was thinking of the young women she was seeing in the outpatient clinic, those returning for follow-up visits because of previous malignancies. She had quietly pulled a few records, and had been surprised at the incidence of youthful cancer victims.

Gordo was startled by the question. "What in the world would make you think that?"

She told him about her observations and the charts, and expected him to be interested and concerned. Instead he reacted with irritation. "What do you think you're going to accomplish doing things like that?" he asked.

"I'm just curious as to why so many mastectomies are done here."

"Are you kidding? That's our specialty. We do the mastectomies because the women have cancer."

She wished she had not brought up the subject. "I merely asked a question, Gordo, that's all."

"I know you did," he responded, an edge of sarcasm in his voice, "but what the hell kind of question was it? I don't think it's very smart for a junior resident to be snooping around, jousting with imaginary windmills." He looked away.

She didn't respond, and after a pause he turned back toward her. "There's nothing wrong here, Carlsie. This is the finest breast hospital in the country, and you know it. You could get your sweet little body in trouble with talk like that. I hope you haven't mentioned this to anyone else."

She stared at him in amazement. She couldn't believe he was taking such a defensive, hostile attitude to her perfectly sincere concern. He had no right to imply that she was rabble-rousing when she was merely posing a legitimate question. "I have not discussed this with anyone else, Gordo."

"Good," he replied. "I wouldn't if I were you. All we need is for you to open your mouth to the wrong person; then we'd really have trouble. The papers would love that one. Walker Barret would fire us all."

His barb found it's mark. How can he be doing this? she thought. "I would like to go home," she said quietly, then went to the ladies' room. She wished she could leave via the window and not face him again.

He was waiting at the door when she finally came out. He seemed to regret his rather hostile comments, and tried to apologize while driving her home. He took a philosophic view of the whole matter, and rambled on about the vulnerability of surgical residents and the dangers of even suggesting that unnecessary surgery had been done. "You and I could be gone in a flash if Walker Barret wanted it. Do you know what it does to a surgeon's career to be kicked out of a program?" he asked.

"That's not the point, Gordo. I'm talking about the possibility of healthy girls being mutilated for no reason. That has nothing to do with anyone's career. It's our obligation to look into it if the stats here are worse then everywhere else. Even one wrong case is one too many."

His voice rose again. "Get off it, Carlsie! It's suicidal to talk like that. Crazy! Ridiculous! Think about where you are. This isn't some Podnuk hospital. This is one of the most famous places in the country. Barret could sue you for slander for just thinking something like this. You would never get out of hock."

They drove along silently for a while. She couldn't understand why he was focusing only on what would happen if her suspicions became

115

known, not showing the slightest concern that she might be right. She had hoped he would help her review more statistics. She told him so.

"Are you kidding?" he practically yelled. "Do I look insane? You know how many years I've invested in this program. Why in the hell, just a few months before I'm a free man, would I want to take a chance on screwing myself up?"

"Because," Carlsie replied bitterly, "women's lives are at stake. Or doesn't that matter to you?"

He parked at the curb in front of her apartment, and spoke more quietly than before. "I'll tell you what's important to me, Carlsie. Finishing up this goddamn lifetime of medical education I've been going through, and finally getting out there where I can earn some decent money before the whole stupid system collapses into a socialized mess."

"So money is all you care about. Who cares if an occasional patient gets the shaft, right?"

He glared at her, fiercely. "Wrong again, Carlsie! We all care about the patients. But it won't do a single patient any good for some green-ass resident to cause an uproar over nothing—absolutely nothing!"

"What if I'm right?" She stared at him intently.

"There are too many safeguards in the system. It couldn't happen."

"But what if it has?"

"It hasn't! The pathologist double-checks the frozen sections by looking at the permanent slides the next day. If a mistake were made it would be obvious immediately. Once in a blue moon that happens

116

in some hick hospital, maybe. Never here."

"Who double-checks the pathologist?"

"Get off it, Carlsie. You're barking up the wrong tree. Don't cause trouble for yourself."

"And don't cause trouble for you either, right?" She was furious. "We don't want to risk you not making a million next year, do we?"

He smiled sardonically. "That's right. So whatever stupid ideas you have in that hard-headed Cajun brain of yours, leave me the hell out of it."

At that moment she hated him, despised him, for his callousness about her feelings and concerns, especially since she had thought they were starting to get close to each other.

"You're an asshole, Gordo. A perfectly round asshole." Her disappointment in him was shattering. Gordo had become important to her. She had trusted him, believed in him. How he could say these things to her? She felt betrayed.

He stared at her, seemingly speechless. After a long silence during which his expression softened into benign disbelief, he repeated her insult. "A perfectly round asshole? Perfectly round? . . . How in hell did you come up with that one?" The earliest signs of a smile appeared at the corners of his lips.

A grin slipped uncontrollably onto her face, but she quickly forced it away. She wasn't ready to stop fighting. He was acting like an insensitive jerk, like so many men she had known — Louisiana men. Gordo was supposed to be different. She wasn't going to let him treat her callously and then laugh it off by teasing her about her choice of words.

117

"That's what you're acting like, Gordo. You're a creep."

He emitted a sound that was half-snort, half-laugh. "A creep? Jesus H. Christ! First you call me an asshole, a perfectly round one, no less—whatever the hell that is—and now you say I'm a creep. What's next? I guess you also think I'm a chauvinistic shitbird, right?" He put on one of his million-dollar smiles.

The situation was hopeless. There was no way to stay angry at Gordo when he turned on the charm. He was too cute and too lovable, and besides, it was stupid to be fighting like this. Of course he didn't understand her fears. She had presented them too bluntly, and in a way that was threatening to a man whose life has been dominated by the institute for years. She needed to move more slowly.

"I don't think you're a shitbird. You're only an inconsiderate ass, that's all." Carlsie smiled meekly.

"A perfectly round one?"

"Yes. Perfectly round."

"Are you sure?"

"Perfectly sure."

He nodded and shrugged thoughtfully, as if he were beginning to see her point. "Well, considering everything, I suppose that if I am one I would just as soon be a perfect one. Lord knows I'm not perfect at anything else, especially at handling hard-headed lady surgeons."

She rolled her eyes and looked at him in friendly exasperation. "What am I going to do with you, Gordo? One minute you hurt my feelings, and the

118

next you're trying to make me laugh.

He chuckled and put his arm around her, drawing her close to him. "You must accept my bad parts along with my perfectly perfect parts, which you so colorfully described. Besides, I think there're a few perfect things about you, too. They're not necessarily round, though. More curvilinear."

Blocking a rebuttal, he pulled her to him and kissed her passionately. She returned his embrace, and they lingered together a moment before he walked her to the door.

"Be careful with all this question asking," he warned her gently as she was entering her apartment. "Don't get worked up over a few meaningless numbers. Just remember you're a much better doctor than a detective."

She clucked her tongue disapprovingly. "Don't be so sure."

"How about dinner tomorrow night at my place with candlelight and music?" he asked.

"Sounds like a setup."

"Maybe. Don't you think it's about time?"

She shrugged teasingly. "I'll think about it. Tomorrow is a long way off. I'll have to see what other offers I get."

She kissed him quickly and closed her door.

She thought long and hard about Gordo and herself that next day, and then she had dinner with him.

As he had promised, it was very nice.

Very warm and intimate.

And he was charming and handsome and sexy. She was almost persuaded . . . almost.

Something held her back, though. Something she couldn't quite define. Just a feeling that she couldn't go too far. Her intuition said this was the wrong time, and she listened to it, though that was very, very hard to do.

"You know I'm falling in love with you," Gordo said when he took her home. He was clearly wounded by her reluctance to be physically closer with him.

She nodded.

"Do you feel anything for me at all?" he asked.

"I feel a great deal for you, Gordo. Don't you know how difficult it was for me to keep cool tonight?"

"You made it look easy."

"It was tough." She smiled. "You are a beautiful man."

"I must not have used the right music . . . or maybe my after-shave was wrong."

"No, that wasn't it."

"Was it the meal? That's it; you hate artichokes, right?"

She laughed. "It wasn't the artichokes."

He thought for a moment. "I've got it; you're having your period."

"Gordo! Wash your mouth out with soup!"

"Soup?" he said. "Don't you mean soap?"

She smiled impishly. "Of course not, Gordo. You're not that bad. Soap is a terrible thing to put in someone's mouth."

Now it was his turn to laugh.

She snuggled more closely to him. "I love you too, Gordo, in a special way," she said softly. "I'm just not ready to commit myself yet. For me sex is a kind of commitment. Please understand me."

He hugged her. "I do, and I'll give you time, honey. However long it takes."

He kissed her again, and she returned the kiss enthusiastically.

Chapter Eight

At the Bloody Goose Show-Bar Debbie Hunter cleared the last empty beer mug from the counter, then wiped it down. The last dancer had dressed and gone, and the club was almost empty. The big spenders had picked out girls — mostly the prettier strippers — and had left. Since it was late and Wednesday, with little hope of any additional high-class customers appearing, the rest of the hookers had lowered their prices and taken off with men who had a few bucks to spend and an empty night to kill.

Those customers who remained, mostly loners with nowhere to go and nearly empty pockets, were a diverse lot. An occasional one was young, but that was rare Youth could usually find what it wanted and seldom had to pay. The young ones frequented the club only because they had nothing else to do and wanted to have a drink or two while eyeballing the girls.

On the other hand, almost none of the hangers-on were old. For easily understood reasons most were middle aged, and had a lot in common. They were tired-looking guys who still worked hard and were going nowhere. Usually divorced and with a bad break or two behind them, they worked at the same jobs as the younger ones, but the pride associated with work had long faded. It was one thing to be blue-collar earning seven to eight dollars an hour at age nineteen, quite another at forty-three.

"What time does this place close?" one of these men asked.

Debbie answered without looking up. "Three o'clock. I'm calling for last round right now. You need anything?"

He chuckled lasciviously. "I need something all right, honey. It all depends on the price. You selling any bargains tonight?"

She cast him a disdainful look and moved on down the bar, taking orders from those who still wanted yet another drink and who had the decency not to insult her.

After ringing up the last sales, she slumped beside the register, wishing they would all empty their glasses and take off. It had been a long and grueling night and she was tired. She had only worked this part of the business a couple of weeks, and found it exhausting. She did it for the money. Bartending at the Bloody Goose gave her twice the take-home waitressing did.

She hadn't always had to depend on tips to live, but she did now. The surgery last summer had ended the big bucks she'd earned as a stripper. She missed having the extra cash . . . and she missed the boost to her ego. Despite the negatives of the profession, she had honestly enjoyed the reactions of the men when she'd been a dancer. And had been a good one. Everyone, from the boss on down, agreed on that.

That was over, though. No one wanted to see her naked now. Her chest was too ugly since the mastectomy. She couldn't even put on a novelty act like the fat pigs who danced sometimes, playing it strictly for laughs — and the money, of course. She wouldn't do that even if asked, but it was another insult to her damaged self-esteem to know that nobody would look at her . . . even as a joke.

An old friend came in and took a seat near where she was standing. Despite her fatigue, she smiled. "Long night, Ken? You're in here awful late." It was the first time she had seen him in months.

"Heard you were back, Deb. Where you been all this time? I asked around about you." He gazed warmly at her. "You're looking pretty good . . . a lot better than the last time I laid eyes on you, anyway."

Ken Redman had been one of the few who had visited her while she was still in the hospital. And he had been her only male friend in those first few weeks after she'd gone home. Everyone else had been too embarrassed or too squeamish to come around. Ken had even taken her out a time or two after she had recuperated. Had tried to bed her, too. She had declined. As far as she was concerned, sex was over for her. No way was she going to be an object of pity to a man with whom she had once

125

made love.

They chatted a while about old times, old friends, and all that had happened in the last half-year. He told her he was still working at the hotel where he'd been for almost five years now, and caught her up on the latest gossip around the neighborhood. Just talking with him made her feel better, and when closing time arrived he offered to buy her a drink at an all-night joint not far down the street — one frequented by the workers in the other clubs and restaurants.

She was tempted. She wanted to go with him, to enjoy his company, but her anxieties were still strong. One thing would lead to another and inevitably the moment would arrive when she had to confront her greatest fear. If not tonight, sometime later it would come. There would be a point when he wanted her the way a man wants a woman — and she wasn't ready for that.

"Can't do it, Ken," she said. "I'd like to go, but I gotta say no."

Disappointed, he shrugged. "Someday you're gonna have to rejoin the human race, Debbie," he said. "You're too much woman to let this thing beat you."

"Yeah. I guess so, Ken. It's just hard, that's all."

He nodded in understanding, and she appreciated that. It was nice to have a least one male friend that had some sense of what she'd gone through.

"Tell you what," he said. "A week from Sunday the hotel's giving their big picnic for the employees. Why don't you come with me. We'll have a few

126

beers, some laughs. It'll be a nice afternoon. A real low-key situation . . . no promises, no obligations. What do you say? I'd really like you to go."

She started to shake her head — no — but he stopped her. "Don't give me your answer now. Think about it. I'll be by in a few days, and we can talk about it then."

He slapped down a couple of bucks for his beer, and she pushed it back to him. "You don't pay when I'm selling, Ken. You know that."

He grinned, picked up his glass, and raised it high. "Here's to old times." He winked at her. "And to picnics on Sundays." He finished off the beer.

She watched him go, and wondered about his invitation. Is he right, she thought. Should I make myself go? Am I strong enough to try it again? She didn't know the answer. She only knew she was bitter about it all. Bitter about her cancer, about what the surgeons at the institute had done to her, and about the way she still felt when she looked in the mirror.

How could any man want me? she asked herself, and then contemplated Ken's friendship. She liked him very much, and it wasn't hard to remember happy moments with him. But they were in the past, in the days before her surgical cure . . . the days when she was whole.

Chapter Nine

During the next week, heavy surgical schedules and the consequent load of new patient workups helped Carlsie keep her thoughts off the tragedy of Melissa. She stayed busy long after dark each night, and she was being given more and more responsibility in the O.R. Having proven to the staff that she deserved the recommendations her previous teachers had given her, she was being put to work. Almost daily, she was assigned teaching cases that rapidly progressed from the simple biopsy with which she had been tested. There seemed to be no question that she had hands which met the standards of the institute. If she was able to stay the course in the other ways required of the residents, no one doubted that she could become as skilled as any of the surgeons trained at the institute.

But being accepted as a worthwhile trainee did not bring her the joy it once would have. A vague sense of foreboding was growing with each passing day. She couldn't stop thinking about Melissa.

On Friday she helped with another mastectomy,

this time on a thirty-five-year-old. Not exceptionally young, although young enough that her age was noticed.

Ed Grossman seemed to be particularly affected. "I can't stand this anymore," he whispered to Carlsie in the recovery room. "I don't know what I'm going to do. I know it's out of my control, I'm only the anesthesiologist, but I won't be a part of it."

She followed him out into the hall. When he realized she wanted to talk, he led her into the stairwell where they were alone.

He was obviously quite distraught. "Don't you wonder about all these girls?" he asked. "I've never seen this many cancers in my life."

She give him the stock answer. "We're a referral center, Ed."

"Bullshit!" He frowned angrily. "Aren't you a little curious about how this place got to be so famous? What made it, out of hundreds of hospitals, get so many patients and find so many malignancies? His voice had a bitter edge to it. "And have you noticed how rich these guys are? They're making more money than any surgeons I know of."

"I'm just trying to learn their techniques, Ed. I don't pay any attention to the money part of it."

"Well, you'd better start, honey pie. Because the money part of it is what it's all about."

"I don't believe that for a minute."

Grossman sneered. "When were you born, Carlsie? Yesterday?"

He started away, but she grabbed his arm. "Wait

130

a minute, Ed. You can't say things like that, then just walk away from me. Quit beating around the bush and tell me what you know. I deserve the truth. I consider myself your friend."

He calmed down. "I don't know much. I just know there's too much surgery going on. Oh, sure, technically the skill level is incredible. Who wouldn't get good with this many patients to practice on? I'm telling you, Carlsie, this place is weird; it's filled with weird people and weird rules. Have you ever seen the way Walker Barret and Oscar Mendel huddle together in the halls, whispering about things. I've never seen a surgeon and pathologist work so closely together. And what about the rule that only one person, namely Val, can carry the specimen? That's odd and restrictive, isn't it? I mean how much skill does it take to carry a goddamn piece of tissue down the stairs?"

"I'd never thought about it that way."

"You had better start thinking, Carlsie. You're in this, too. You know, Val's had a mastectomy, and she's very bitter about it. And you ought to see the house she lives in. It's damned fancy for someone on a nurse's salary." He paused. "Everybody here has money—I mean big money."

At that moment someone entered the stairwell several floors beneath them. From the footsteps Carlsie could tell at least two people were below. She recognized Mendel's voice, but could not understand what he was saying.

"We'd better get out of here," she said to Grossman and opened the door.

131

He nodded. "You go ahead. I'm going down to put in my resignation. I'm going to tell them what I suspect, too."

"Don't be so impulsive, Ed. Think this through a little bit." She wasn't sure he'd heard what she'd said. He had already started down the stairs toward whomever it was that was coming up.

Carlsie spoke to no one about the exchange with Grossman. Around six o'clock Gordo came up to her ward and asked if she was interested in having dinner with him. She told him she was too tired.

"Did you hear about Grossman?" he asked. "He got fired this afternoon."

She feigned ignorance.

Gordo continued. "Apparently, Barret called him in and fired him on the spot."

Though shocked by Gordo's version of the story, Carlsie didn't know what to say, but when Walker Barret arrived to start rounds, she asked him about Grossman.

Barret appeared unconcerned. "Dr. Grossman is an immature and unresponsible physician. His conduct is very unprofessional. We can replace him easily. Anesthesiologists are a dime a dozen."

"What did he do?" Carlsie asked.

Barret gazed at her. "I imagine he would prefer that I do not discuss the details of his situation so I will keep them confidential for his sake. I will say this much, however: the man has psychological problems. He was hospitalized once for treatment, and I suppose the stress here rekindled his illness. It was my unfortunate duty to discharge him."

Carlsie's mood soured at the lie. "He didn't re-sign—he was fired, kicked off the staff?"

Barret looked at her more intently. "Well, techni-cally he did resign. I allowed him to do that, of course. We came to a gentlemen's agreement. If he went quietly and called no attention to himself—did nothing to sow seeds of discontent as discharged workers are prone to do—then I promised to say nothing of his problem to anyone inquiring about his qualifications." Barret's voice took on a more ominous tone. "However if he discredits this insti-tution, I vowed to make sure that he never works in any hospital in the country. I think he got my meaning."

I'll bet he did, Carlsie thought. She wondered what had really been said. Grossman's view of the hospital and its staff had certainly seemed odd, per-haps even delusional. But she had her own doubts about the incidences of cancer. At the very least she was going to look into the numbers, she owed that to Grossman.

Physically and emotionally exhausted she went straight to bed when she got home. What she dreamed revealed the extent of her concern about what Grossman had said.

There was a young girl, nude. Her body was painted with wild, unusual designs and colors. Bright red spirals encircled each breast in everwid-ening patterns, and her face was covered with a white powder, except for elaborate purple shadings about her frightened eyes. Her mouth was frozen into a panicked scream, which had been silenced by the tight binding across her neck. Above her danced a witch doctor, moving to the rhythmic chanting of the crowd that surrounded the altar. In each hand he held a gleaming blade. Carlsie struggled to break through the mob so she might stop the coming sacrifice. The crazed natives restrained her, ignoring her admonitions to help the terrorized victim. She pushed and shoved and did everything in her power to break free and save this innocent child. She had to stop this, she had to! When at last she was released and she climbed the steps to reach the girl, it was too late.

Then everything changed. There was no painted body, no binding around the girl's neck, and the man standing above the pleading girl was not a witch doctor. He wore a green surgical scrub suit, and he did not wield ancient, sacrificial knives. It was a scalpel that he thrust into one breast and then the other.

Carlsie cried out as she pulled herself from the dream. It had been a terrible nightmare, and its symbolism was obvious. The tiny ember of suspicion she had been harboring had been fanned by Grossman's statements. She realized, of course, that there was probably very little truth to them. The odds overwhelmingly favored the doctors being as outstanding as they appeared to be and the institute being the ultimately professional place it seemed.

The time had come, though, for her to resolve this once and for all, so she could free her mind and concentrate on the task at hand: doing a good job in this fellowship. Carlsie decided to quitely look into the stats—*quitely*. She certainly was not going to become a crusading zealot. She would proceed calmly and professionally, and keep herself emotionally in check unless she found some objective evidence of misinterpretation of tissue samples.

In the meantime, her life would go on because, though she was not taking this lightly, she did not intend to become another Grossman and crash without accomplishing a thing.

Chapter Ten

She'd been invited to a big party on Saturday, in Gordo's words: "A real posh Palm Beach affair."

Continuing his campaign to win her heart, he took her first to dinner at a restaurant which she knew cost ten times what a resident could afford . . . even a chief resident. But it didn't help his cause. For one thing he wasn't the doctor she wished him to be. He wasn't as dedicated as she was. Carlsie loved medicine so much, she knew she couldn't love someone who didn't share her reverence for the profession. And Gordo didn't have the overpowering charisma she wanted in a man. In many ways, likeable though he was, Gordo was not as attractive to her as a man like Hank Ritter. Indeed, Ritter had been in her thoughts more and more lately, and he seemed to be giving her more attention too. Her respect for him was growing, and if she could only put her doubts about the institution aside, she'd acknowledge that he was everything she thought a doctor should be. She really did not believe Hank could be involved in any wrongdoing or medical carelessness. He had become the ideal she wished to emulate. She wanted to learn everything he knew. To her, he was the master, the near-perfect teacher. And a very attractive man.

At the party that night, she encountered Ritter in a social situation for the first time. The hostess was one of the ultrarich heiresses who took great joy in outdoing each other in providing lavish entertainment during the social season. There was a large orchestra, freely flowing booze, food, and drugs if one desired them. Already feeling the bourbon she'd been drinking, Carlsie stood alone while Gordo went to fetch more of the same. She was watching a young man in a silver-sequinned jump suit puff busily on a joint.

"Try some," he offered. "It's good stuff."

She just said no.

"Are you sure you don't want a little toke?" he urged. "It's Colombian."

"That's what you guys always say," she teased. "It's probably from Okeechobee, Florida."

The dude shrugged and moved away.

"Pretty streetwise, aren't you, lady?" said a familiar voice behind her.

She turned to face Hank, who was looking outstandingly good. He had removed his jacket and tie, and was wearing a maroon velvet vest over a silk shirt unbuttoned enough to reveal a bit of his muscular chest. His well-tailored pants had a slight Western cut to them. "You look great," he said. His eyes swept down from her curly black hair, over her one bare shoulder, and across chest and hips sleekly

138

outlined by a skin-tight, white evening gown—the only one Carlsie owned. His appreciative appraisal of her figure pleased her.

"Some party, huh?" She gazed warmly into his friendly brown eyes and studied the features of his cowboy's face. Even after working with him all these weeks, she still saw him as a good-looking bandido.

He nodded as he glanced at the throng around them. "They have one of these shindigs every darn year. Gets wilder and wilder, too. Last one turned into a skinny dip around four o'clock in the morning." He grinned. "I mean, that's what I hear. I was long gone by then."

"I'll bet," she answered.

"I guess this sort of affair is pretty old hat to a New Orleans girl, right? I hear they party all the time over there."

"Every big city is a party town."

"For me Houston didn't seem that way," he said. "At least not while I was in training. I guess I need to go home someday and check that part of it out again, see what I missed."

"Too late, now. 'You can't go home again.' "

"Oh, yes you can," he replied. "Who was it that wrote 'home is the place where they have to take you in'? It gives me a feeling of security to know that if all this falls apart there is still somewhere to go."

She sipped the last of the water, residue of melted ice, in her glass, and thought about what he had said. Could she really go back to Slidell if all else

139

failed? She wondered if she would fit in. No, she decided, not Slidell. New Orleans, maybe, but her niche there was only due to her education. When Papa died, she would have no reason at all to be there, except it was the only place she had ever known. The realization made her sad. Momma had had the bayou. It was a place that had truly been home to her, not only because of family, but because it simply was home.

Just then the band changed the pace and played a slower number. Hank asked her to dance.

"Yes, I would like that," she told him. "Does Dr. Barret allow his senior staff to dance with residents?"

"Until this moment, I don't think it has ever happened. I figure he'd probably prefer to have me dance with you rather than Gordo." They smiled at each other, enjoying the absurdity of his remark.

He pulled her toward him, unexpectedly close, and she found pleasure in being in his arms. Willingly, she allowed herself to be brought snugly against him, and for several minutes they moved as one.

As the slow throb of the music rose in intensity, Hank's embrace grew stronger, their physical contact increasing. His arms, his chest, his thighs — all of him rubbed against her. She laid her head against his neck, and his strong smooth fingers caressed the curve of her back. She was enjoying the feel of him even more than she had anticipated.

When the music ceased, his embrace held for a moment. Only when she pulled away did they part.

Gordo was approaching, drinks in hand, and Carlsie wondered how obvious the surprisingly passionate overtones of their dance had been to those around them.

"Nice dance, Carlsie. Thank you," Hank said quietly.

Gordo finally reached them and delivered her drink. She tried hard to act perfectly normal as the three of them struck up a conversation about the party. Gordo did most of the talking, while she and Hank did most of the listening. Still flushed with emotion, she continued to wonder if the others had witnessed the specialness of her encounter with Hank. It seemed impossible that it had not been blatantly apparent to everyone, but Gordo seemed oblivious of it all.

Gordo winked at her. "I was afraid one of these rich potheads would abscond with you. Good thing Hank was here to keep an eye on you for me."

Carlsie agreed, feeling guilty, and Hank quickly excused himself.

Gordo gazed after him as he departed. "Hank's some kind of guy, isn't he? If I ever had a brother, I'd like it to be him. He's been great to me these past few years. If I could be half of what he is, I'd be happy."

"Nobody's perfect, Gordo. Nobody." She stared numbly into her drink then led him to the food table, where they could occupy themselves with nibbling and not have to converse for a few minutes. He clearly had no idea what had happened between Hank and her. She cast a sidewise glance at Gordo.

He was more than enough man for any woman, she thought. She should be glad to have him.

Trying to get herself back into a festive mood, she danced the next several dances with him, acting out a lie. She did it for him.

She caught a brief glimpse of Hank and his Maria, a very attractive Mexican girl, and, according to Gordo, a wealthy Houston socialite who maintained a condominium in Palm Beach strictly to facilitate occasional visits with Hank. The two had been lovers off and on for years, and their relationship had survived the long-distance commuting both had to do. For reasons unknown to Gordo, marriage had never been planned, although Maria very much wanted Hank to return to Houston to open his own breast institute to serve the Southwest. Carlsie noted that Maria was beautiful and danced very close to Hank.

Once, he turned toward Carlsie, and for a brief moment their eyes met. In that glance, she received a message no words could ever deliver. He wanted her.

The knowledge kindled a sensation of fear. She foresaw pain. Pain for herself and Hank, and for Gordo and Maria. She didn't want that, hadn't sought it. She had no room for complex emotional entanglements. If the timing and situation had been different, a relationship between her and Hank might have been feasible. But not now . . . certainly not now. She fought back emotions she didn't want to feel.

Putting her arms around the attractive Gordo,

she whispered, "Hold me, please."

He responded enthusiastically, innocently misunderstanding her embrace. "I love you, Carlsie, now and forever. You've swept me away, girl."

"No. Don't say it," she quickly responded. "You don't mean it. It's too soon."

He tried to pull back his head to look at her, but she clung to him tightly, not wanting to see his face. "I do mean it, Carlsie. I do. I love you more than I've ever loved anyone." He waited, hoping for a response.

She remained silent, distraught because of her situation.

"You love me, too," he continued. "I know you do. We're just right for each other. We can have a great life."

"Please, Gordo, no."

"It's okay, Carlsie." His voice was happy. "You do love me, don't you? It's all right if you say it. I'll never hurt you."

She said nothing.

"Carlsie, I know you love me. Don't you?" His voice carried a plaintive hope. "Don't you?"

"Yes," she finally whispered meekly, and regretted the word the instant it slipped out. It was wrong. She shouldn't lie . . . but she didn't want to hurt him. She believed he loved her more than anyone before him had. She tried to modify what she had said. Too late. He swooped her up and, beaming happily, whirled her around the floor.

He was at the peak of joy, and she didn't know what to do. She wouldn't cause him pain, because she did love him in a way. He was a wonderful man, and did not deserve unhappiness.

She hardly slept that night for a new reason. Thoughts of the two men in her life had displaced, at least for the moment, her concerns about the frequency of surgery. She worried about Gordo and the mistaken impression she had given him. And she thought about Hank. Despite every effort to prevent doing so, she could not stop thinking of him. He filled her mind—his face, his voice, and most of all his sheer masculinity. She longed for his touch.

The rumor that she and Gordo were a couple spread rampantly the next week. She didn't know how it had started but there was now widespread belief that the friendship between the two of them had rocketed into one of those hot flings for which Gordo was infamous.

Everyone assumed they were in a real scorcher, this time with a difference. The word went around that Gordo was the same ol' romantic boy throwing himself fearlessly into a relationship, as he always did with a new love, but this time something had happened. He had actually fallen for this warm-blooded Cajun girl. Now he found himself really hooked, frighteningly hooked. By his own admission to one of the other residents, for the first time he was having anxiety about an affair and wondering how he would handle it if things went sour.

The great Gordo had been snared, and the whole hospital recognized it, including the nurses who had had brief flings with him. Even Walker Barret picked up on it, and let it be known he didn't care for it. In his usual dictatorial manner he pointedly asked Carlsie, in private, one afternoon after she had scrubbed with him on seven augmentations in a row, if she didn't think it was somewhat unprofessional to be so "morally loose," particularly with the other staff members.

His attitude about what she did on her own time caught her by surprise, although she realized it shouldn't have. He considered everything at the institute, including the lives of his staff, to be his domain.

"I don't think the friendship between Gordo and me is anyone's business except our own." She hoped he would drop it at that.

"Friendship? Is that what you call it?" He looked at her contemptuously. "I'd say it was more like shacking up."

That was untrue. Carlsie was angry about it and furious at Barret for trying to insult her. It was uncalled for. Nonetheless, determined to stay calm, she responded as politely as she could. "Whatever you call it, it's doing no one any harm. We are good friends, that's all."

The chief responded more viciously than she'd expected. "Of course this sort of thing causes harm. You are supposed to be concentrating on our patients and on improving your surgical skills, instead

145

you're perfecting your pelvic thrust, and no telling what else, and distracting my chief resident as well."

The cut went deep, and she could see that Barret knew it. Without additional comment, he walked out of the surgical lounge, leaving her alone with her fury and dismay. She had faced this kind of double standard all her life. Barret would not have considered a male physician sexually immoral even if the guy screwed every female in sight. Apparently, he had thought it all right for Gordo to have numerous girlfriends, and had even joked about that. Now, in addition to his other antifemale biases, he found her immoral for having an affair with a well-respected man — one man — and the ironic part was that it wasn't even true!

It was hopeless, she decided. Unless she was willing to live her life the way men around her expected her to, she was going to receive the brunt of their disdain . . . even for things they would condone in a fellow male. She wished that — oh, delicious moments — she could put selfish fools like Barret into a woman's harness and watch them squirm. They would undoubtedly find their own notions of feminine duty and morality unreasonably stifling.

The more she thought about her situation with Gordo and Barret's condemnation of it, the more depressed she became. Yet she didn't know what to do about it. She had to quiet this down, but wanted to minimize the pain for Gordo. He was still ebullient over what he considered to be the strengthening of their relationship, while she dreaded popping his bubble and suffered guilt for having let him build it up in the first place.

Hank, on the other hand, maintained an absolutely professional demeanor with her. So much so that at first she wondered if the electricity that had flowed between them at the party had been one sided. She scrubbed with him frequently during the week, and nothing seemed changed. He was technically perfect as usual, and as untalkative with her during surgery as he had always been. However, on the few occasions when he allowed his gaze to meet hers she knew she hadn't imagined what had happened that night. His eyes were sending messages that only she received.

It was a tantalizing situation. Their conversation never strayed from work. They never touched. They never exchanged secret smiles. There were only brief lingering glances. She knew the attraction was there, and she knew he was aware of it. That showed in the way he looked at her, the gentleness of his voice when he spoke, and the softness of his touch when he guided her hand through a new procedure. The desire was unquestionably bilateral.

It was not good thing, tough. For a lot of reasons. He was teacher, she was student. He was Gordo's friend, she was the woman Gordo loved. And Hank was already seriously involved with a woman.

Try as she might, though, Carlsie couldn't completely control her feelings. From the very beginning she had admired Hank's dedication and desired his abilities and knowledge. Now she wanted even more. Despite the many reasons she did not want an emotional entanglement complicating her life, it was threatening to happen. In addition to everything else she coveted about Hank Ritter, she had come to want the man himself.

Chapter Eleven

On Friday Beth Ainsley was scheduled to undergo a biopsy. She was a stunningly beautiful blond socialite who was married to a wealthy man much older then her thirty-two years. Rumor had it that Beth had once starred in a soft-core porno flick. According to Gordo, no on had ever come up with a copy of the film, so the tale remained only scuttlebutt. Carlsie had done the H and P the night before, and had found the delightful woman to be remarkable healthy. Her tumor, clinically benign with a negative mammogram, seemed likely to be a benign fibroadenoma since aspiration had failed to show it to be cystic.

At the scrub sink, while Carlsie waited for Beth to be anesthetized, Barret continued the harassment he had begun earlier. When he expanded on it, Carlsie learned why he had been on her back so much lately. "Dr. Mendel tells me you have been going into the lab after hours and viewing the slides without proper supervision.

"I looked at one set. Melissa Bates's."

"Learn anything?"

"No."

"That's what I thought. From now on when you want to see a patient's slides, schedule it with Path personnel so someone will be there to teach you something. We can't have people fooling around with that material. Those slides have great medico-legal significance. Losing one might present a serious problem if litigation arose."

"I understand."

"Dr. Mendel was understandably quite disturbed by your intrusion."

"That was an overreaction. All I did was ask the tech to show me the slides I wanted to see. I didn't break in there, you know. There were a lot of the lab people still around."

"That's beside the point. You did not have permission to do it." He glared at her. "Do you get my meaning?"

Spare me this bullshit, Carlsie thought. Of course she got his meaning. She was to do her scut work, keep quiet, and not bother anybody else — and to hell with worrying about whether anyone was checking on the pathologists, to hell with anything other than getting the surgery done on time and in huge amounts.

"And another thing," he added, as he started into the O.R. "I would appreciate it if you would stop independently checking the charts of our post-op patients. If there is any information you require about them, all you need to do is ask."

Carlsie said nothing. She understood perfectly. She got "his meaning."

The biopsy went routinely. In less than a half-hour a dressing had been placed across the tiny incision and Carlsie stood with the others awaiting the Path report on the specimen Val Ryan had taken downstairs. The anesthesiologist would not awaken Beth and transport her to the recovery room until the result was in.

Carlsie's mood had not improved. In fact she wished she had a good excuse to leave the O.R.

The crackle of the intercom brought news that made everything worse. Dr. Mendel announced, very matter-of-factly, that this patient had cancer of the breast, intraductal papillary type. It was an unexpected development. Carlsie had been so sure the specimen was benign. The message was relayed to Barret who quickly returned to the O.R. It would be his task to remove the breast from this attractive woman. The senior surgeon offered no comment. He immediately rescrubbed his hands, and assisted in the redraping of the unfortunate patient.

Carlsie broke the silence. "Are they sure? Maybe it's a mistake. Did they double check?"

Barret responded caustically. "Don't start that. Denial never accomplishes anything." He continued the preparations, then, as if he had been thinking

151

about it, added: "Mendel's never made a diagnostic error on a frozen section in all the years he's been here. That can be documented."

"There's a first time for everything," Carlsie muttered, then wished she hadn't.

Barret paused just long enough to cast an irritated glance toward her. "You are going to regret that remark, young lady." He thrust the blade deeply into Beth's firm breast and brought the long elliptical incision across her chest and into the axilla.

Carlsie felt sick. This wasn't cancer. She was certain a mistake had been made. Something was wrong. This beautiful woman was being disfigured for no good reason.

Her head was pounding, her stomach hurt, and she was nauseated. The room felt abnormally cold, but she was perspiring profusely. The people around her seemed far away, as if she were in a tunnel. Her vision was blurry. Her hands were difficult to control. She didn't know what to do. She had no demonstrable proof that this was all wrong, but every cell in her brain was screaming out disbelief that this was actually happening.

She struggled to continue to do her job, trying hard to keep up with the rapid pace Barret was setting, but it was impossible. She was too slow at clamping the bleeders and retracting the tissue. Her hands didn't seem a part of her. Twice Barret told her to pay attention. Twice more she fell behind.

152

And then he was speaking to her, but she couldn't hear. His eyes glared angrily at her, but his words didn't reach her brain. She felt isolated and alone, confused and frightened.

This was wrong. Horribly wrong.

She became afraid . . . so terribly afraid. She was unable to go on. She had to stop. This operation had to stop. Something inside her was telling her to prevent this from happening.

But she couldn't move.

She couldn't think.

Even breathing was difficult. She thought she might be having a stroke, or even a heart attack. It was bad, so very, very bad.

Her hand reached out and clamped on Barret's wrist. "Quit!" she muttered. "Stop this now while we still can."

He stared at her in disbelief.

Gordo was suddenly in the room, and Val Ryan was leading her away while the chief resident replaced her to help Barret complete Beth Ainsley's operation. Other O.R. personnel watched curiously as Carlsie walked weakly down the hallway, then collapsed in a chair at the front desk. Slowly her anxiety abated. She drank the juice one of the nurses brought to her, and sat, bewildered by her experience.

She was scared. More than scared. She didn't understand what had happened to her, or why, or how. But she was convinced that Beth Ainsely did not have carcinoma of the breast, no matter what any-one said. It seemed irrational to be entertaining such a thought, but she could not dismiss it. The pathologist was in error, she knew it. She had a sudden overpowering urge to go to the lab and ex-amine the slides herself.

She left the O.R. by the back stairs.

Oscar Mendel delivered his message about the frozen section and turned away from the intercom. He recorded the woman's name in his small log-book. "Beth," he murmured. It was such a pretty, soft word. So feminine. How unfortunate it was that this woman had chosen to indulge in such lewd behavior.

He filled and lit his pipe, then turned to gaze out over his lab. There was nothing unusual. The tech-nicians were busy preparing specimens or working with their machines. The hustle and bustle was in its first surge of the day. He noted with satisfaction that all was in order.

The door, which led to the stairs to the operating rooms, suddenly opened, attracting Mendel's atten-tion. What he saw irritated him. An angry Carlsie Camden walked defiantly toward him.

"I would like to see the frozen section on Beth Ainsley?"

"I asked you not to bother us," Mendel said firmly.

"I just want to look at it."

"What makes you think you would understand what you were looking at?"

"Come on, Dr. Mendel. I rotated on pathology in my second year, just like every other surgical resident. I know what a straightforward cancer looks like.

Her self-confident indignation further irritated the pathologist. He wanted to tell her to go to hell, but caution prevailed. "I don't have time to teach you how to read these slides just now. Besides, frozen sections are very difficult to interpret. Just this once, you may come back tomorrow when I have the permanents ready. You will learn more from them."

Carlsie stared at him suspiciously. "I don't want to come back tomorrow. Beth is having her mastectomy today, and I want to see her cancer today."

Her attitude infuriated Mendel. His eyes narrowed into angry slits as he frowned at her insolence. He wanted to pop her one right then, the trouble-making bitch. "I said tomorrow."

A trace of an arrogant smile came to Carlsie's lips. "Are you afraid to let me look? Are you going to complain again to Walker Barret that I'm invading your private turf?"

Her blatant rudeness amazed Mendel. He turned toward her and moved to within a few inches of her face. Then he spoke softly so no one else could hear him. "Nothing about you scares me, you little cunt."

Although offended by his choice of words, Carlsie was not surprised. She had already heard plenty about his crude behavior when angered. The language was in character, for him.

"I assume you know no one had the slightest suspicion this would be malignant," she said.

"What a pity." He continued to glare at her.

She kept after him. "I find your lack of compassion unbecoming in a physician, Dr. Mendel."

"Compassion?" He sneered. "You expect me to have compassion for someone like her? That woman is trash, pure and simple."

"I can't believe you said that." She thought the man's callousness outrageous.

He smiled, contemptuously. "God punishes in mysterious ways, doesn't he, my dear? Your Beth should have thought about that before she lived her life the way she has. People usually get exactly what they deserve. I assume that's the cause here."

The remark revealed more to her about the state of his mind than anything else he had said or done. He was obviously not normal. Never in her career had she heard of anyone in the profession make such a foul remark about a patient.

"Someone would have to be crazy to think that way," she said. The expression on his face and the weird squint of his eyes verified her opinion.

Although her remark enraged him, Mendel retained enough control to respond quietly. "You say

156

that again, and I'll jam these slides right up your ass, inch by bloody inch."

Her slap reached his face before he could withdraw. He didn't flinch. He stared steadfastly into her eyes as a clamor arose from the lab techs who had been observing the encounter from an appropriate distance. He smiled faintly, in victory. "You lose," he whispered, then turned away.

Tears welling in her eyes, Carlsie quickly retreated to the stairs, while the room buzzed with comments on what appeared to be an unprovoked attack upon a senior staffman.

Mendel watched her go, then harshly commanded his people to get back to work. Enraged by her insolence, he closed the door to his office and paced incessantly about. He needed to calm down. His heart was pounding and he was sweating profusely. His goddamn headache was starting again. He would have killed her right then, if given the opportunity.

Carlsie rested in the surgeons' lounge. Emotionally exhausted, she stretched out on the big sofa. Now she had a real problem: how to explain what had happened in the lab. She didn't know what to say. The truth wouldn't do any good. There was no way she could justify losing her temper so badly she'd actually hit him. And he was sure to deny everything. No one would believe her version of what he'd said about Beth, nor would anyone believe he'd insulted her as he had. She wished she had not gone downstairs at all.

One thing, though. She now knew beyond a shadow of a doubt the man was a psychopath. She didn't care what anybody else thought about him or how many books and articles he had published, Mendel was a deviant who should not be allowed to practice medicine. Her first impression of him, the day she'd arrived, was absolutely accurate. There was something fundamentally wrong with him.

Carlsie felt frustrated, and angry at the other surgeons for the pressure they were putting her under and for letting this happen. She didn't know who to blame, but she wanted to yell at someone. Why didn't any of them realize that Mendel was sick?

Ritter was the first to come in and check on her.

"What happened?" he asked softly.

She told him she didn't know.

"Ever happen before?" he inquired.

"Never. I have never experienced anything like this."

He smiled sympathetically, then walked over to the big window and stared contemplatively out to the river. "Well, don't worry about it. Maybe your blood glucose was too low. Did you eat breakfast?"

"Two cups of coffee."

He turned back to her, gazing inquiringly into her eyes. He seemed to want to give her an easy way out. "Not a very substantive beginning for a hard day's work." Ritter held her wrist, palpating her pulse. "You're not starting a period, are you?" The question was annoying. Why did men always assume that periods made all females fragile and weak?

"No. It's not that. I don't have problems with that."

"It's no great crime if you do, you know." His expression told her he wanted to help. "You know how people are, Carlsie. I don't want anyone to use this against you." He looked at her thoughtfully. "Next time, let us know if you're tired or didn't get enough sleep or whatever. You don't have to push yourself so hard."

It was obvious that he didn't know about her encounter with Mendel. "I slapped him," she said. "He implied that Beth deserved her cancer."

He had no idea what she was talking about.

She told him about the incident, emphasizing the crudeness of Mendel's insult. Hank was speechless.

"I didn't mean to do it." Carlsie was about to cry. "It all happened so quickly. I was so furious at what he was saying. The man's a psychotic, Hank."

"You hit him? You actually hit him in the face?" Ritter was having a very hard time comprehending what she was telling him.

"He's looney! Can't you tell from just talking to him? It wasn't my fault!"

Before the conversation could continue, Gordo bounded into the room, anxious to see how she was. "Jesus!" he exclaimed. "I thought you were going down for a minute there, girl. Are you pregnant or what?" He grinned—one of his big friendly ones—and rustled her hair. His presence made her feel better. It was hard to worry about anything with Gordo around.

Ritter turned to him. "She had a fight with Mendel. She slapped him."

Gordo instantly became serious. "I hope you're joking. You don't need that kind of trouble, Carlsie."

Carlsie's gut tightened and she blushed. No one was going to be on her side. She suddenly felt very sick. She rushed past Gordo into the dressing room where she emptied the contents of her stomach into the sink and onto the surrounding floor. Her insides struggled to erupt into her burning throat. Her entire body was in pain. And she was trembling with fear. What had she done? God, how she wanted this to be a dream.

She closed her eyes and tried to sort it all out. The others were soon beside her, calming her down, wiping her face.

In a little while she felt better and was regaining control of her emotions. The consensus being that she was not well, Gordo agreed to take her to her apartment, where he got her to eat a little and made sure she was all right.

She was fine, she assured him. She promised to rest. And she agreed to sleep late the next morning,

160

which was Saturday.

He told her he was convinced that she was going to be okay. It had all been a matter of overwork, low blood glucose, and the stress of being new . . . and female, besides. For good measure, he also said she was probably coming down with a virus or something. No big deal. No one was going to blame her for the Mendel incident. It was just one of those unfortunate things that would soon blow over.

He was undoubtedly correct, she told him, and also very kind for being so concerned. She gave him a little peck of a good-by kiss and waved him off. She was going to be just fine, she insisted. He should not worry about her. Everything was all right.

Moments later, Hank called to check on her and to make sure that whatever had happened to her had subsided. She told him it had and that she was prepared to face the consequences of the incident with Mendel.

He was on her side, Hank assured her, and she shouldn't worry because everyone would believe her story about the argument. After all, the entire staff knew Mendel was difficult and had funny religious notions about cancer. Hank said he would do whatever he could to help. He'd make sure that the incident was downplayed. Besides, he added, everyone in the lab had seen that Mendel was unhurt by the blow.

She was totally unconvinced, but thanked him for

161

his efforts.

Then, finally, she was alone to reflect upon what had happened and to contemplate the change it could make in her life. Fear gripped her like a vise, squeezing the joy from her as a boa crushes the spirit from its victim, breath by punishing breath. Alone, she must reach an emotional and intellectual accommodation with her irrepressible belief that there was an insane pathologist in control of the lab and that something was wrong with the biopsy results.

With no solid evidence to support her, she now believed that the most outrageous thing she could imagine was not just a nightmare, but was fact: at the most renowned hospital for surgery of the breast, women were being mutilated because of errors made by an incompetent pathologist.

It was hard for her to deal with this. She disdained all things unscientific, but she found herself completely convinced of wrongdoing at the hospital without having one piece of hard evidence to prove that some of her patients had been erroneously diagnosed. True, Mendel had acted and spoken inappropriately — probably psychotically — and there were a large number of young mastectomy patients returning for follow-up visits. But that wasn't enough. To have suspicions based upon such scant observations was one thing, but they were certainly not proof.

Her studied ability to remain calm about all this

was now gone. No longer could she carry on life as usual while she proceeded with a rational investigation of the institutes statistics. She had now become the possibly paranoid zealot she had tried not to be.

As to why she seemed to be the only remaining staff member who suspected the truth, she had no explanation. She pondered the basis of intuition, and tried to remember everything scientific she had ever read about it. She recalled reading in one of Jung's books on psychoanalysis that he had believed the human mind might occasionally make great leaps in judgment that seemed to defy rational explanation. Could it be possible, she asked herself, that this had happened to her? Was this all due just to intuition?

Had poor Grossman made the same leap? And what about his notions regarding the strange attitudes and conduct of Val Ryan and Walker Barret, and the inordinately large amount of money he claimed everyone connected with the institute was making.

Had Farber thought the same thing? Was that why he had been so interested in her study of young cancer patients? Was that why he had been fired?

Suddenly, a connection between the two dismissals seemed possible. What if both men had known something, or at least suspected it, and been foolish enough to make their suspicions known to the wrong person? The implication was staggering. What if Farber's death had not been accidental as everyone believed? After all, he had had access to all the specimens in pathology. What if he had discovered something? What if he had seen proof of what she and Grossman suspected? She was both frightened and intrigued by this possibility.

What she had to do now was obvious. She needed facts: she needed data. If what she feared about the diagnoses was true, surely there was information in the institute that could verify it. Carlsie's task was to find it. She would start with the medical records . . . and then she was going to have to gain access to the lab in one way or another.

She needed Gordo's help. Somehow she had to convince him.

Chapter Twelve

As he had promised, Gordo arrived early to take her to breakfast. He was happy to see her feeling well, but dismayed when she persisted in what he considered to be her absurd fixation on the cancer statistics. She wanted him to authorize an audit of the surgical results of all biopsies done in the last few years.

"That's crazy, Carlsie. Of what use would it be?" he asked. "And besides, Barret would have my neck for doing that without his okay."

"Please, Gordo. If you've ever been willing to do a favor for me, do this one. I promise I'll stop bugging you about all this pathology business if nothing unusual shows up."

"It's too risky. The tissue committee keeps track of all that stuff anyway. Why don't I get you copies of their minutes? That should be enough to convince you that this whole idea of yours is off-base."

"It isn't. Don't you know who the chairman of

the tissue committee is?"

"Who?" Gordo inquired. "Mendel?"

"Right. If he's trying to hide anything it would be a cinch for him."

Gordo sounded exasperated. "Carlsie, sweetheart, love of my life, when are you going to get it through your thick Cajun skull that nobody's trying to hide anything? Mendel's strange, I'll grant that, but he's far from insane. He's just got some peculiar beliefs, that's all. Lot's of people do. Let me say this in Louisiana language: there ain't nothing to hide!"

"I'm not the only one who's thought of this, you know. Grossman believed something was wrong, too."

"Grossman? Who gives a damn what he thinks?"

"He's been around, Gordo. He's seen a lot of surgery."

"Crap! He's seen a lot more bottles. He's an alcoholic, Carlsie. Barrett told me. He blew a good chance here."

"Then what about Farber. Isn't his story a little strange?"

"So what? I've never met a pathologist who wasn't a little strange . . . or an anesthesiologist, for that matter. They're all weird. I mean what kind of doctor wants to take care of patients who are either dead or asleep?" He laughed at his own remark.

"Okay. Forget about them." She spoke as sweetly as she could. "Gordo, indulge me just this once.

166

Please, help me."

He frowned at her sympathetically and seemed to be weakening.

She turned up the heat. *"Please* . . . I'll do anything."

"Oh, lord . . . how can I fight you, Carlsie? All right. I'll do it this once, but if I get stung on this, you'll have to pay me back with the services of your body. Fair enough?"

"It's a deal."

He smiled his most charming smile. "I'll have it done by Monday; you can plan on it. If you're wrong, shall we use my place or yours?"

She gazed into his boyish eyes and wondered just how he would react if they found what she was convinced would show up. Using the audit information Gordo had promised to get for her from the medical records department, Carlsie planned to compare the hospital's statistics with national data to see if she could verify her impression that too many young women were having mastectomies. If the results matched what she suspected, it would throw a shadow across the entire institute. Gordo, of course, was assuming she was focusing her attention exclusively on the work of the pathology department. She let him. At this point she would accomplish little by telling him Grossman had implied that a much greater conspiracy was involved. Just how widespread was difficult to imagine. Carlsie found it hard enough to believe that a demented pathologist could do something like this. In no way could she understand the involvement of apparently normal surgeons and, perhaps, nurses.

She knew she'd lose Gordo's help if she even breathed a word about a possible connection with Farber's death. That accusation deserved a lot more thought before she mentioned it to anyone, though her suspicions did make her want to lock her door a little more securely, particularly now that she had picked a fight with Mendel, a psychopath if she had ever seen one.

Chapter Thirteen

After having gotten through a tense weekend, Carlsie was already in the dressing room on Monday morning when Val Ryan, her hostility very thinly veiled, said she was not to bother changing into a scrub suit. Walker Barret had left strict orders for her to come—immediately—to his office.

Carlsie's mood plummeted. "Is it about my argument with Mendel?"

Val frowned. "Get serious. You know what this is about. Gordo's in trouble, too. Something about some statistics."

Carlsie nodded in understanding. Nothing got past Barret. He had eyes everywhere. Too bad he doesn't have a few watching the pathology department, she thought. Then maybe this all wouldn't have been necessary.

Val followed her down the hall. "What are you trying to do, Carlsie? Stir up trouble? I think you spent too much time with that bigmouth Grossman."

Carlsie ignored her and continued on her way.

Val wouldn't let it go. "That's right. Don't talk to me. I'm not important like you, right? Well, let me tell you something. You're just like all the rest of the doctors. Got it?"

Carlsie whirled around, surprised at the woman's vitriolic tone. She had never had as much as a cross word with her, and now, out of the blue, came this attack. "What is your problem, Val? I've not done a damned thing to you, so get off my back, okay?"

The nurse glared at her. "Anything you do to hurt this hospital hurts me. I need my job, and lots of other people here need theirs."

"I'm not threatening your job."

"Are you sure?" Val stared pensively at Carlsie. "Think about what your doing. Just think about it. One hint to a newspaper about trouble here and it'll be blown so out of proportion we'll never see another patient. I mean never!"

Val Ryan walked briskly away.

Surprised that the nurse seemed to know so much about her audit, Carlsie went to Walker Barret's office, determined to speak her mind. Part of what Val had said was true. Investigative reporting could ruin a place like this, even if there wasn't the slightest thing wrong. It made sense that people would get nervous if anyone seemed to be rabble-rousing. But that was no reason not to look into this situation. If everything was fine, the numbers would show that.

It was going to be interesting to see Barret's reaction. Carlsie was sure he would be upset, and the degree of his unhappiness would be enlightening. A resident at her level of training had the right to perform chart reviews of interesting topics—was expected to, actually, in academic settings. Doing it was nothing she should get flack for, if everything was on the up and up.

She hoped Barret had taken time to assess her results. If there was anything amiss, it might turn out better if he'd reviewed the data by choice—assuming, of course, that he didn't have anything to do with the problem. What's more that way she wouldn't have to present the bad news to him, and thereby incur the wrath directed at whistle blowers. One thing was sure, if Mendel was responsible for the work of the tissue committee, all the official records were undoubtedly lily white. That could explain why no one had ever noticed anything unusual about the results coming out of the pathology department. It was a classic case of the fox guarding the henhouse.

Barret's secretary immediately led her into his ostentatious inner office. He stared at her somberly, as if he were trying to decide what this was really all about and what he should do.

"I understand there was some trouble between you and Dr. Mendel last week," he said.

She grimaced. "We disagreed on whether I could look at Beth Ainsley's slides."

"I thought I asked you to stay out of his way."

She shrugged. "I wanted to see her tumor for my-

171

self. It wasn't a big deal."

"I'm afraid I don't share that viewpoint. I think it is a very big deal, to use your phrase, when one of my residents behaves inappropriately. Your conduct in the O.R. was inexcusable. You complicated matters further by going to the lab, though you were obviously in no state of mind to be there."

"I can't deny that I was not feeling well."

He seemed mollified by her admission that something had been wrong with her. "Rumor has it you tried to slap Mendel. Fortunately for you he has said nothing about it to me, so you are going to get off lightly on that count."

"Thank you. I can assure you it won't happen again."

"Good. I hope you are as cooperative on this other matter—the statistics. You never mentioned you were going to do a study such as this." He held up manilla folder from medical records to emphasize his point. "I thought I asked you to drop the project Farber had proposed."

"This has nothing to do with Farber. In the post-op clinic, I've seen so many young girls who've had mastectomies, I wondered if we were above the national mean. So I asked for the statistics."

Barret's expression remained unchanged. "Why do I get the feeling there is more to this than meets the eye? I just can't imagine what you would want to demonstrate with such data."

"What does my data show, if you don't mind my asking?"

172

"That is not the issue. I'm less interested in your results—which are inconsequential, I assure you—than I am in your motives. Why would you spend your time on something like this? A question directed to me could have resolved any curiosity you may have had. Of course we do more cancer surgery on young patients than most hospitals. We are a referral center. Gordo—I am also displeased with him—says he told you that."

His tone and expression revealed his hostility. Because Carlsie knew he wouldn't have cared if the study had shown nothing bothersome, she wanted access to the numbers more than ever. "I would like to know the answers to my questions about the spectrum of clinical pathology we see here in young women," she responded.

"And what are these questions that weigh so heavily upon your inexperienced mind?" Barret's irritation was becoming even less veiled.

"As I said, the problem is we do a lot of mastectomies."

"So you see the number of cases we handle as a problem, do you? Initially you indicated this study was of purely academic interest. What are you trying to prove, Carlsie?" He was certainly manipulative. Already he had her in a defensive posture, and she hadn't even seen the data. What she really wanted to do was tell him to give her the results and let the numbers speak for themselves.

But caution prevailed. She spoke politely, although her façade of professional subservience was weakening. She had done nothing more than look at the sort of thing the institute itself should have been keeping track of. Every major academic center compares its statistics with those of others. To do so assures competency and aids cancer epidemiology. She reminded Barret of that, trying hard to conceal her disapproval of a pathologist functioning as a watchdog over his own work.

He gazed at her contemptuously. "It is such a pleasure to have a well-informed person with your vast experience tell me what we should be doing. I wonder how we got along so well prior to your arrival."

Carlsie did not respond, for he seemed to be considering his next remark. He rose and stood behind his chair, still glaring at her. She really didn't care at the moment. She was tired of his attitude, of his blatant belittlement of her, of her ambition and her morality. If he did fire her it no longer mattered; things had changed. What she wanted most, right then, was to see the data she had put together; it had upset Walker Barret so much he wanted it to simply go away—along with her, probably.

"Why can't you be like any other resident, give proper attention to your work?" he asked. "The trouble with women like you is you never accept things as they are. Your kind is always looking behind doors and underneath carpets. You assume that if you can't see dirt, it must be hidden somewhere."

"Are you going to allow me to see my study or

not, Dr. Barret? I am aware of your feelings toward me, and I'm sorry about that; however I don't care to wallow in remorse."

"I would hardly say you wallow, young lady. You activist women aren't even willing to discuss your shortcomings, must less wallow in them."

"Not everyone has as low an opinion of me as you do, sir. If you are finished with me, I would like to leave." Continued discussion with him was pointless, and Carlsie was afraid an ill-conceived remark might make the situation worse if he pushed her much more.

Exasperated, Barret appeared to give up on her. "Numbers can be very misleading in uninformed hands. I will not tolerate any additional abuse of your academic privilege where the records of these private patients are concerned."

"I can't see the data I'm interested in, is that it?"

He raised his voice to an angry pitch. "Who cares about your silly data! Of course you can see it if it's that important to you. We have nothing to hide. The information was available for the asking. You didn't ask. Following the rules would have been offensive to you, right? You had to sneak around like an investigative reporter." He threw the folder into her lap.

His secretary's voice came unexpectedly over his intercom. "O.R. called and Dr. Greer needs Dr. Camden to scrub in right away. Apparently they're a little short-handed."

Barret pointed at the door. "Get out of here,

Carlsie."

As she rose to depart, he got in one more well-placed jab. "You know, the sad thing about your behavior is that I once thought you were going to fit in with us. You are a very talented young surgeon. I was ready to start making plans to build you a name." He shook his head in disgust. "I can never understand why some of you young ones let mental problems ruin your potential for greatness. I wonder how Tulane is surviving without your help."

She glared at him defiantly, but refrained from telling him what she thought about his screwed-up institute, his bizarre pathologist, and him. Pouring gasoline onto his smoldering anger would accomplish nothing good. She still believed that he was not a part of the problem. He was too great a surgeon for that. It didn't seem possible he would cancel out all the good he had done for so many years with an act such as this. Money couldn't be that important to him at this stage of his career. Besides, though he was angry about her actions, he did not appear to be trying to hide anything.

She was beginning to understand, though, how this terrible thing could have happened, whether he was involved or not. It could happen at any hospital where surgeons considered themselves the single most important element and let their inflated egos blind them to weak links in the chain.

Her real concern now was whether the system — even if these were the actions of one man — was capable of recognizing and dealing with its own failure. If shown that unnecessary surgery was being done, would this group of famous men admit it? Carlsie was confused and troubled by what she was seeing in Barret. She hoped the others would be more willing to examine the possibility of wrongdoing, but she was worried. It would shatter her trust in the profession if these doctors weren't willing to admit what had gone wrong. It was one thing to have a weed spring up in a garden, quite another to refuse to acknowledge its presence and thereby allow it to strangle flowering plants.

Could this system be trusted to analyze and purify itself?

Back in the O.R., with no time to study the data, Carlsie scrubbed with Fulton Greer prior to a long and complicated operation, during which the surprisingly skilled fat man said very little except that it was nice she was now feeling well.

She had not yet had a chance to talk privately with Gordo, but he soon came to observe, ostensibly. He grimaced at her, rolled his eyes, and, putting an imaginary gun to his head, pulled the trigger to tell her something had gone wrong with the audit.

"Tell me about it," she mumbled.

Gordo had something else to say, however. "Remember you promised to pay me for it. I never forget a debt."

"You're kidding!" she exclaimed. "You're not going to hold me to that are you?"

"Does a bear crap in the woods?" He smiled, then frowned. "I paid a price. You'd better make it worthwhile."

Greer looked up, irritably. "Come on, you two! Can't you see I'm trying to do a little surgery here? I think true love is grand and all that, but give me a break."

Carlsie concentrated on finishing the day without attracting additional attention to herself. She was concerned that Gordo had been so cavalier about the data. Was it possible it had not revealed what she thought it would?

On her way out she dashed into the cafeteria to get a cup of coffee to take to the lounge, and happened upon a strange trio. For the first time in all her weeks at the institute she saw the chief of staff, the head nurse, and the chief of pathology together. Barret and Val looked up quickly after Mendel noticed her, but they immediately resumed their conversation. Only Mendel continued to stare at her until she left.

At home Carlsie reviewed every detail of the study. Compared with the national statistics, several factors stood out, all regarding women thirty-five years of age or younger.

First, for patients at or below thirty-five the rate of positive biopsy was three times greater at the institute than in the rest of the nation.

178

Second, the data on systemic spread and reoccurence of cancers in patients who had undergone mastectomy below age thirty-five showed that patients at the institute were found to have cancer spreading to the axillary lymph nodes only one-fourth as often as patients at other hospitals; and there was almost a total absence of metastases to brain, liver, bone, or lung. Other hospitals had a significantly higher incidence.

Oddly enough, for patients older than thirty-five the results of the institute closely matched the national pattern.

With young women, the conclusion drawn at the institute was that it was doing a terrific job. More cancers were being diagnosed, and they were being diagnosed at a much earlier stage than at other hospitals, the result being that these young women were operated upon before their cancers spread to other areas of their bodies. Seemingly many, many lives were being saved.

It was a miracle. If made public, this was news that would make headlines across the country, and would cause a great deal of excitement in the medical world. The famous institute would become even more renowned, even more in demand. This was data to make Walker Barret proud indeed.

There was just one little problem.

It was too good to be true. Much too good. The data was exactly what one would expect if many of the patients had not had cancer in the first place.

As Carlsie went deeper and deeper into the de-

179

tails of the analysis, her spirits sagged. Her discovery held no joy. It was as if she had opened an abscess. The foulness enveloped her, overcame her and sickened her. In her bedroom, alone and sad, she contemplated the horror of these bloody crimes against the healthy flesh of innocent young women. She envisioned the pain and tears of mothers, of sorrowful husbands and lovers; the agony of mutilated young women ripped apart unnecessarily by doctors they trusted, and in a hospital supposedly dedicated to their care.

What she had uncovered was a much more extensive crime than she had imagined possible. This was not the case with a few unfortunate victims as she had expected. Scores of women had been maimed. This was sadism at its worst. It. was the most despicable medical abuse she had ever heard of — worse than violence. An evil. Yes, an evil that had been allowed to flourish.

How could this happen? she asked herself. How could something like this occur in the midst of what had been intended to be so noble, so caring? Why had this little hospital with such talent and dedication to healing become such fertile ground for nurturing something so foul. What fatal flaw had allowed incompetence to thrive instead of being rooted out and destroyed by the excellence around it?

She refused to answer the phone, which rang incessantly — Gordo's calls — nor would she go to the door. She wanted to be alone. She had to think.

180

The tragedy was greater than she had anticipated.

She passed a difficult night, knowing now that the worst was confirmed but still uncertain as to the extent of the staff's involvement.

Chapter Fourteen

Carlsie didn't have the heart to go to the hospital the next day. Around noon Gordo pounded on her door, calling out her name and threatening to get the police unless she let him in.

He was dismayed by her intensity when she tried to explain the situation. He reviewed the statistics with her, studied the cases, and listened to her conclusions. Still, he wanted to convince her to consider other explanations. "What makes you focus so exclusively on the negative?" he asked. "What's wrong with the idea that we are an exceptionally efficient hospital? Why not believe the obvious? This place is the best, and we get the best results. What's so terrible about that?"

She wanted him to understand, badly. How could he be missing the point? she wondered. It was obvious that the institute was doing nothing innovative or different in the area of cancer screening or early diagnosis. There was no reason cancer should be detected earlier there than at other hospitals. Its expertise was in surgical techniques, not in preoperative evaluations or case-finding procedures.

She explained that to him again and again, becoming increasingly frustrated by his stubborn reluctance to face reality. Why wouldn't he see the point? Mendel was insane, he was making mistakes and nobody had realized it until recently.

"The only believable explanation is that we are doing mastectomies on women without cancer!" she argued. "It's easy to have great cure rates when there is no tumor to begin with."

"How the hell would Mendel be pulling this off, Carlsie? And why?" Gordo was becoming angry because of her persistence.

"It would be easy for a pathologist to hide things like this. Who ever double-checks them?"

"Carlsie, be reasonable. Why would he do such a thing?"

"He's crazy, Gordo! How many times do I have to say it? We don't have to know why he's doing this. We just have to check on it, if that's possible."

Gordo sighed and sat down beside her. "Okay, Carlsie. Just for the sake of argument, how would it happen? Forget the motive. How could it be happening?"

She spoke calmly, happy to get the chance to describe a possible scenario. "What if he is overzealous in his diagnostic criteria? What if he calls tissue cancer when it's really not?"

Gordo grimaced. "Carlsie, get serious. He's a nationally recognized expert. He wouldn't make such mistakes. Be practical, for Christ's sake."

"You don't understand what I'm getting at, Gordo. Because he's so famous, he has supreme confidence in his own opinions. He's on a power trip. Who would dispute him, right? So unconsciously he widens the definition of malignancy. Because of his own diagnostic zeal, he slips into calling borderline cases cancer. Next thing you know he's seeing cancer in everything. He's human. People find what they are looking for. It happens all the time. Don't you see?"

Gordo did not. She realized it even before he told her he thought she was building a case out of nothing. "No way, Carlsie. He wouldn't make that many mistakes. He just wouldn't."

His stubbornness infuriated her. "What if he's doing it on purpose? What if he's a sadist?"

"Come on! Look at what you've got. Some stats that show the good results of the surgery done here, and that's it. Everything else is just bullshit. You don't have any evidence that he's doing this. You don't even have a motive. Think about it for a minute. What possible reason could Mendel have to do something like this? It simply doesn't add up." He put his arms around her. "I think you're making a big mistake, honey, unless you know something I don't know. Why don't you forget all this for a while? It's just numbers."

She went to the window and looked out at the lights glowing in the early Palm Beach evening. It was fruitless to continue arguing with him. He didn't see her point, and never would at this rate. If he didn't believe her, who would? She had been certain that the numbers would tell the whole story. It had seemed so obvious to her, but she'd said, people see only what they are looking for.

Barret had seen something. She was sure of that. The numbers had, at the very least, made him nervous. There was no other explanation for his anger over what she was doing. She wondered what he had concluded? Surely he knew their cancer detection efforts were no better or worse than those made elsewhere. What was he thinking now? Was he just nervous because the numbers could be misinterpreted by the uninformed, or was he frightened because there might be some truth in what she believed?

Grossman's accusations came into her mind again. Was there any possibility that Barret was alarmed because she was closing in on a crime in which he was involved? That seemed unlikely to Carlsie. And so did the involvement of anyone else — Val Ryan for instance, despite her recent display of hostility.

Gordo stood behind her, placed his hands upon her shoulders. "Carlsie," he whispered quietly, sympathetically, "relax, baby. You've gotten yourself all worked up over this. You need a break."

She turned angrily toward him, pushing away his hands as he tried to hold her. "A break?" she cried. "I don't need a damned break! This is real, Gordo.

What I'm saying is true and nobody cares." Tears streamed down her cheeks. How could he be so insensitive? It was outrageous. She moved away from him, to the other side of the room.

He stared at her helplessly. "Carlsie, be reasonable. Talk to me. I want to help you." His voice carried a plea for her to come back to reality.

She knew he had not believed anything. He thought she was the only one who was crazy. She was suddenly terrified at being so alone. No one understood her situation. No one would even try. She turned wet eyes on him. "Gordo, what am I going to do?"

He smiled, humoring her. "Oh, baby. You don't have to do anything. I'm going to get you some help. A psychiatrist can help sort this out. You've been under too much stress, and it's partly my fault for not recognizing it. I'm sorry." He stepped forward, intending to embrace her.

As she watched, he seemed to come toward her in slow motion while her mind raced through a thousand thoughts. This situation was unbelievable. Had he nothing better to say than that he would get her a psychiatrist? What was wrong with him? Hadn't he been listening to her? Couldn't he see beyond the end of his nose? Her frustration with Gordo's inability to comprehend what was going on drove her into a rage. "Get out of here!" she shrieked. "Leave me alone!"

He attempted to put his arms around her but she pushed him back forcefully. "Don't touch me!" She shouted, glaring angrily at him. "You're as bad as the others. Maybe even worse because you know the facts and you're still denying everything. Maybe you're in on it."

"Cut it out, Carlsie. You're getting a little freaky now."

"Maybe you're all in it! You, Barret, Val, Mendel . . . everybody!" She couldn't bring herself to include Hank in the list. She spoke more softly now. "Just get out of here and let me alone! Go on over there and finish up your residency so you can get to the big money quicker."

Hurt, he stared at her for a moment. "You're blowing it, you know. You had a chance to do something really great with your career. Walker Barret is giving you a phenomenal opportunity and you're crapping on it."

She regretted her outburst. "Gordo, I'm sorry. I didn't mean to imply anything about you. I don't really think anyone else is involved. Grossman tried to make a case that Val was doing something wrong, but it doesn't fit. And Barret wouldn't gain from this either. If he'd been doing something, he would have distorted the numbers, and he wouldn't have let me see them. I know that. I'm sorry I said what I did."

Gordo gazed at her, a profound sadness in his eyes. "You should be."

She waited in silence while he went to the door. He turned back to her just before he left, and his voice carried the hurt of a far worse wound. "I

188

thought I knew you. I was wrong."

After he had gone, she considered everything, in a troubling blur of quickly changing mental images. She thought about Gordo, Mendel, Hank; about her own uncertain future and about the fact that she didn't want this task. Gordo was right, in a way. The opportunity of a lifetime was being blown. It seemed impossible that all her years of hard work had come to this. "Why?" she mumbled. Why has this happened? No matter what resulted from it she was finished here. If she was right, the place would be a shambles, and if she was wrong, she would no longer be welcome.

Carlsie collapsed on her bed and cried. Without Gordo's, or anyone's, support she felt so isolated, so alone. She needed someone who would understand her, sympathize with her, and give her some emotional support. She needed somebody on her side, somebody who was like her and thought the way she did. So much was at stake.

For lack of anyone else to turn to, she dialed Ed Grossman's number, back in Detroit where he'd said he still owned a condo. Miraculously, she caught him at home. He sounded depressed. She told him about her statistics, but he didn't want to talk about them.

"The numbers look bad, Ed."

"It doesn't matter."

"How can you say that? You're the one who put me on to this."

"I was probably wrong. You'll be better off if you

just forget about it, Carlsie."

"Now you sound like Gordo." Grossman's reaction was not what Carlsie had expected. He had originally been so upset about the situation she didn't understand how he could be so unconcerned about it now. "What's changed you so, Ed?"

His voice took on a sterner tone. "Look, Carlsie, I can't talk about this. It won't do any good. You're only going to do your career harm by pursuing it."

Now she understood. "Do you have another job yet?"

"Maybe. They're waiting for my references to come in."

"I see . . . and you're worried about Walker Barret?"

"He's a very influential man. I'm sure you know that."

"Ed, are you an alcoholic like he said?"

After a long silence, he answered. "I don't know how Barret found out about that. Two years ago I took an extended vacation and went for treatment. As far as I could tell, no one knew. Now, he's threatened to ruin me with it."

"If you're not drinking anymore, how can he hurt you?"

"Be realistic, Carlsie. I take people's lives in my hands when I administer anesthetics. No surgeon or hospital administrator would want to chance it with me if Barret puts the hex on me . . . not with the malpractice situation the way it is."

"Sounds like blackmail."

190

"Call it what you wish. I know I'm weak. I just don't have any weapons to fight him with."

"You have my data. Blackmail him back."

"No deal, Carlsie. Count me out. I know when I'm outclassed."

"Is there anything at all you know that would help me?"

He sighed. "No."

"Do you really think I should drop it . . . I mean really?"

"I can't make that decision for you, Carlsie. It's hard enough living with the decision I made. I can't cure all the ills of the world, and neither can you."

"I am going to try to cure this one, though," she responded softly.

"I just can't get involved. If I lose my profession, I lose everything. I'm not a young man and I have a blemished record already."

"You're wrong, Ed. If this is really happening, there's no excuse for not stopping it, no matter what the professional cost."

"Carlsie, you've got no proof."

"Then help me get it."

"You're messing with some very powerful people. Lots of money and lots of reputations are on the line."

"So what?"

His voice was strained. "Be careful, Carlsie. I really mean it. Now, I've got to go."

"Ed, you're disappointing me."

"Good-bye, Carlsie."

After hanging up, she checked her door and window locks. Grossman had obviously been intimidated, and that made her afraid. He was right. A lot of money and a lot of reputations were on the line. If the worst was true, there was no telling to what lengths someone might go to protect the status quo.

Chapter Fifteen

Oscar Mendel cruised slowly past Carlsie's condominium. Satisfied that the evening parade in and out of the building had waned, he circled the block once more, noting that the neighborhood was quiet and the streets were empty. The night was dark, with only a rim of a moon visible on the Atlantic horizon. The moment for action had arrived. It was time to play hardball with the Camden slut — his newest enemy.

He wondered if Bernie Farber had played any role in bringing about the so-called statistical study she had done. Perhaps Farber had wanted to bring her here to harass him. In retrospect, the timing of her arrival could hardly have been a coincidence. Damn you, Farber, he thought. Damn you for doing this to me!

In the beginning, when he had first suspected his colleague had discovered what was going on, he had decided that Farber hadn't had time to tell anyone.

The man had had no family and no close friends. Certainly he wouldn't have discussed his suspicions with anyone at the Institute — not without more proof, anyway. It would have been Farber's style to avoid acting hastily; he would have worried about not knowing who else was involved. But lately, as Mendel had pondered the situation, it had seemed more and more obvious that Farber might have confided in a woman. He was weak in that way. He must have told Camden, Mendel concluded. Why else would she have come here?

Fortunately, Farber himself — the clumsy oaf — had been easy to handle. Since everyone knew what a chain smoker he was, it had been easy to make the fire in his apartment appear to be a tragic accident.

But silencing this Camden woman was not likely to be such child's play. He wondered if she was a nun. He knew she was Catholic. What confidence she exuded, what conceit! She hadn't even bothered to conceal her origins. God, how he hated Catholics.

He turned his Mercedes into the parking garage, and found a visitor's space on the mostly deserted second level near the stairwell. Sitting in the silence, he rethought his plan and checked the equipment in his briefcase. It contained two pairs of surgical gloves, a couple of scalpels with new blades, a syringe and needle, and the most important item — a full ampule of Anectine, the muscle-paralyzing drug used by anesthesiologists. The proper dose, given intramuscularly, rapidly blocked the ability of

194

nerves to conduct impulses to muscles, thus rendering the patient — or victim, as it were — totally paralyzed, unable to move a muscle, including those used for respiration.

Mendel enjoyed the thought of having Carlsie at his mercy, completely helpless. To him the intriguing part was that the drug did not affect consciousness. Anectine only paralyzed the muscles. The brain was not sedated or anesthetized in any way. Eventually there was an effect on the brain, of course, because as respiration ceased a lack of oxygen developed. That caused a loss of consciousness — a permanent loss of it. This would take a while, perhaps as long as four or five minutes, and during that time Carlsie would be aware of what he was doing to her but completely unable to fight him . . . or breathe.

For Mendel it was an ideal situation. His anger was so intense that he wanted to be sure she suffered before she died. He wanted her to know what he was doing to her body as she faded away. He wanted her to feel the blades tearing into her breasts, to know that her own warm blood was running down her chest. When he had found out about the statistics she'd gathered, he had realized that she must be stopped. She was hard on his heels, trying to hang the blame for all this on him, and there was no time to waste. Her continued existence was incompatible with his happiness.

Armed and prepared, he entered the stairwell and moved quickly to the fifth floor. Because he thought he heard voices in the corridor, he waited for a while to make sure he was not seen. Finally he cracked open the door, and saw that his path was clear.

Carlsie's apartment was about halfway down the hall, just across from the elevator. Quietly he passed the other doors, then stopped just outside her doorway, put his ear to it, and listened. From inside came faint noises as if someone were moving around. Then he heard a cabinet being shut. Mendel listened carefully for voices: he wanted her to be alone. He was not prepared for any surprises.

Hearing no one speaking, he was satisfied that all was the way he wanted it. He could hardly wait to see her startled expression when she opened the door and he drove the needle deep into her, injecting her with Anectine. He planned to tell her exactly what shot she had received before it had time to work. He wanted her to dread what was coming. She would know what the effect of the drug was going to be — any surgeon would — it was used often enough in O.R. But in surgery patients were rendered unconscious before being paralyzed, and an anesthesiologist was there to "breathe" for them. Tonight there would be no anesthesiologist, only a pathologist and amateur surgeon, who usually operated only on the dead.

Mendel's pulse was racing, and he was trembling with anxiety and anticipation. He realized that he was hyperventilating. Forcing himself to breathe more slowly, he stepped past her door and leaned

196

against the wall. As he tried to calm down, he sensed the beginning of a headache. He had been worried that this stress would induce one. Not now, he thought. God, not now. He fumbled through his pockets and brought out the bottle of codeine, swallowed three tablets immediately. Two wouldn't be enough this time. His discomfort was threatening to worsen.

He waited for the throbbing and ringing to ease, determined that nothing would stop him now. He was so close. He concentrated hard, trying to overcome the pain by willpower. The codeine would help, but the drug didn't stop the dizziness or the noise. The roar filled his consciousness and threatened to take permanent command of it. Only the antiseizure medicines Dilantin and Tegretol could do that. Mendel hated taking them. He disdained the capitulation that implied.

He put his fingers to his temples as the discomfort grew, confirming his fear that he had procrastinated too long before taking the pills. He should have taken them before leaving home.

Goddamn it, he thought. He didn't want to go through this again. He didn't need this misery.

Screw you, Farber!

Screw you, Camden!

Somewhere in his brain, the temporal lobe the neurologists had said, he perceived the awakening anger of his new consciousness, his new personality — the one that called itself Belail. He tried to fight it, but knew that was futile. It was starting now and would go on and on like it always did.

Panicked by the impending loss of control and consciousness, he stumbled noisily toward the elevator and pressed the button.

The grinding, squeezing, nerve-shattering pressure grew until his skull seemed to be breaking like a melon dropped on a concrete floor.

His head was exploding now . . . coming apart . . . bursting open. Spilling out blood and gray matter, nerves and brains. He wanted to scream from the agony. He was exploding all over the floor! The pain! . . . The goddamned pain! Something please stop the pain! Please!

Leaning forward, his head sinking into his hands, he moaned softly, totally incapacitated.

The elevator opened and he tumbled in. The door closed automatically.

Then came the rage.

As usual he was not able to control it. For one brief minute he wanted to tear the cage apart. Smash the goddamn hell out of it—burn it, piss on it, stomp it . . . and burn it again!

He slammed his fist into a glass display panel on a side wall of the elevator car. Shattered pieces showered down onto him. He hit the panel again. This time, blood erupted from his hand, splattering his shirt and face.

"Goddamned surgeons!" he roared, and kicked the door. "Somebody needs to kick their asses . . . straighten the dumb sons of bitches out."

"And this new bitch . . . he would have to

straighten her ass out — for good. The whore! Even as he clamped his mouth shut to keep from further revealing his torment, profanities were ricocheting about in his mind. He hit the wall again. And again.

Then, finally, it was over.

The pressure was gone.

The pain was gone.

The rage gone.

Wet with perspiration, he waited gratefully as the last remnants of the seizure ebbed slowly away. Once more he, Mendel, had survived. In that private portion of his mind still untouched by this bewildering disease, he thought: "I want more time. I deserve more time to just be myself."

He realized where he was, and was glad that the closed elevator was not moving.

Silently, desperately, he pressed the button for the second floor. When the elevator stopped he pulled himself up and went as quickly as he could to the garage exit. His gait was unsteady, and he left a long, spotty trail of blood on the way to his car. Breathing heavily, he lay down on the back seat, safe now from prying eyes.

For three years he had secretly fought this battle. At first, he had turned to his own profession for an explanation. Using an assumed name, he had traveled to Boston to be examined. The specialists had done everything they could — CT Scans, arteriograms, EEGs, NMRs. No diagnostic possibility had been overlooked. He had undergone the most comprehensive workup for headaches and seizures that modern neurologists could devise.

In the end psychiatric evaluation had been recommended, and Mendel had made the mistake of telling the truth. When he'd revealed the existence of this new awareness within him — this Belail — his doctor had wanted him to stay on for prolonged treatment. Their diagnosis of temporal lobe epilepsy with associated schizophrenic psychosis had been disappointing. They had said he was paranoid, that Belail was his own creation, merely a part of his hallucinatory and delusional symptomatology.

He had taken the drugs prescribed just to see, but they were of no use. He didn't like the way they made him feel. Finally, he had abandoned them because he knew his problem was not psychiatric. There was nothing wrong with his mind, for Christ's sake. This wasn't a weakness, it wasn't his fault. Someone had done this to him. It was some kind of new infection that they hadn't recognized. Why couldn't they see that?

He knew when it had begun, and where. It had started when the young lab tech had entered his life. How naïve he had been when she'd first come to him, her voice sweet as honey, her skin like silk. What irony that pleasure such as she had given him had been instrumental in shaping his destiny. Who could have guessed how unclean she was? She had been loving, tender, and for a few short weeks had brought him joy surpassing the sum of happiness he'd known previously. How was he to know she would turn out to be infected—a whore?

His initial headache had come after their first night together. Three days later the second had followed, worse than the initial one. Only then had he realized what she was doing. The seeds she was putting into him were foul. And most inappropriate of all, it was during the act of love, when he felt so tenderly toward her, that the contamination was occurring. Her body was a source of exhilaration for him, yet he was being soiled by the very contact that was so pleasurable.

Seemingly alone, on the run from a broken marriage, and needing a job, she had come to him. He had comforted her, and given her succor. His reward had been the pains in his head. The headaches she had induced had never stopped.

Sadly, it had been necessary to sacrifice her when her deed had been discovered, God only knew how many others she had already damaged. Mendel had been forced to punish her when she'd tried to leave. The voice of Belail had guided him.

Later, he'd pondered the weakness that had made him so willing to do what Belail said was right. It had been so easy to take her life. Clearly, he remembered her screams, her anguish. The bloodstains on his bed had necessitated burning the mattress and sheets along with her body. The instructions had come from Belail. He had heard them quite clearly.

He kept her breasts for a while, but eventually they, too, had been destroyed. Because with those bountiful breasts she had tempted him, it had seemed appropriate to cut them from her as she'd writhed helplessly and painfully, pleading for mercy while her punishment was administered. The torture of bilateral mastectomy without anesthesia had helped her understand the significance of what she had done. As she lay dying, while blood from her mutilated and breastless chest spurted wildly about her, he had dangled the amputated organs before her and explained her role in what had happened to him. He hoped she understood that her debt was paid, and that she was happy now, at peace and forever quiet. The vase in which she permanently rested was above his fireplace.

It was during her mutilation that he'd first understood the profound meaning and inherent justice of carcinoma of the breast — it was a way of punishing women for the wanton use of their bodies. It was natural. It was just. Belail had shown him that, together they had implemented the plan.

And now this Camden woman needed a lesson. Since she claimed to be a surgeon, it seemed appropriate to let her suffer by the blade. He knew she would appreciate his unique technique of bilateral mastectomy.

Not tonight, unfortunately. He needed rest now. It would be all he could do to drive himself home and get cleaned up. There was blood all over him, and his hand hurt like hell. Gently he examined it. The wounds seemed superficial. Thank God, the tendons were all intact.

He must get Camden soon. He had no choice. There was so very little time. When he came for her again, he would take the medication first — before he experienced the stress.

Carlsie came out into the hall at the sound of excited voices. Someone had smashed up the elevator and blood was everywhere, her neighbors told her. The police were in the lobby taking fingerprints.

Carlsie wasn't interested. She had more weighty concerns than vandalism. Mutilation was on her mind. Still, it was weird that such a thing had happened in her building. The wanton destruction fueled her generalized anxiety.

Chapter Sixteen

For Debbie Hunter, the picnic hosted by Ken Redman's employers was a special event. It was the first time in a long while that she had been able to relax and enjoy the company of a man. She took the day off and pushed the problems of her job at the Bloody Goose to the back of her mind. She had decided, finally, to take Ken's advice and start living a normal life again. The two of them drank beers, ate hotdogs, and walked along the beach. Later in the afternoon they joined some of her old friends in a volleyball game.

It was a grand day. Ken was nice and easy to be with. He wasn't the handsomest man on earth, nor the most debonair; but he was sweet and pleasant and, most of all, nonjudgmental. Behind his wire-rimmed glasses were warm friendly eyes that made up for thinning hair and a slightly overweight body. The fact that he knew all about her made it even more comfortable being with him.

When the day was over and he took her home, she invited him in. She had known she would, if all went well. It was part of the deal. If she was going to try to be normal, then she had to do it right. Asking him to stay awhile, have another drink and maybe watch a little TV or something, was the thing to do after a day such as that. It was not a decision she had made lightly, however. She had struggled with it, considered all the consequences, and had finally made herself get up the courage to do it.

They talked awhile about the picnic and the staff politics at the hotel where he worked. Then they had a friendly argument about which was the best soap opera. They both watched them, since they had evening jobs.

She mixed some frozen daiquiris, and he was impressed; so they had another round. They snuggled together and watched a late movie; then he kissed her. She had a moment of self-doubt right then, but she fought it, overcame it. She wanted to be normal, to make love again, and she wanted to do it with this man. She trusted him.

As their passion rose, he led her into her bedroom. Slowly, tenderly he began to undress her, and she helped him from his clothes. Eventually all that remained was her bra. He made no attempt to remove it.

She started to unsnap it at the back.

"It's all right," he said, softly. "You don't have to take it off."

But Debbie wanted it off. She didn't care to make love partially clothed. She continued loosening it.

He put his hands on hers. "No, don't do it. I want to remember you the way you were." He peered deeply into her eyes.

His words sliced into her confidence. She didn't want him to feel that way. She needed acceptance of her body as it was now. "Ken, I need you to want the real me, to see the real me. It's not that bad."

He said nothing. She took away the bra.

His eyes never left her face. The sudden strain in the air grew worse. They tried to hold each other. They kissed, he ran his hands over the normal parts of her body, they did all the things they were supposed to do.

It didn't work.

Debbie grew progressively more tense. He could not bring himself to look at her chest, and, in his nervousness, became unable to function as a man. Her sense of self-worth plummeted.

In the end, they both were sad. They stood together at her door, not knowing what to say or do. Their failure was devastating to her, and embarrassing to him. "I'm sorry, Deb," he said. "I don't usually have this problem. Please forgive me."

She knew he wanted forgiveness for more than his impotence. He wanted to be excused for his inability to cope with her disfigurement. "It's okay," she responded. "You probably had a little too much to drink. Don't worry about it; we'll try again sometime." She knew that was a lie.

"Thanks. I had a great day," he said, and turned away. He had taken only a few steps when he looked back. "I'm really sorry . . . so very sorry."

For a few minutes she sat alone in the darkness of her apartment, trying to shake off her depression. She couldn't. She cried as hard as she had in the days just after surgery, maybe even harder. This was failure at its worst. Things weren't going to get better. If this man who had been a friend for so long couldn't face her, then what man could?

She decided that night never to try again. She would turn her heart to stone as far as men and love and sex were concerned. She didn't need it anyway. Most males were unfaithful bastards in the long run, and could almost never be depended upon. She decided it had been stupid of her to weaken and think that a man could understand her. That had been a bad mistake. She promised herself she would not make it again.

She spent the night wondering why she had gotten cancer. No one else in her family had, and she'd never met anyone as young as she was who'd been through this hell. What had she done to deserve this punishment? She knew the doctors at that hospital had been trying to do the right thing, but she hated them. They had ruined her. It might have been better if they had just let her die.

Chapter Seventeen

The weekly surgical staff meeting began in the usual way exactly on time, at seven A.M. There was a moment of awkwardness when Carlsie entered and everyone turned to stare at her. Hank caught her eye, and watched her sympathetically for several minutes.

Barret, in fine form, was pompously berating the residents for not getting their paperwork done, for occasional failures to keep the flow of patients in and out of O.R. moving smoothly, and for ineptness in general. Dressed in one of his finely tailored thousand-dollar suits and a custom-designed silk tie, which had tiny scalpels carefully embroidered along its edges, he looked the million-dollar surgeon he was, and seemed to be enjoying his game of intimidation.

He was irritated about a minor wound infection in one of his augmentation patients. It had necessitated removal of a silicone breast prosthesis, albeit temporarily, in order to allow the antibiotics to work more effectively. The patient would be fine, but would have to live with one small breast and one quite a bit larger for several weeks. It was no big deal — occasional wound infections are a fact of life for all surgeons — but he was raising all kinds of hell with the resident involved.

Fulton Greer, clutching the last of the jelly doughnuts that had filled the tray in the center of the conference table, munched happily away, nodding in good-humored appreciation of the chief's sarcastic criticisms. Greer was one of the biggest proponents of the theory that residents were supposed to eat a little crap everyday.

Hank seemed to be ignoring the whole diatribe, preferring to stare at the table in front of him and cast quick glances at Carlsie.

Gordo, who had been purposely avoiding eye contact with her all morning for reasons Carlsie well understood, was displaying sympathy for the resident under attack, but he seemed unable to find a graceful way to divert Barret's cuts. This was one of those rites in surgical training in which a senior staff man periodically removed a testicle from an errant trainee. Barret, capable of the most caustic remarks, actually took pleasure in embarrassing the resident as much as possible. Carlsie found the whole scene disgusting and absurd.

When, finally, Barret seemed to tire of the tirade, she decided to act. Rising from her chair at the side of the room, she stood at the opposite end of the long table and cleared her throat noisily several times. She suspected that Barret would attempt to stop her from talking, and was prepared to shout him down or do whatever was necessary to be heard.

"Gentlemen," she said forcefully, "I need your attention. I must share with you some statistics I have put together in the course of my clinical research. What I have found is not going to make anyone happy."

She couldn't have surprised this particular gathering more with this sudden interruption had she climbed onto the table and disrobed. She saw more slacked-jawed expressions of disbelief than she had the day she'd arrived, a full-blooded female. Fulton Greer paused in midchew, exposing a mouthful of horrible-looking lemon-lime jelly. Hank appeared totally amazed.

Only Gordo understood her purpose. Breaking his self-imposed isolation from her, he silently mouthed the word "no" and shook his head warningly. She ignored him.

Walker Barret uttered a furious grunt and started to rise. "Look here, young woman—"

"Excuse me, Dr. Barret. I must say—"

"You will do nothing of the kind," he interrupted. "I demand that you take your seat or leave this instant!"

"No, sir. I won't! Listen to me now or read the figures in the newspaper. One way or the other, I'm going to be heard."

Barret fixed a challenging stare upon her while the rest of the men sat back, curious about what this little lady could possibly say that was so damned important. Carlsie paused for a moment to guarantee their attention, and then laid the foundation for an accusation more vile than any of them had ever thought they would hear. Next she shattered the smug confidence and delusion of superiority that had enfolded the institute and its surgeons for almost two decades.

She described her statistical analysis of the breast biopsy results, emphasizing the startlingly high percentage of positive biopsies in the younger group of women and the equally amazing low number of cases that metastasized.

Barret, who had been listening although obviously annoyed, now leaned forward. Everyone else seemed to be anxious to hear what she had concluded from her findings, but Hank appeared to be more concerned about what she was doing rather than what she was saying.

As she prepared to deliver the conclusions she'd drawn from the data, Carlsie was interrupted by a soft-spoken but firm Gordo. "Carlsie, I think you've said enough. Why don't you stop now? We can discuss this in more detail later, in a more appropriate forum."

"An excellent suggestion," Barret said.

"No, Gordo," she declared. "This is the place and now is the time."

"As your chief resident, I'm ordering you to sit down. You are only going to get yourself in trouble," he retorted.

"I'm going to finish what I have started."

"I'm asking you to stop. I'm your friend." His eyes pleaded with her. "There is no need to do this."

She felt a rush of affection for him, and gratitude

for his concern; but she was committed. "I'm sorry. You are my friend, Gordo. You are all my friends, but so are some of our victims."

The uneasy atmosphere in the room became palpably tense. Gordo looked hopelessly to the floor. Ritter stirred nervously.

"Are you involved in this, Dr. Keene?" Barret asked.

Gordo shook his head but didn't look up.

"Speak up, man!" Barret roared, startling almost everyone. "What do you know about this? You're the chief resident, aren't you? So what the hell is this all about?" He had risen to his feet, and was leaning across the table alternating his menacing glare between Carlsie and Gordo.

Gordo spoke softly, almost inaudibly. "I have nothing to do with it. I tried to convince her to stop. She's acting on her own. None of the other residents have any part in it or even know what she was doing. Her conclusions are hers alone." His voice carried a sense of defeat, betrayal, and despair. His eyes remained fixed upon the floor.

Barret stared unwaveringly at Carlsie. She did not turn away. "Are you finished?" he asked. "I advise that you should be."

She spoke deliberately and in an unemotional monotone, much like a judge rendering a capital sentence. "I believe we have performed unnecessary mastectomies upon innocent young women who did not have carcinoma of the breast. I suggest that, at the very least, this institution has been complacent while its pathologist made error after error, leading to the mutilation of dozens of patients. I accuse

213

this institution of failing to monitor its own statistics, and I accuse each of you of performing more and more surgery with almost no regard to assuring fail-safe procedures in a department not nearly so glamorous as our own."

"You bloody bitch!" Barret roared, and came around the table in a rush. "You ungrateful little whore!" He was pushing his way behind the chairs of the others, his face mirroring his hatred and uncontrollable anger. Ritter and the others restrained him while Carlsie stood her ground, her faced filled with defiance, confidence, and willingness to sacrifice everything she had worked for.

The room was alive with the shouts of outraged men and the heavy, dull sounds of bodies and furniture in collision as the others struggled to keep Barret from reaching Carlsie.

"I should break your neck for those lies!" The chief surgeon bellowed, still trying to loosen himself from the grip of his colleagues.

"Read the numbers!" she retorted, waving her papers in his face. "You should have known this two years ago. You should have been more careful. The data speaks for itself!"

"You're a bloody liar!" he ranted. "A muckraker, trying to destroy what you could never be!"

"You are destroying yourself by not caring! You worry more about this institution's reputation and the money it brings in than you do about the patients." In defiance, she had moved closer to him, the fire in her eyes glowing more fiercely than ever.

Ritter pushed himself between the two. "Shut up, Carlsie! You've said enough."

She ignored him, stepping sideways to get a better view of Barret. "Don't you ever look at Mendel?" she asked. "Don't you hear the things he says? It's written all over him. He's a madman. Everyone knows it. Hank. Gordo. All of you. How could you have let him do this?"

"Let go of me!" Barret grunted, and with a mighty heave, he freed himself and lunged toward her, swinging.

"It's criminal, that's what it is!" she screamed, raising her arms in front of her to block his attack. A glancing blow caught her high on the forehead and she stumbled backward into the wall.

Screaming obscenities, Barret bore down on her again.

Carlsie sank to the floor, covering her head with her arms, prepared to receive the full force of his blows. She was frightened, not panicked. She wished she could fight back. She wanted to push him, hit him, punish him for doing this to her.

He stood over her, fists poised, but at the last instant he suddenly seemed to gain control of himself. He stopped and remained motionless, his face still contorted in anger. The shouting ceased; all movement toward him stopped.

Carlsie rose to her feet, eyes focused on Barret.

"Are you all right?" Hank asked her.

She nodded as Gordo came to her side.

"I want you out of here right now," Barret ordered. "And don't come back. If you ever say anything like that again, I'll blast you with a slander suit you'll never get over, and I'll make sure you never practice surgery anywhere in this country." He frowned at her. "Now, get out!"

But Carlsie was not quitting. She had not come this far to be intimidated. She refused to move.

Barret turned to Hank and Greer. "Get rid of her. Call security if you have to. She wants to destroy us."

Greer grabbed Carlsie by the arm and pulled her toward the door. "You heard what the man said, Camden. Why don't you leave peacefully?"

Hank spoke firmly. "Take it easy, Fulton. Let's just handle this calmly. I'm sure Carlsie will cooperate, so keep your hands off her." He stepped between her and the fat staff surgeon, who glared angrily at his colleague and then at Carlsie.

"Somebody call security!" Barret grunted.

"Why don't you do that?" Carlsie put in. "I'd just as soon discuss my findings with the police and the press as I would with you. I'm sure they would be very interested in what I have to show them."

"Don't be ridiculous. They won't print your lies. Not in a million years. I'd sue the hell out of them, and they know it."

"Can we chance it?" Hank asked. "What if they believe her? It could mean real problems for us. The numbers could easily be misinterpreted.

Barret frowned. "So what do you think I should do, pander to this maniac?"

"I don't think we have to do that," Ritter replied. "On the other hand we don't need to be so defensive about this. We've done nothing wrong." He turned to Carlsie. "You've said your piece. Now, what is it you're after? Why are you doing this?"

Barrett spoke before she could. "Publicity, that's

why. She thinks she can make a name for herself by dragging us down. She's not worth the time of day, and we're foolish for bothering with her."

Ritter showed signs of impatience and irritation with his chief's hostility and unwillingness to hear Camden out. "Walker, why don't you be quiet a minute and let her talk. We need to know what her point is."

Barrett shook his head in disgust but said nothing.

All eyes were on Carlsie now. She stood before them, wondering how to phrase her conclusions so they would realize she was not trying to harm them. She desired only to stop the mutilation, to compensate the victims . . . and to put an end to the crimes of Mendel and whoever else might be acting in concert with him. She wanted these surgeons to recognize what the pathologist had done to them and their patients, and to put an end to it.

She spoke slowly, choosing her words carefully. She had to take time so they might understand what her evidence really meant. She wanted to allay their bitterness, to have them join her effort to eradicate this evil, even if the price of doing so was high. She wished she had taken a softer, more gentle approach at the beginning, but she had failed to anticipate the animosity her words would arouse.

Carlsie outlined her findings in a quiet, supportive manner, noting that everyone now listened carefully, pensively. She, as well as they, realized there was no happy resolution to the problem she had presented. If she was correct, which none of them believed she was, it meant disaster for the institute.

If she was wrong, as they all hoped she was, it meant disaster for her. She would be banned from the institute and probably from all hospitals. No one wanted a troublemaker around, no matter how well intentioned. She perceived that despite everything most of those present liked her. They had come to be as fond of her as she was of them, and they hated to see her self-destructing.

Gordo's pain seemed more than he could bear. And Hank was equally hurt. His eyes saddened as she spoke about her interpretation of the statistics. Then he attempted to rebut her conclusions just as Gordo had done previously. The institute is a referral center, he pointed out. We get the most intricate cases, and we have the best cure rate because we do better surgery. He and the others came up with many explanations for her data.

But there was no satisfying Carlsie. Too many girls with small pre-op chances of having malignancies were receiving positive biopsies. An unbelievably low percentage were found to metastasize to the lymph nodes in comparison to every other published study on cancer statistics. Only one conclusion explained that satisfactorily: some of these girls did not truly have cancer. Mendel was making mistakes.

How could he? she was asked. She was reminded that he was a renowned expert.

It was because of his expertise that mistakes were possible, Carlsie explained. In his zeal to be perfect in his diagnostic skills, perhaps he had imperceptibly pushed the diagnostic criteria beyond the limits used by others.

Finally there was no rebuttal. Begrudgingly they accepted the possibility of what Carlsie had outlined . . . barely. Everyone made it perfectly clear that he believed she was wrong, was shooting at shadows, and was endangering the reputation of the institute with only a shred of evidence.

"What can we do to show you that you are wrong?" Hank asked. He had taken over the leadership of the meeting, Barrett, still furious, was refusing to talk with her.

Now that she had had a chance to explain herself, Carlsie quickly answered. "I want an outside pathologist to review the permanent slides of the presumedly malignant biopsies of patients under the age of thirty-five, those taken at the institute during the last several years."

No one spoke immediately. They were all considering the consequences of her request.

"Anything else?" Hank asked.

"Yes. I want no additional mastectomies done without verification of the diagnosis by an outside source until this review is completed."

Hank glanced at Barret, as did the others.

The chief, continuing to glare at Carlsie, decided the time had come to negotiate. "If I order this done, and Dr. Mandel is vindicated, as he surely will be, will you abandon this absurd theory, surrender all your research to me, and apologize to him and to the rest of us?"

"I will."

His expression became even more scornful. "And will you then quietly resign, disappear, and never discuss this institute or your demented suspicions

219

with anyone else? Will you get out of plastic surgery forever?"

The old man was going in for the kill. Carlsie's eyes misted over. If by chance she was wrong, this was too severe a price to pay for attempting to carry out her duty. But she had no choice. "I accept your terms." She rose to leave.

"Then so be it." Barret turned to his associate. "Hank, take care of organizing this review a.s.a.p. I'll inform Oscar myself. I'd like it finished by the end of the week, so we can get back to taking care of patients instead of catering to the imaginings of"—he looked at Carlsie who was standing in the doorway—"a hysterical, paranoid, out-of-place woman. Consider yourself suspended from all clinical activities, Camden, and I suggest you begin packing your bags. I understand they need doctors in Ethiopia."

Carlsie walked out into the empty hallway, and someone closed the door behind her. By the time the elevator arrived a few minutes later, she had heard angry voices several times. None of the others had come out of the room.

She felt alone, homeless. Yet in addition to the vast, painful emptiness within her, there was a sense of increasing personal strength. She was right, she knew she was; and she was ready to take the heat until everyone was convinced of it.

Chapter Eighteen

It became the longest day of her life. Leaving behind the institute and everything she had ever cared about in medicine, Carlsie wandered away, on foot, into the beautiful fall day of Palm Beach. The air was crisp with the fresh scent of an ocean breeze, and the island was lush and verdant. The full-time residents as well as the tourists were out in force. The streets were crowded with expensive cars and richly dressed people.

She tried not to think of the consequences she must face whether she had been right or wrong in her accusations. Either way, everything had changed for her. There could be no returning to the old dreams and career plans. Those were gone forever, no matter what followed. There would be no breast-surgery fellowship, no hope of a rewarding academic career at the institute. But she didn't care anymore. Not now. Not after everything that had happened.

* * *

Carlsie wandered along beside the surf enjoying the frivolity of the beach-goers. She talked for a while with a toddler who offered to bury her feet in the sand, and watched a zany Dalmatian playing Frisbee with his master, a blond Adonis reminiscent of Gordo.

Eventually she settled down in her favorite spot, beneath the overhanging boughs of an ancient banyan tree just south of the inlet, where she could watch the sportfishing boats come through the channel. After a while she closed her eyes and in the warmth of the afternoon almost dozed off.

A familiar voice awakened her. "I thought I'd find you here," Gordo said.

Carlsie peered upward at him, seeing only an outline against the bright sun. Sitting up, she shielded her eyes from the glare and gazed at him without speaking. She didn't want him here, not now that she had such mixed feelings about him. She loved him but not in the way that he wanted. "Why did you come?" she asked.

"I wanted to talk to you."

"There's nothing more to say, Gordo. You know how I feel."

"There's a chance I could convince Barret to forget everything you said. We could blame it on overwork. I could send you on a little vacation. Hell, I'd take time off and go with you. He'd buy it. I know he would. You could start all over. Things could be just like they were." He pleaded with his eyes and his handsome face. "Come on, Carlsie. Do

222

it. Let me go talk to him."

He was so sincere, so honest and concerned, she wanted to cry. He sat down beside her and took her hand as he spoke. "I understand why you're doing this," he said. "Forget everything I said before. I was just being stubborn, that's all. It's just that I love you so much I can't stand watching this happen to you." He looked away, out over the ocean, hiding his pain. "You're all I care about anymore. I've never felt this way before. You've got to straighten out, Carlsie. You've just got to. It's killing me."

He paused, grimacing, emotionally exhausted.

It broke her heart to see him suffering. He was so innocent and filled with love . . . and she felt so guilty. She should have broken off the relationship weeks ago, when she'd felt a rising interest in Hank. His pain was her fault, but she wouldn't allow that to go on. She had to put an end to his hopes, now and forever.

She held his hand. "I will never know a better friend than you, Gordo. I love you dearly. I truly do . . . as a friend."

He turned away, his voice wavering as he spoke. "No, Carlsie. Don't say that. We can make it. I know we can." He looked at her again. "Let's forget this place. We can go away. I know some hospitals in California that are begging for residents. Let's go out there and leave all this behind. It'll be great." He swallowed and blinked hard. "I don't think you know how much I care about you."

She shook her head. "It's no use, Gordo. It won't work. We can only be friends." She clasped both his hands and smiled warmly. "I'll never forget some of the moments we've had. They were the best, believe me. It's just that . . . well, how else can I say it? People change. It would be wrong for us to hold on now that so much has happened." She rose, pulling him up with her, and put her arm around his waist. "I know I'm the one who's changed, Gordo, not you. And I'm sorry about that."

They began walking slowly down the beach, holding each other close. There was no conversation as they moved along, and after a while they came to where he had parked his car.

"I think I'll walk on alone," she said separating herself from him. "I have a lot of time to kill nowadays." She grinned at her light-hearted reference to her suspension, and he tried to smile back.

"Take care, sweet girl," he murmured. "Be careful and let me help in any way I can."

"You can count on it."

He turned away, but after a few steps he hesitated and glanced back at her. With both arms held up imploringly in front of him, he told her he could not give up this easily. "No matter how long it takes, I'll wait until you want me back," he said. "Because I know that eventually you will. Somehow we are going to end up together. It's in the stars, I'm convinced of it. This love was meant to be."

Their eyes met for a long silent moment. She didn't know what to say to this man who loved her so.

"When you need me, will you call?" he asked.

She nodded.

"I'll be ready, baby. When that day comes, it will

be the happiest one in my life because you are all I think about. I couldn't care less about this other stuff, I just want you to be all right."

"I love you for that," she replied. "I won't forget."

"Just send for me any time you want — any time at all. Meanwhile I'll let you alone. I know you need space now." He held up one hand in a gesture of good-by and started off again.

Her heart aching, Carlsie watched him go. Finally she turned to the water. Through teary eyes she watched an old cargo vessel plow out to sea, and tried hard not to cry. She remembered the first time she had met Gordo, then glanced back in the direction in which he had walked.

He had disappeared over the dune.

Chapter Nineteen

Oscar Mendel sulked in the darkness of his bedroom, contemplating the consequences of Camden's declarations. Once again her boldness had surprised him. He was furious that her demands had been granted. In his view, Barret was making a major mistake by allowing this ineffective little audit. Nothing would be found, of course, but it was an admission that something might be wrong. Despite Barret's lame explanation that it would be good to clear the air and get her off his back, the audit called too much attention to the department of pathology and would inevitably create suspicion. It was something else she must be punished for.

As he changed the bandage on his hand, applying a light layer of antibiotic ointment in the process, he thought about the blood he had washed out of his shirt, and wished it had been hers.

Chapter Twenty

Hank's visit was unexpected. Carlsie had skipped supper, choosing instead to pass the evening on her balcony, watching the lights of Palm Beach come to life and musing over her present situation as she tranquilized herself with tequila and orange juice, but at a little after nine he arrived, apologizing for not calling first.

"I thought you'd want to know—everything is set," he said immediately. "Dr. Sparkman, the chief of pathology at St. Joseph's, has agreed to do it. He can start tomorrow, and will probably finish up within a day or so."

She was glad and told him so, adding, "It'll be good to get this over with." Then she offered him a drink, he accepted, and they went out to the balcony. He seemed to be waiting for her to talk.

"You don't really understand why I did this, do you?" Carlsie said finally.

"No, I am afraid I don't." He sipped the tequila and stared out to sea. He appeared somber and introspective.

Carlsie wondered why he had come. Surely it was not merely to pass on word that her plan was in motion. He could have done that by phone, or had his secretary do it. There was more to this visit. He didn't seem to want to interrogate her, though, or to give her a hard time. She got the impression that he wanted some place to relax and think. The tenseness evident in his face was easing as he quietly finished off his drink and continued to study the dark void of the Atlantic. There were no questions, no criticism, no disapproving vibes. Only silence and a sense of retreat from what had undoubtedly been a trying day. He seemed completely at home sitting next to her, sharing her space, drinking her drink.

"Will you have another?" she asked.

"Might as well. I've never tried this combination before, although I've put away a lot of tequila over the years. Potent stuff."

"Potent situations call for potent solutions," Carlsie responded and went inside, to return soon with two more tall glasses.

"Used to drink mescal back in Houston," he said. "Now, that was strong. Came straight in from Mexico. Still had the worm in it. It would cure what ailed you." For the first time he smiled a little and his eyes met hers and lingered.

"You've been gone from Texas a long time. Think you'll ever move back?"

He smiled again. "Who knows his future, Carlsie? Maybe I should never have left. I was really at home there, you know. People understood

230

me. Here, they think of me as some sort of wild cowboy who just happens to know a little bit about surgery. Palm Beach tolerates me more than anything else. They know I don't exactly fit." He seemed to sadden a bit as he thought about that. "Yeah," he added. "I think that's what I'd do if something here didn't work out. I'd just trot right back to Texas. Wouldn't be so damn bad, either. Set up my own clinic, buy a ranch, raise a few head of cattle."

"Me too, I guess. I'd probably go back home. Dear ol' New Orleans, here I come. I don't have anyplace else to go. I imagine I should start making my travel plans, don't you think? One way or the other, I'll be on the road." After she said it, Carlsie wished she hadn't. She hadn't meant to; it had just slipped out.

He took another big sip of his drink, and changed the topic. "You know, I was out in Houston during the heart transplant craze a long time ago. It was a sight to see — more transplants being done than appendectomies, weekly press conferences, TV film crews all over the place. It was something."

He was smiling broadly, reminiscing over the old days. The little wrinkles around his eyes gave him a warm look, despite his sun-baked toughness. He settled back into his chair and continued his story.

Carlsie, intrigued by the tale and the man telling it, watched him intently as he spoke. He had such a lively glow of intelligence and humanity, all within the framework of a folksy, country sort of personality.

As she responded with stories of her own, she could see that he was not merely following her comments. He was drinking all of her in. He seemed to hang on every word. Supremely capable of drawing her out, he savored the things she told him, wanting to know everything about her—her family, her old loves, why she was still single. He roared with laughter as she explained the failure of her first serious romance and the dilemma caused by two medical students sharing the same apartment, each too busy to take care of the place.

Most men just wanted to tell their own stories, but Hank was a great listener. He was fascinated with her. That was obvious. And Carlsie felt drawn to him, spellbound by his charm, his charisma. It was easy to forget the problems of the day, in each other's company to seek relief from the potentially damning reality they were caught up in.

After a long while, when there was a lull in the conversation, he glanced at his watch. "You know, it's getting pretty late and I'm feeling a mite hungry," he said. "How about you? Think you could force down a bite or two? I know a place that stays open late and serves some great fettucini." He held out his hand to her. "One cannot live on tequila alone, you know. It's an old Texas truism."

"I didn't even know Texans could say fettucini, much less eat it," Carlsie joked, to buy time to think about his invitation.

"Not only do I eat it, I sometimes cook it."

"Wow," she said in mock disbelief. She was losing the will to resist. She started to say no, then hesitated, growing weaker with every second that he smiled at her.

"So. What do you say? Are you hungry?" His expression told her how much he wanted her to go with him.

She smiled, finally. "I've never been able to resist fettucini."

He nodded. "I thought so. My momma always told me the way to a woman's heart is through her stomach."

They gazed at each other in a way that made her think, *So this is the beginning . . . what happens next?*

Just off Worth Avenue was a small Italian restaurant popular with the late-night crowd. The maître d' recognized Hank immediately and showed them to a booth in the far corner of the room.

Hank ordered a red Italian wine Carlsie had never heard of and the fettucini, of course. The wine turned out to be sweet and tasty, and the pasta as delicious as he had promised. Their conversation was easy and spontaneous, and time slipped by. When the waiter brought the check, she didn't want the evening to end.

As they lingered over their cappuccino, Carlsie told more stories about New Orleans, but Hank seemed to have stopped listening. He was fascinated by every movement of her face, her lips. He stared uninhibitedly into her eyes. Finally, he leaned forward and brushed a few curls back from her face.

"You are a flower among thorns, Carlsie. You are about people. From the beginning I've known

233

you are special."

She was basking in his attention. His voice . . . his charm . . . all of him was enchanting, and she wanted to hold him as close as she had when they'd danced that night so long ago.

"I'll never forgot the day I met you," he said. "You came strolling into my lecture like some kind of cool-school medical student. I said to myself, I'm gonna fix her little red wagon, and I'll be damned if you didn't blow me away when I tried to." He smiled and laughed quietly. "You fooled me."

She smiled back. "I trekked all the way across the country to study with you people, thinking I was linking up with a bunch of ivy-league types, and what did I find but the most handsome cowboy I'd ever seen. Even wearing boots. I was in a state of shock."

He leaned back, savoring the moment as they both reflected upon that first encounter. Then his eyes suddenly lit up. He took her hand in his, a new enthusiasm in his voice. "Come on. I want to take you somewhere else. I want you to see some of my best work."

"Where?"

He grinned mysteriously. "You'll understand when we get there."

Crossing the river, they left the island and headed to West Palm Beach. The Bloody Goose Show Bar was garishly lit up, and quite popular judging from the size of the crowded parking lot.

"This is the wildest strip joint in south Florida," Hank explained, as he paid the five-dollar cover for himself. Ladies were admitted free. The doorman, perched on a high stool and holding a big wad of bills, smiled at Carlsie and then stamped their right hands with an undistinguishable red insignia. Beyond the front door was a small foyer, divided from the main room by a pair of swinging doors through which the thunderous beat of rock music reverberated.

Entering the larger hall, they were immediately swallowed up by the raunchy atmosphere of big-time exploitation of feminine flesh. On Bourbon Street Carlsie had seen nothing to compare with the Bloody Goose. The room — filled with smoke, flashing lights, and glitter — had purple walls slashed by diagonal, red stripes. The tables were jammed close together and packed with appreciative spectators. At one end was a large stage upon which, gyrating rhythmically, were a pair of totally nude and well-endowed females. At the opposite end was an unclad female, on a pedestal about six feet above the floor. Scattered randomly throughout the club a half-dozen or so nude women danced provocatively on tabletops. And topless waitresses were all over the huge place, serving drinks and beer as fast as it could be delivered.

Loud whistles and catcalls filled the air as the dancers worked the audience into a frenzy. The music was deafening, smoke enveloped them like fog, and the strobes and light effects were dazzling. For security, Carlsie entwined her arm through Hank's, holding on tightly as he led her to a small table near the stage. He said something, but she couldn't hear it; so he just grinned, and they sat down.

As her eyes grew accustomed to the scene, Carlsie looked at those seated around her. Mostly men, but with a fair scattering of couples. In a corner near the stage was as group of six or seven young women. They were barely watching the show, mostly talking and laughing among themselves. Office pals on a night out, Carlsie concluded.

Absorbing the sights and sounds of this pulsating place, she watched everything going on. When the music ended, the crowd gave a roar of approval, and the dancers, donning minimal coverups, scrambled from their perches to be replaced by other equally energetic, uninhibited young women. Openly displayed breasts and buttocks were everywhere. Carlsie, who thought she had seen everything in the French quarter, was truly amazed.

"So, what do you think?" Hank asked, grinning from ear to ear. "This is my type of joint."

She nodded and gave him a sheepish smile. "I should have guessed. Now I know why you're so dedicated to your surgery. Self-indulgence, right?"

He chuckled. "Maybe you know more about me than I think."

"I'll bet I do. I've been watching you for quite some time now."

"And what have you concluded during this period of observation."

"That you really have great hands."

"There are parts of you that I think are really great, too." He glanced up and down her body. "You've got this excellent pair of . . . eh . . . feet."

His way of flirting with her was adorable. She was flattered that he was continuing to give her his almost undivided attention despite the flock of beautiful naked women dancing around them.

"So what is it you want me to see here?" she asked. "Do they have some male strippers?"

"I wanted you to see her," Hank pointed to a tall statuesque dancer just taking center stage. "She's my masterpiece. The best augmentation I've ever done. I'll never do better. I'm sure of it."

Carlsie studied the unusually attractive girl who was beginning a strange sort of dance to slow hard-rock music with an especially throbbing beat. The woman had a graceful erotic style of movement and smooth artistically understated rhythms. Although she was several inches over six feet, she was built like a ballerina. Long blond hair hung to the middle of her back, and her breasts, perfectly symmetrical and of generous size, moved fluidly with her body. They were perfect.

"I did an augmentation on Joni about a year ago," Hank said. "Since then she's become the star attraction — Joni St. Cyr — worth big bucks at the door. They did a spread on her in *Penthouse* a few months ago."

Carlsie watched silently as the sexy girl swayed and stretched, turning and bending to the music with the approval of an enthusiastic audience. She admired the dancer's shameless acceptance of the beauty of her body and her willingness to share it so openly with this crowd of hyped-up men. Hank was justified in his pride in his work. The surgery was totally undetectable. The woman's perfection seemed natural.

Carlsie glanced at Hank, whose eyes were shifting

back and forth from her to his patient. It was a suprise to her that he considered this particular patient one of his biggest successes, because her surgery was not clearly as complex as many of his operations. As she watched him, he seemed to be enjoying the audience's admiration of his work and she realized that, like any artist, he loved the approval of experts. Certainly these men were proba bly about as expert on the subject of young women's breasts as any group she had ever seen.

She leaned toward Hank, whispering into his ear. "Good work, doctor. Your results seem very functional."

He put his arm around her. "It's fun to see this. You understand, don't you?"

She kissed him quickly on the lips. She enjoyed his company so much it was dangerous, she thought. His easy openness and irrepressible masculinity captivated her. She wanted to take him home, keep him in a box and not let anything change him. The thought reminded her of the trouble ahead. They had very little time before something happened one way or the other.

As if he had intercepted her unhappy thoughts, Hank pointed to the pretty, fully clothed, young woman working behind the bar. "There's a sad story," he said. "Debbie Hunter. She used to be a real popular stripper here. Joni sent her to me last year. Carcinoma of the breast. A real shocker. I had to do a mastectomy."

Carlsie stared intently at the morose barmaid, the irony of the woman's situation weighing heavily upon her. She glanced quickly at the frisky, sexually

238

inviting dancer and then turned back to the more tragic figure. What a different lot life had given them! One had been made more sexy by a surgeon and one had been scarred. Now here they were, not thirty feet from the man that had carried out their sentences.

"I didn't know she had come back to work here. I told her to do something else if she could," Hank mumbled through the din of the music. "I don't think this is a good environment for her." He became silent, gazed off into a distant corner of the smoke-filled room. Carlsie knew he was thinking of the accusations she had made. She felt badly for him. He was suffering, too. She understood that. If he felt there was even the slightest chance that she was right, he had to be feeling terrible.

She glanced again at the barmaid, who looked up at that moment and made eye contact with Hank. The woman's unkempt brunette hair and sparse makeup gave the impression that she cared little about her appearance, but she nodded in recognition of her surgeon, though there was a noticeable absence of warmth or friendliness in her expression. Hank smiled faintly and gave her a thumbs-up sign. Debbie nodded again and went back to her work.

Carlsie, experiencing a deep sorrow for the young woman, had a feeling that this patient was one of the victims. It was unfair. Joni St. Cyr was so perfect. Debbie Hunter so incomplete.

Again almost answering her thoughts, Hank said it had been especially rough for the young bartender. He told her how hard he had worked to get this patient to accept what had happened and to

239

recover emotionally. He had sent her to a psychiatrist, he had maintained contact with her for an extended period after the surgery, he had counseled her, he had done everything he could to make her well; all to no avail. He said that a reconstruction was planned soon, but she showed no enthusiasm for it. "Sometimes I think she's a lost cause. She comes into the clinic in old worn-out clothes. She won't fix herself up. It's like she doesn't care about herself anymore. She doesn't even wear the breast prosthesis we gave her to use until we can rebuild her. I feel real bad about her." He clutched Carlsie's hand. 'It was just one of those unexpected things. Sometimes I get the feeling Debbie blames me, but what else could I do? I mean, the slides showed she had cancer. I had no choice."

Neither spoke. Neither had to. Each understood the anguish of the other.

The mood of the evening being irreparably damaged, he called for the bill. When they reached the exit, Carlsie turned back to look at Debbie one last time. The girl was watching her. Their eyes met and Carlsie felt a rush of empathy for her.

The drive back to her apartment was quiet. She sat close beside him, his arm around her, her head resting upon his shoulder. She wanted to forget the sadness that had overtaken them but didn't know how. Apparently he didn't either.

Good nights were exchanged at her door. She had decided not to invite him in, realizing as he surely did that the moment was not right. She wondered if there would ever be a time for them, however brief.

He turned to leave and then, as if realizing that it

was now or never, looked back to her. "I think I'll take tomorrow off," he said. "I doubt if I'll be able to get much done anyway, considering the audit and all. I was wondering if you would like to go boating with me? The weather should be nice. What do you think?" His expression told her more than his words. He really wanted her to go, needed her to. He seemed to acknowledge that this was it for them. A day or so when they could drift out of sync with their environment, and briefly forget that reality would inevitably reclaim them. His eyes and gentle smile conveyed a hope for serene bliss if even for a short while.

She knew she would say yes but spent a moment weighing the consequences. The situation presented a terrible dichotomy. The better the hours they spent together, the stronger the passion that developed between them in these few days, then the greater would be the pain of the ending. For every second of joy and ecstacy they shared the price would be hours and days of loneliness, of regretting what could no longer be. The involvement they so desired could only be followed by the inexorable hollowness and anguish of the unavoidable separation their destinies demanded.

All of this she considered while peering into the dark eyes of the handsome man who had already moved her more than any other male and without benefit of the more physical parts of the male-female interaction. What she would feel when they became truly close was beyond her ability to imagine. It was a temptation she was not strong enough to turn away from despite potential suffering and the terror of withdrawal. She had to give it a try, if only for a little while.

She agreed to meet him at his house the next morning, where he would have a Texas-style breakfast cooking, and his boat ready and waiting.

Oscar Mendel had waited a long while for Carlsie to return home. He had parked so that, from the comfort of his Mercedes, he could see both the entrance of the building and the garage. On this night he was only trying to become more familiar with her movements, because the immediate urgency to silence her was gone. Whatever minor damage she could do had been done. Now he had time to pick the place and circumstances to meet his needs. Unfortunately, though, his task had become infinitely more complicated. Because her accusations were already known to many people, he had to make certain she appeared to be a random victim. Her death must never be linked, not even in the slightest way, with him or with the charges she had made at the institute.

Finally he spotted her approaching the front entrance in the company of Ritter. That surprised him. He had thought it was Gordon Keene who was getting into her pants, not Ritter. What on God's earth could she see in that hick cowboy? he wondered. Keene was twice as good-looking and ten times smarter. It only proved once again how stupid women can be when it comes to picking men.

He pulled out of the condo parking lot, grinning at the ridiculousness of the Ritter-Camden pairing.

In a way this was better. Because of her association with this particular surgeon, he was going to take even greater delight in "fixing her up." He just needed a little more time to work out the details. The plans he had for Camden required prolonged privacy with her.

Chapter Twenty-one

For breakfast Hank went all the way. They dined aboard his yacht on eggs Benedict, broiled brandied fruit, Bloody Marys, and Southern-style grits with bacon served on custom-designed china and crystal. The boat was larger than she had imagined it would be. A sixty-two-foot sportfishing craft, it had every possible amenity in its spacious interior. Equipped with complex electronic and navigational instruments, it seemed built to please someone who loved expensive toys.

The dock to which the *Jubilation* was secured stood off Hank's three-acre estate which was located in the center of the most expensive part of the island. After they ate he showed her around the place. The Georgian-style home was formal yet open and comfortable. Despite its size, it was not intimidating. It had balance and grace: colors, shapes, and spaces guided the eye and pleased the heart. The terraced pool and patio were provided with a tented bar, beyond which was a putting green that looked onto the beautiful intracoastal waterway which spanned the half-mile across to West Palm Beach.

Carlsie stood on the balcony of the second-floor master suite, surveying the magnificent view and expressed amazement that a doctor could afford such a palace. "Your father is an oil baron, right?"

He shrugged. "You know, Carlsie, I never thought much about the money when I came here. I just took the deal Walker offered me and signed on. He never realized how cheaply he could have had me. A third as much would have been more than enough."

"You would have had to settle for a smaller boat."

"Now that would have been bad. That's the only part of it I would really miss. I love that boat. Helped design it. Had it furnished and powered just the way I wanted."

They talked for a while about the economics of medicine and the business setup of the institute. Hank was a full partner, along with Greer and one other staff surgeon, in the corporation headed by Barret. His personal income the previous year, based upon his share of the surgery that had been done, was twenty times what she expected to make at the peak of her career. Carlsie was staggered by the sum but believed it, considering the style in which he lived.

They spent the day aboard the *Jubilation,* fishing for sailfish and marlin, catching two of the former and none of the latter, which did not surprise Hank who explained that marlin were relatively rare in these waters. "On the other side of the Gulf Stream in the northern Bahamas I've hooked up with more of the big ones. The best place is Cozumel. Billfish are a dime a dozen down there."

Carlsie liked talking about his hobby. It revealed a side of him she had not seen. Aboard his boat he was a salty, suntanned fisherman who concentrated as hard on rigging perfect bait as he did on closing a surgical wound. Hank was an intense man who did everything at full speed, not seeming to differentiate between fun and work. If he was going to do it, he was determined to do it as precisely as possible. He did appear to be enjoying himself more than in the O.R., though, and if something wasn't right he didn't get quite as uptight about it. He merely persisted until he was satisfied and only then did he pop open a couple of beers.

It was a great day filled with adventure and stories about fishing and boating in the Caribbean. By late afternoon when they returned to the dock, Carlsie's troubles seemed far away. The biggest decision facing them was where to have dinner and thereby begin what promised to be the best night of their lives.

They had an incomparable meal at Cappricio's, followed by a few drinks and a moonlight stroll along the beach near the Breakers, where they also did a little dancing in the grand Florentine Ballroom. They returned to his home well after midnight. After hours of conversation and soul-searching discussion, they found themselves strangely quiet with each other. There was nothing more to say.

Perhaps it was the unspoken understanding of the

inevitability of their separation that fueled their desire and made them both willing to be as open and as intimate as is possible between male and female. The moment belonged totally to them. It wouldn't and couldn't last; they knew it very well. But this night was undeniably theirs. Feelings flowed between them, and they made love as it was meant to be. These two desperate people, plagued by the knowledge that this was the end as well as the beginning, merged without reservation in the sweet world of each other. And passion consumed them.

Carlsie had never been happier or more secure. She understood bliss, fulfillment, and the meaning of femininity. She knew joy, she loved life, and she loved this man. She wanted to be with him forever.

And then—too soon—it was over.

Morning came, and she awakened alone in his bed.

The joy of the night was offset by a sense of loss. On the table beside her was a still-warm cup of coffee Hank had left for her, and a note saying he had gone to the hospital.

A sense of foreboding crept over her. Today was the day of revelation at the institute. It would be a time of anguish when Mendel's crimes were proven. But she didn't want anguish. She wanted only to love Hank again.

Fear became her dominant emotion, fear of losing something she had just discovered—a joy that outshone all others.

Chapter Twenty-two

While Carlsie showered and dressed in Hank's bedroom, a beautiful young woman was placed on a hospital stretcher. Her husband kissed her good-by, and the frightened girl was wheeled toward the institute's operating room.

Carlsie was still brushing her hair and studying her reflection in the full-length mirror in Hank's bath when the anesthetist in the O.R. induced a state of anesthesia and the nurse performed a surgical prep of the patient's bare chest. The orange Betadine scrub solution flowed down the patient's cleavage and across her large breasts. Her eyes were taped shut as surgical drapes were placed across her body.

Carlsie drove down Hank's long driveway and turned onto the street for the ten-block ride to the hospital. She wondered what everyone there was doing on this third day of the moratorium on surgery; and she was apprehensive about the reactions of the surgeons when they saw proof of what they had done.

In the surgical suite the first of many operations scheduled to be done that day was begun. A scalpel was plunged into the soft periareolar tissue of the woman's breast and a tiny benign-appearing nodule was cut out. The wound oozed warm, bright red blood, then skillful suturing was begun. Walker Barret operated while Gordo assisted. The two surgeons talked quietly to each other as they awaited the results of the biopsy.

Oscar Mendel was at his microscope, examining the biopsy. He was smug and confident. He had received the specimen, made the frozen section, and determined that it was benign. He now spoke authoritatively over the intercom to the O.R. "It's malignant, all right. An adenocarcinoma.

Barret thanked him and Mendel turned off the intercom.

The pathologist glanced back at the original benign specimen, examining it once more under the light before wrapping it, and the slides he had made, in paper towels. After verifying that he was not being observed, he dropped the entire package into the receptacle for biological wastes. It would be incinerated by noon.

He unlocked the bottom drawer of his desk, and from behind books and papers pulled out a small bottle. It was full with formalin and contained bits and pieces of carcinomas of previous patients. He swished them around, extracted an appropriate-sized piece, and replaced the bottle in its hiding place. The substitute specimen was dropped into the container brought from the O.R. bearing the patient's name, and was placed on the rack marked Incoming specimens. Permanent diagnostic slides would be made from it the next morning. The switch would be untraceable. Mendel had made it departmental policy never to keep frozen-section slides. The permanent slides made from the substituted specimen of real cancers would be the only ones in existence. This was a slight deviation from routine lab practice, but he could justify it because the permanents were of better quality. And besides, he had never been questioned about the policy. He was, after all, an acknowledged expert.

He washed his hands, added this new name to the list — all bitches and whores who, in his opinion, deserved the punishment he had prescribed.

That one is for you, Camden, he thought, pleased at how foolish the woman surgeon now appeared. Her stupid audit had cleared his department of all suspicion. His work was safer from criticism than it had ever been. In the eyes of the institute the correctness of his diagnoses had been verified.

Still thinking of the woman upstairs, whose breast was being severed from her body, he crossed the lab to his personal office. He wished he could find some plausible excuse to watch the operation.

Even if he didn't get to participate in the surgery, he enjoyed receiving the whole breasts later in buckets, as final specimens to be evaluated to determine the extent of the cancers. In the privacy of his office he squeezed the nipples until blood oozed out and the dark pigmented skin broke open. It was a thrill, and difficult to get a live woman to allow no matter how much she was paid.

But he would soon get any pleasure he wanted from Camden. She would be unable to deny him. He would especially enjoy her desecration now that he knew about her and Ritter. Perhaps he should mail a little piece of her to the surgeon. He wondered which part Ritter would like to have as a permanent memento. Maybe he should give some of her to Gordo, too, and to her other boyfriends. It might be interesting custom-cutting samples of her to give away.

Mendel found the grotesqueness of his own humor very amusing. He was getting an erection just thinking about it. He wondered if Camden's friends would fight over her best parts.

As Carlsie parked her car and entered the hospital through the doctors' entrance, the surgeons in the O.R. were frowning unhappily and their patient's chest was being redraped for a mastectomy.

A gleaming silvery scalpel was thrust into the upper outer aspect of the right breast and brought down in a wide elliptical incision below the organ, then swung back upward to complete the circumscription around the soft, globular, now-bloody feminine appendage. Yellow fat erupted from the wound edges as the cut was pushed deeper, almost to the muscles of the chest wall.

Completely unaware that surgery was underway, Carlsie wandered around looking for everybody on the floor below the O.R. Not knowing quite what to expect on this day of turmoil, she was surprised to find the usual hustle and bustle of a midweek day. She went first to Hank's office, figuring he would have the latest news about the audit and what was going to happen now.

His secretary greeted her in an ordinary way and informed her that he was in surgery. The news surprised Carlsie, but she assumed he was doing some cosmetic procedures while awaiting the results of the audit.

Not knowing what else to do, she went up to surgery to see what was going on. She didn't want to go to Barret's office to find out about the audit. He was undoubtedly fit to be tied, and trying to decide how best to deal with the impending crisis.

In the surgeons' lounge she poured a cup of coffee and then glanced at the surgery schedule posted there. It was surprisingly large, and not made up of only cosmetic or reconstructive cases as she had assumed it would be. This can't be, she thought, noticing the biopsy with possible mastectomy on a thirty-two-year-old, Barrett as surgeon. Her first impression was that it was a mistake, an old schedule, or one printed up several days ago, before everything was postponed. But the date was correct!

Something was wrong.

Still hoping this was some sort of error, but beginning to feel a little panicky, Carlsie rushed out into the O.R. hallway. "What room is Barret in?" she yelled to the front-desk nurse as she started down the hallway into the surgical area.

"Room four. You can't go in there dressed like that, Dr. Camden!" the astonished woman blurted out, jumping up from her chair. "You're in street clothes! You don't even have a mask!"

Carlsie heard nothing except the number. Rushing past a handful of shocked O.R. personnel she slammed into the operating room door, swinging it open so hard it slapped against the wall behind it. She couldn't believe what she saw. They had promised to wait! Barret had promised! Surely the results of the audit were in, proving conclusively what she knew Mendel had been doing.

In near hysteria she shrieked at them from the doorway. "Stop it! Stop it, you bastards! You lied to me!"

The startled Barret turned a puzzled stare on her just as he lowered the severed breast, now bloody and greasy, into the plastic bucket held by the nurse.

"Oh no," Carlsie moaned, realizing she was too late. "How could you do it? She might not have cancer. Don't you know that?" She felt totally defeated.

For a moment no one spoke. The only sounds were those made by the bucket hitting the floor after sliding from the hands of the dumbstruck R.N. and those coming from the nurses, doctors, and orderlies running down the hall to respond to the disturbance she was causing. The amputated breast slithered from the upside-down container and slid several feet across the tile floor, coming to rest with its oxygen depleted, bluish gray nipple upright.

Everyone was watching Carlsie, Gordo in a state of dismayed disbelief. The nurses were frightened. Barret's face was contorting into an expression of hatred. "You sorry bitch!" he roared. "I told you to

254

stay the hell out of this operating—"

She didn't allow him the pleasure of finishing. Her dejection turned into uncontrollable fury, her wrath into an impassioned storm of revenge. Eyes ablaze with resentment, she swiftly crossed the room and, catching him off balance, flung him onto the floor. He lay bewildered and stunned a few feet from the symbol of his crime, the ugly specimen taken from his patient.

"You sadist!" she raged. "You callous, vulgar sadist!"

She gazed in horror at the large gaping wound across the newest victim's chest. The red muscle of her pectoralis major was displayed in glistening perfection. A faint wisp of steam rose from the warm tissue into the cold air of the room. The woman slept in quiet repose, black hair carefully tucked beneath her neck. The carefully controlled violation of her body seemed so legitimate, so common within the context of where she lay.

Quiet tears of grief rolled down Carlsie's cheeks. Surgery had always seemed such a holy thing during her years of training. Now it had become debased, foul. This patient had come to these doctors in faith and trust, and they had mutilated her—perhaps destroyed her—all in the name of compassion and good medicine. The bastards . . . the foul bastards!

Barret was getting to his feet, looking shaken and gray. A hush had fallen over the entire suite. Eying her carefully, everyone moved away as she turned her harsh glare back to the surgeon, who stood trancelike before her. All signs of his willingness to fight her were gone.

"You lied to me!" she screamed. "You butcher! You should be destroyed like a rabid animal." She advanced threateningly toward him and an expression of doom came onto Barret's face. He backed slowly into a corner and lifted his arms defensively.

"Carlsie!" Gordo's voice broke the silence. "Please stop. Please!"

She glanced at her friend.

"Please, Carlsie," he said again. "Think about what you're doing."

She took a series of deep breaths.

Gordo continued to speak quietly, almost soothingly. "You need to ease on out of here now. On top of everything else we don't need a wound infection."

She nodded, backed away and went out the door. She started down the hall toward the exit, as the others cleared a wide path. Doctors and nurses looked out of each of the remaining O.R.s, curiosity in their eyes.

She desperately wanted to talk to Hank, but he was nowhere to be seen. As she passed beyond the doors to the surgical suite, they were immediately shut behind her and locked. She could hear the excited chatter of upset nurses.

Taking the stairway, she bypassed the lobby and descended to the floor below. Straight down the hall and around a corner was the Path lab. Mendel would still be there, gloating no doubt over his latest triumph. She moved slowly, her desire to punish him right then and there increasing with every second that passed. It was his time to suffer.

She entered through the main door of the lab. A hush went over the room and Mendel noticed her immediately. He came confidently toward her, making no effort to conceal a contemptuous smile. "Did you come to say good-by?" he asked, sarcastically. "I understand you'll be leaving here now. Such a pity. You haven't had time to sleep with every one of the surgeons, yet. I've noticed that you're working on it, though."

His confidence was infuriating. He obviously knew she was on to him, but he believed he was invulnerable. He seemed to have no fear whatsoever of anything she could do.

"I'm going to stop you," she said softly. "I don't know why you are doing this, but you will definitely be stopped. And you are going to pay dearly for it. I promise you."

He laughed. She had never heard him do so before. The sound was rude and rough. Uncultured. It carried a tone of derision and disrespect. It was the laugh of a man who was not indulging a sense of humor. "You are the one who is going to pay, you foolish bitch," he whispered. "You can count on it. I want to teach you something about your own specialty." Mendel made that coarse sound again, the laugh of a mad man.

Frustrated by her inability to deal with him, Carlsie retreated. Fearing that Barret might attempt to have her arrested, she ran to her car and drove west, across the intracoastal waterway.

Despite her distrust of Barret, she'd never believed he would break his word like this and persist in doing mastectomies without waiting for the

257

results of the audit as he had promised. But she had seen the proof. It was business as usual at the institute. It crossed her mind that she had been conned. Perhaps there was to be no audit. Maybe they had decided to ignore her, label her as crazy, and get her out of there as quickly as possible. If so, she had played right into their hands. It would be easy to characterize her as demented, considering how many people had witnessed her unusual behavior.

As she thought about what she had done she become more frightened. What had happened to her judgment? It had been a horrible mistake, barging into the O.R. She began to question her own sanity. Had she misjudged all this? Could she possibly be wrong? No, she decided. She wasn't wrong, something else was. She wanted desperately to talk with Hank to see if the audit had really been done.

What if the slide study had been completed? she wondered. What if Barret had waited, as he'd said he would, and the audit had shown nothing? If that were the case, it was a disaster for her; Mendel had won again. Somehow he might have managed to escape detection by the professional most likely to uncover his manipulations: an honest and knowledgeable pathologist.

If that were true, if he had been able to pull this off, then her problem had been made much more difficult, for he was doing all this purposely. It was not the work of an insane pathologist making mistakes. These were the actions of a demented man cleverly misrepresenting tissue results to cause unnecessary surgery.

This meant that any attempt to expose him to his peers would probably fail. His deceptions were so perfectly devised there might be no satisfactory solution to her problem. Mendel might be uncatchable.

The mere thought of such a catastrophe sickened Carlsie.

She couldn't let him get away with this. She had to reveal his crimes to the medical world so that they could never happen again — here or anywhere. All surgeons had to be alerted. Every physician must be made to understand that the unthinkable was possible: there might be individuals within the profession who practiced the reverse of first doing no harm.

She tried to phone Hank. His secretary wouldn't put her through, and she was too scared to identify herself or leave a number — she didn't trust anyone, except Hank himself. Even he might not understand why she was doing this, yet she knew he would never do anything to harm her. She believed that with all her heart.

She needed time to think, to work all this out. She needed a plan, and she needed help that obviously wasn't coming. The system had failed. The bad guy had won, and she was the only one who knew. This was her battle now. Her own private war. She, alone, understood the tragic consequences of allowing Mendel to continue these heinous acts.

No matter what, she had to stop him. . . .

For her patients.

For herself.

For her profession.

* * *

Mendel watched her go, then retreated quickly to his office and into his private bathroom where he could be assured of being completely unobserved. He suddenly was not feeling well. Closing the door, he slumped against the wall, worrying about his racing heart. He should not have provoked her. It was a dangerous mistake to antagonize Camden before he could shut her up permanently. He was so unsure about her abilities, what she knew, and the level of her willingness to retaliate against him. Surprised by the level of anxiety he was experiencing, Mendel sweated profusely. Oh God, he thought. It's starting again.

"This can't keep happening," he muttered. The spells seemed to be getting worse, not better. And they were coming more frequently. He was afraid they were going to make him die if he didn't somehow stop them.

He inhaled deeply, trying to overcome a sudden shortness of breath. His skin tingled with piloerection. He needed his codeine. The pain was returning. The part of him that was Belail was aroused.

He began to experience the aura that foretold one of his episodes. Remaining calm was hard because of the rising sense of disaster within him. His head was starting to pound: he needed his medicine. Then the seizure overtook him.

He imagined Carlsie's voice, her disgust, her disdain. She wanted to destroy him!

An aura of death surrounded him, and he rebelled. His muscles trembled as he squeezed his head in a vain effort to mitigate the pain.

He slid onto the floor, paralyzed by fear, seemingly enveloped in a cold mist. He was confused, terrified, and angry beyond words.

He tried to shout out his defiance of this thing, but no sound would come. The shrillness of Camden's imagined voice increased. She was in his head, his ears, his very soul. She screamed and wailed, and shrieked his name until he thought his eardrums would burst.

All his senses were assaulted, his very essence was threatened. A crushing ache within his chest drew his attention to the irregular rhythm of his heart, and he prepared to face death.

Every nerve ending discharged a message of doom. Noxious impulses flooded in from his skin and joints, from his intestines and bladder. He felt pain in its totality. His spinal cord discharged neuronal impulses at maximum rate. Angina seized him, and cramps. He was burning, yet cold. Gangrenous death seemed to penetrate inward from every portal. The stench of decay apparently came from his own rotting flesh.

He became blind and deaf, and sank into a void of isolation. He no longer felt his own body. His nervous system transmitted empty messages from functionless sensory organs to an unresponsive brain. He seemed to be dying an electric death caused by sensory overload. Breakers were tripping, circuits burning out. The central computer was shutting down.

Darkness came creeping in as the sensations from around Mendel slowly faded away. His spinal cord went quiet, his thalamus ceased to function. All willingness to resist ended.

He lay silent, motionless and painless, upon the cold hard floor. Deep within his withdrawing brain lingered one lone image: a steel blade was being thrust into the breast of an innocent girl. Her blood ran slowly from her as a mastectomy was begun.

And then the flickering light within him burned out, and he went far away into a lonely black emptiness.

The half of his personality that had become Belail awoke and commanded him to plan retribution—to plan sacrifice. Camden must die.

Chapter Twenty-three

Certain that she was being pursued, by the police and maybe by Mendel, Carlsie spent the day on the run. She drove south to Fort Lauderdale and mixed with the tourists along the strip. Sitting at the back of a cheap bar, she passed the hours thinking and wishing there was a happy solution to this horror. But there wasn't.

She figured out how Mendel was doing it, finally. It was so obvious it was ridiculous, once she'd thought of it. What he'd done had been so blatant, so sadistic, that she had never considered it possible anyone could be that cruel. He had to be purposely switching tissue at an early stage of the pathological evaluation—an almost undetectable procedure.

Almost.

Now that she knew how he was doing it, proving what he'd done would be no problem. The solution lay in tissue typing.

The whole amputated breasts were always preserved and kept in the lab for several years. Bits of tissue could be taken from them and typed. The results could be compared with the tests done on the permanent slides of the supposed cancers that had been removed. If Mendel had substituted real cancerous tissue for benign specimens, the tissue typing of a removed breast would not match the tissue found on the same patient's slides. The jig would be up.

Carlsie was sure she had Mendel this time. This was the only way he could cover himself that had not already been checked. It was foolish of her not to have thought of it sooner. Her problem, now, lay in getting the tissue typing done, since she had already blown her credibility with one serious and seemingly false alarm.

And there was a new obstacle. Hank's disgrace had become an unacceptable result no matter how sweet the victory otherwise. If she proved her theory, it would become public immediately. The institute would be destroyed by outraged public opinion, and along with it Hank's career and everything he had ever worked for. Carlsie wondered how she could destroy Mendel without harming any of the innocents around him? Although he had to be stopped and restitution should be paid, the scores of women he had already damaged could not be restored, and she did not wish to inflict additional pain upon the victims that had already suffered so much. Instead, she desired a quieter solution, and for that she needed Hank's help and cooperation. Before she did anything she wanted to see him, to explain how it had happened, and to get him to understand why she was doing this.

Hank's house was dark when she turned into his drive that evening. After parking so that her car could not be seen from the street, and determining that he was not yet home, she found a sliding door, on the back deck by the pool, which had been left unlocked. She went into the den and settled down to wait.

He arrived about an hour later. It was almost ten o'clock. "Thank God you're all right," he said. "We've been trying to find you all day." He immediately embraced her.

"I tried to call you." Carlsie attempted to smile bravely, but her despair showed through.

He went on and on about how worried he had been and how everything was going to be okay and how she should just leave everything to him. Still, she noticed immediately that something was different about him. He was not the same man who had loved her the night before. His attitude had changed. His words seemed strained . . . as if he were uncomfortable being with her. The more she attuned herself to his mood, the more distressed she became. He feared her. The insight was startling. After what had occurred between them, it seemed impossible that he could feel anything but extreme closeness and affection. She'd believed he was the one man who would understand her and believe her.

"What is it?" she asked. "Why are you afraid?"

He didn't answer immediately.

"Come on, Hank. I have to hear it."

He looked away. "I don't know how to explain it." He spoke hesitatingly, his voice filled with emotion. "You see, Carlsie, I knew all along that Mendel was right. I had to believe it. So, of course, I was happy when the audit proved that he was doing nothing wrong." He peered hopefully into her eyes. "I didn't want to discover that I've done what you say I have. Not after all these years of trying so hard to do the right thing. For my survival Mendel had to be right." He clutched her in his arms. "Please understand me, darling. Please. I'm falling in love with a woman who is trying to ruin me. Can't you imagine how I feel?" He pulled her toward him and they clung tightly to each other.

She knew, in that instant, it was her last time in his arms. She realized that telling him what she had finally concluded about Mendel was not going to help. Gordo's reaction had proven that even when a man loves a woman he won't believe something he can't justify with his own experience. Hank wouldn't do it either. He just wouldn't. Carlsie didn't have the strength right then to let him slip away from her completely. And he surely would if she started talking. She knew that very well.

After a long silent while of being close, he rose and walked slowly to the window overlooking the pool. He spoke softly and earnestly, his voice filled with affection and love. "Last night was wonderful. It was like a dream or something. I couldn't describe it if I had to, but I know one thing: for me it's never been like that with a woman before."

She made no response, only wanting to listen, to

hear what he felt.

He sat beside her. "I love you more than I thought I was capable of loving. I'm forty years old, and have never felt anything like this. Never, sweetheart. The thing is, though, I don't understand what drives you. It's like you're against me or something."

"I'm not against you, Hank. I could never be."

He gazed sadly at her, his frustration and unhappiness evident. "It seems like it sometimes, with all these accusations . . . regardless of the evidence against it. We have given you every proof that the institute doesn't do unnecessary surgery, and still it's all you think about."

She felt him slipping away from her. "Just tell me, Hank. Why do you think I'm doing it?"

He sighed and looked away. "I don't know. It's just that the others think . . . well, they think you've gone off the deep end on this."

"They think I'm crazy. Is that it?"

"I wouldn't exactly say crazy, but maybe there is something distorted about your thinking on this issue."

"I know it seems that way," she replied pleadingly. "But don't give up on me, Hank. I know what he's doing now. I've finally got Mendel figured out."

"Carlsie, cut it out! I don't want to hear it. Nothing is wrong with our surgery. Give us a break, goddammit!"

"Just listen to me a minute, will you? He's switching tissue! We can prove it with some tissue typing. It'll be so simple to do this time."

He was staring at her in disbelief. "I don't think

you're hearing me right, Carlsie. There won't be any more tests. It's over, got it? Over! Mendel is a good pathologist and we're not going to destroy him and the institute by pursuing your games."

She stood petrified. Everyone was against her. It had all gone wrong. With the loss of Hank's trust, her rational attempt to end Mendel's reign of terror was over. She had failed to gain the confidence of anyone—Gordo, Hank, one single person. She now found herself totally alone, and reduced to fighting everyone . . . even this beautiful man that she loved.

Something started changing inside her right then. She watched Hank, who was continuing to talk to her, but she didn't hear him anymore. He was out of her life. She didn't love anyone . . . didn't even know what the word meant. And she didn't care. She just wanted to do what was necessary and be gone.

She walked to the door.

"Carlsie! Wait."

She ignored him.

"Carlsie! We're not through talking. You're not being fair."

She stepped out into the night air.

He was following her now. "I'm sorry I said all those things. I didn't mean them. I want to help you."

She didn't look back. In a moment she would be in her car.

He spoke softly, yet firmly. "Whatever else you do, stay away from the hospital, okay? Barret has hired some guards. He thinks you're going to try something crazy. And so does Gordo and everybody else."

She stopped suddenly, turning to glare at him. "Gordo, too? And how about you?"

"Carlsie, get off it, okay? We're running scared. You seem to be hell-bent on wiping us out. Gordo was pretty shook after what you did in the O.R., and he talked to me about it. You've got to admit it was a little freaky. Mendel says you even went down to his lab again, for God-knows-what purpose. We discussed the whole situation, and we all agree that we need to put all this behind us. Barret and Mendel don't think you're going to stop, though you've been proven wrong. Even the experts think you have some sort of vendetta against us."

"What experts, Hank? Who do you mean?"

He answered quietly. "It doesn't make any difference. We just want you to calm down and be all right."

"Who else is in on this, damn it? Don't sweet-talk me, it's too late for that. What experts?"

"If you insist." He spoke very slowly. "A psychiatrist . . . the police chief . . . the chief of your residency back at Tulane . . ."

She nodded in disdain as he spoke. "You guys don't pull any punches, do you?"

"Our main concern is to make sure you're going to be all right," Hank was saying. "Believe it or not, we're worried about you."

Her dismay and fury were intense. Mendel was winning. He had successfully turned her entire environment against her. It was her own fault, she realized. She had made a lot of mistakes; that was evident. Still, she didn't understand how Hank

269

could be so against her. Her bitterness toward him was just beginning. Without another word, she turned and started across the porch and down the stairs.

"Wait a minute. I want you to come with me," he said. "I'm going to get you some help."

She kept walking.

"Carlsie, I can't let you hurt yourself like this. I promised them I would bring you back if I could find you. I'm going to take care of you."

His voice was much closer, and she was startled by a strong grip on her shoulder. "Hold up a minute," he said. "You can't leave like this."

Angrily, she faced him, "Don't touch me, you bastard!"

Hank took away his hand and became silent.

Their eyes met and lingered for a long while. Despite everything, she perceived his love for her, his despair at what was happening. He was, at the same time, adoring of her and filled with passion and desire but plagued by suspicion and fear.

Carlsie's guilt was immense. It had been unfair of her to allow this thing between them to have come about. She had selfishly taken his love, knowing that only pain would come of it.

"I love you, Hank. Please remember that, no matter what happens to me."

"I believe that."

She broke the eye contact and started away. His parting words cut into her like a blade.

"Don't hurt us if you don't have to . . . please." His face remained in the shadows while the rest of him was illuminated by the moonlight. His posture

270

radiated defeat and fatigue.

"I would never harm you, Hank," she replied softly, knowing full well that she must, in this situation. There was no way to save those she loved from being caught up in this. Whatever happened from here on, they were at risk.

He came slowly down the steps, hands in his pockets, looking more to the ground than at her. Seemingly filled with emotion, he stood near her. "You're hurting me now."

"I don't mean to."

"Maybe not . . . but you're sure doing it." He looked off into the trees again, shrugging his shoulders as if he needed more proof of her intentions. "I don't see how you can just walk out like this."

She watched him struggle to talk to her, and she understood his dilemma. Although he realized the hopelessness of their situation, he wasn't ready to let her go. He wanted more from her. He desired a renewal of that sweet flow of positive emotion between them. And he needed time to adjust to the reality of what had happened. He wanted to try to understand her, to be close to her again even if only for a little while. "Can't you stay a bit longer?" he said finally. "Don't you at least owe me that?"

She spoke softly and sympathetically. "What's the use? We're in different worlds now. I'm afraid we would just keep arguing about this over and over. I don't want that."

"Well, I've been thinking." He paused, considering his words carefully. "Maybe we ought to just forget all this for now. It'll still be there tomorrow. We don't have to solve everything tonight, you know."

"It won't work, Hank. It's all turned bad for us."

"Only if you let it. We can get stuck in it, or we can pull ourselves up and salvage what we can." He wanted to calm things down, to change her mind about him and the situation.

She knew that was impossible. "We can't deny reality."

"Reality will take care of itself, like it or not. We sure don't have to rush it. Even people as snake-bit as we are can use a little break from the sadness." He was gazing at her with affection and trust now. Even his aura had changed. His fears seemed to have dissipated.

"There is something you must believe, Hank, or I cannot talk to you anymore."

"What is it?"

"I'm a good person, Hank. You must have faith in that."

He nodded slowly. "I don't honestly see how you could intend to be anything but good."

There was a long silence. Neither knew what to say or do. He held out his hand to her and she grasped it. His voice was tired and sad, yet filled with desperate hope. "Please stay, Carlsie. Just for a little while. I'm hurting bad . . . real bad."

He loved her; she could feel the intensity of it. This man who never did anything less than all the way had been as caught up by her as she was by him. There was already a bond between them. What possible harm could come from spending a few more hours together? Hank was right. Why not postpone the pain? Tomorrow was coming soon enough. She wanted to be near him just a little longer.

Seeming to understand her decision, he put his arm around her and led her into his house.

They lay together a long time without speaking. He held her gently, tenderly stroking and caressing her with long smooth motions that swept down from her neck and shoulders and across her lower back. She snuggled into the security of his embrace, listening to his heartbeat when he pulled her as close to him as was physically possible. Then they slept together for a while, holding each other.

She awakened in the night, relieved to find herself still beside Hank, and kissed his lips. His eyes opened. "I love you so much," he whispered, and his hands once more moved up and down her body.

"I love you, too." His attention was now the only thing in life that gave her pleasure. At last she felt calm again, and she wanted to please this wonderful man one last time. After hours of closeness she was ready for his love.

This time it was even more special than before. Hank was at once gentle and strong, compassionate and passionate, willing yet totally dominant. He was everything she needed. The strength of his legs and shoulders contrasted with the delicacy of her own. His broad chest touched her breasts, and her body was held tightly against his. In his arms she felt gorgeous. His face was the face of every hero she had ever envisioned. He was the best of all men: rugged, ruthless, superior, independent, without fear, filled with an unquenchable fire yet tender and sweet. He was a smoldering ember that became a raging inferno because of her and only her.

Together, they knew love.

Chapter Twenty-four

Before daybreak, while Hank still slept, she slipped quietly from his bed and went to her favorite place. In the calmness of sunrise the surf was, like her, uncertain, lapping timidly against the edge of land. As she passed the hours, again dodging the authorities she feared were seeking her, a plan was beginning to crystallize. The first step was to prove to the surgeons that what she believed was, in fact, true. That meant only one thing: she had to get some tissue typing done and show that some of the slide specimens did not match the removed whole breasts. Since she could not do such a study legitimately, she must gather up the slides and preserved breasts herself, and convince a pathologist somewhere to do the tests.

Since she was obviously persona non grata around the institute, the only possible way to do this was secretly. She had to get in and out of the hospital unrecognized. It was a task that frightened her, but one from which she did not turn away. Carlsie believed her time had come to be brave. This was her chance — one most people never get — to show more than ordinary courage. She would have her best shot to get into the institute after the evening shift change. People less familiar with her would be in the building then, and the lab would be shut down for the night. She decided to wait for the dark.

Hank awoke contented, reached for Carlsie, and became immediately distraught upon discovering that she was gone. He was disappointed to find she'd left no note or message. Thinking she might be at the hospital, and fearful of what she might be doing there, he dressed immediately and went in. She was nowhere to be found. His anxiety grew by the hour as he waited in his office for her to call. She never did.

At noon Walker Barret came by to attempt to get him to get back to work. Hank had not done any surgery since the day before the audit, and Barret wanted the institute to get back to normal now that "that psycho," as he called Carlsie, was finally gone.

Hank refused, and an argument ensued about how long he was going to allow this "incident" to upset him. "If you want to sulk about her, go ahead," Barret told Hank. "Just remember that there are patients that need our help. Life doesn't come to a halt just because one resident drops out of sight." He stood in Hank's doorway, contemplating the mood of his best surgeon. He knew, of course, that there was more to the relationship between Hank and Carlsie than Hank was revealing. He wished he could convince his friend that trouble-making women like her were simply not worth getting emotionally involved with. They never seemed to be an influence for good.

"Look, Hank," he said. "If it makes you feel any better, I'll not do anything to damage her professionally as long as she stays away from here and doesn't do anything else to us."

Ritter nodded in understanding. He did not wish to discuss it anymore, though. Barret, still unhappy with his associate, finally left after again urging him not to let this get blown out of proportion.

A while later Gordo came in to see if Hank had heard from Carlsie. Ritter gazed at the young surgeon and contemplated telling him the truth.

In the end he decided that he needed Gordo's help and so did Carlsie if she was to be found and taken care of. It was going to be painful for all three of them to face the consequences of what had happened, and it was only fair that Gordo know the truth.In a subdued voice Hank related the whole story, going all the way back to the first time he had danced with Carlsie at the party weeks earlier. He told Gordo how hard he had tried to fight his growing affection for her, especially since she and Gordo had had an ongoing relationship. Then he asked Gordo to forgive them both and to help him find her and make sure she was all right.

Gordo listened quietly, tears forming in his eyes. In the end he said nothing for a long while, preferring to bite his lip and stare out of the window into the afternoon sun. "I never suspected," he finally said. "I always knew she was fond of you. I mistook that for admiration and friendship. How could you two do it? How could you let me go on and on not knowing what was happening between you?"

Hank sighed. "I don't know, Gordo. We never wanted to cause you any unhappiness. I guess we thought it would never come to this. I consider you a friend. I know she does, too."

Gordo nodded, accepting that as truth. He cleared his throat and swallowed hard, removing emotion from his voice. "Where do you think she is?"

"I have no idea, and I'm worried."

"She's not going to stop now," Gordo said. "I don't know her as well as you do, I guess, but I know her enough to be sure she'll keep the pressure on. She's not a quitter."

Both men silently contemplated the situation for a while. Then Gordo spoke again.

"I think we need to look at all sides of this, Hank. Just for the sake of argument, what if there's some truth to what she's saying?"

Ritter, surprised by the statement, shook his head. "No chance. We've checked it out. We did everything she asked."

"Wait a minute. I'm not saying she is right. I'm saying 'what if'?"

Ritter listened solemnly as Gordo went on.

"What if something has gone wrong in the lab like she says, and there have been a few—maybe even a lot—of misinterpreted specimens."

"It would be a disaster for us . . . you know that." Hank answered. "The thing is, we've completely checked it out. We know for a fact the slides have not been misinterpreted. There wasn't one error in the lot. Carlsie's wrong. It's that simple."

"Then why do you think she's so convinced—convinced enough to throw her entire career down the drain if necessary?"

Ritter frowned. "I don't know. I simply don't understand it."

"Neither do I." Gordo looked into the eyes of his teacher. "I'm starting to wonder about it, though. I've never met anyone more dedicated to medicine than she is. She'd do anything rather than lose the opportunity to practice this profession. And she's not ambitious just because of the money to be made either. She wants to work at surgery for the pure joy of doing it." He paused, then added. "Her dedication reminds me of yours, Hank. She loves surgery as much as you do."

Ritter watched him quietly, obviously affected by what he was saying.

Gordo went on. "I've been thinking . . . if she's willing to sacrifice everything she's ever wanted from her career, then can you imagine how incredibly powerful her feelings about this must be?"

Hank ran a hand through his hair and rubbed his eyes uneasily. "Go on, Gordo."

"Well, as I see it, all we've really checked out are

279

the diagnoses of tissue actually on slides. There seems to be no doubt that shows cancer."

"I agree. So what's your point."

"Carlsie keeps saying Mendel's crazy. What if she's right?"

The two men gazed at each other silently. The implication of what Gordo was suggesting was staggering to Ritter who had never seriously considered Carlsie's accusations. If Mendel really was psychotic, then anything was possible. Everything they had done to verify the accuracy of the diagnoses was based on the assumption that no covert attempt to misdiagnose had occurred. If Mendel had purposely done something wrong, all bets were off.

"What made you change your thinking on this?" Hank asked. "We have no evidence at all that it could be true."

"Not much, I agree. It's just that if she happens to be right it would be terrible for us not to recognize it. I started thinking about it. Mendel works all alone, just like she says. We hand him the tumor. He evaluates it and only then delivers it to the lab techs. He has the specimen totally under his control for quite a while."

"You're suggesting he could be swapping tissue?"

"We would never know it if he was."

Ritter went to his window and stared out at the river. Gordo noticed a new slump in his posture. He finally turned back with a despairing sigh. "I can't believe this is happening. Now two of you believe this. I guess if it's possible he could be doing that, we have to check it out. Carlsie mentioned something about tissue typing."

Gordo nodded. "It would be the only way to catch him." He saw fear in Hank's eyes when the senior man asked him a final question.

"Do you really think it's possible, Gordo?"

Keene waited a long time before answering. "He's always seemed a little weird, Hank. He never regrets a positive biopsy."

"That doesn't prove anything," Ritter said, grimacing and clenching his teeth. "If he did it, though, I'm going to kill him. I swear it."

Gordo did not doubt that. If Mendel had ruined this hospital, he was a dead man.

Chapter Twenty-five

Oscar Mendel was beside himself with rage when the two surgeons descended upon his previously insulated domain. When Ritter explained, rather matter-of-factly, what they intended to do, he turned white with shock. For a moment he seemed to consider punching Hank. Instead, he unleashed a torrent of profanities regarding what they could do with their insulting, son-of-a-bitch idea. "You can't touch one goddamn slide in this lab, you insolent brainless bastards!" he railed.

He positioned himself between the two intruders and the histology storage area. Frightened lab techs evacuated the immediate vicinity quickly, without regard to the glass containers and slides that were shattered during their wild escape.

Ritter, flanked by Gordo, did not retreat: Mendel gave no ground. Gordo attempted to act as mediator. "Dr. Mendel, we only want a few specimens to match up with the original breasts. You have nothing to worry about if they're okay."

The pathologist directed his reply to Ritter. "I have nothing to worry about from you two assholes no matter what!" He called out to a lab employee to get Walker Barret down to Path immediately. Then he turned back to his tormentors. "Nobody's taking any materials out of here ever again. I've had it with your absurd tests. If you want to test something, try testing the feel of my foot right up your ass!"

The lab techs buzzed with amazement.

Ritter spoke calmly. "Oscar, I told you we don't want trouble over this. We just want to verify what you've been telling us about these tissues. It's a very simple proposition. You should have nothing to fear."

Mendel sneered at the suggestion. "You can have all the verification you want — over my dead body!"

Ritter was now becoming angered by the pathologist's obstructive attitude. "Oscar, these are our patients. You have no right to deny us the opportunity to evaluate your work. We are the referring doctors. You serve at our pleasure . . . or don't you remember that?"

Mendel glared at him. "All I remember, asshole, is that you are a dumb shit who could do nothing without me!"

Ritter became furious. "Get out of my way! I'm taking those slides."

"You heard me. I said 'over my dead body'!"

Although Hank spoke softly, he spoke firmly. "That can be arranged, Oscar."

Gordo again interrupted the conversation which was swiftly going downhill. "Calm down a minute, would you, guys?" He looked at Mendel. "We're going to ask the pathology department of the University of Miami to type these tissues and verify the matches, so why not give us some representative samples and get it done and over with?"

Mendel became even more incensed. "Those jerks don't know anything about breast cancer compared to me. I wrote the book! I suppose you've forgotten that!"

"We just want to check," Gordo said softly. "Please don't fight us."

Mendel's truculence suddenly faded into strained defensiveness. He touched his fingers to his temples and seemed to be in pain. Then he gazed around the room as if those in it were his jurors. "This is wrong. Don't you see it, everybody? I couldn't make any mistakes. I wrote the book! I wrote it, don't you see?"

In that moment he looked so wild, so bizarre, that no one in the lab failed to see him in a new light. He rushed to a bookcase and began frantically pulling volumes out and throwing them to the floor. Finally he held one aloft. "See!" he screamed. "See this? This is it! This is the book, and I wrote it." He began flipping through the pages. No one moved or spoke. Mendel's composure had come unraveled. He was on the verge of degenerating into a blithering fool. He slumped into a chair, still holding the famous text on breast cancer which had rocketed him to the peak of his profession. "I wrote

285

the goddamn book," he muttered. "You can't accuse me." He leaned forward, clutching his head with both hands. Something was happening to him, everyone could see it.

The observers remained still and quiet, their eyes on the pathologist in his moment of deterioration. Walker Barret, who had entered just as Mendel had fallen apart, sat beside him.

The pathologist, seemingly oblivious to Barret's presence, continued to press the palms of his hands to his temples. He was grimacing as if in great pain.

Barret, casting a disapproving eye toward Keene and Ritter, then supportively put his arm around Mendel. "I believe you, Oscar. I've always trusted you, and you did write the book. I've read it."

Mendel, disoriented and confused, gazed at Barret. A peculiar expression came to his face. "It's my head again," he grunted. "My fucking head." Then he extended his neck backward as far as it would go and uttered a guttural growlish noise. Suddenly his back arched and his legs gave way. He fell from the chair, crashing heavily to the floor. His arms and legs twitching, weakly at first, then spasmodically in a coarse rhythmic pattern.

Saliva frothed from his mouth, and he gnashed and gritted his teeth, biting his lips and cheeks repeatedly. Blood poured from his lacerated tissue, and he grunted intermittently as his head and neck convulsed in powerful thrusting movements that brought the back of his skull against the floor.

He urinated upon himself, soiling his pants.

"My God," roared Barret. "He's having a seizure.

286

Somebody get a bite block!" Barret and Hank knelt beside Mendel, protecting the back of his head, restraining him, and preventing him from injuring himself any further.

A few moments more and it was over. Some of the lab techs were crying. Most of the others stood about in disbelief.

Barret glanced around the room. "Did anyone know he was an epileptic?" There was no response. "Has he ever passed out before or done anything like this?" Heads were shaken — no.

Mendel rested quietly, breathing irregularly, his head supported in the lap of his longtime colleague Walker Barret. A stretcher was brought in, and he was lifted carefully into it and taken from the room.

The three surgeons huddled together, watching as Mendel was taken away and the lab personnel began to clean up the mess. Barret's eyes were moist; his voice was soft. "I've never known him to have a seizure, and he's been my friend for a long, long time. This must be recent, he wouldn't keep such a thing from me." Barret peered at the others questioningly. "What the hell was going on down here, anyway? Why didn't someone call me earlier?"

Hank explained what they were trying to do. Barret, whose irritation was obvious, criticized the poorly thought-out plan. "Don't you think I have a right to be told of such a thing?" He paused for effect. "Or did you clear it with Carlsie instead?"

"Wait a minute, Walker," Hank said. "We only want the truth. I care just as much as you do about what's happening here."

Barret sneered. "That's not true, and you know it. This place is everything to me. I'm old, this is my last stop. I won't get another chance if we're ruined by Carlsie's lies and innuendos. You can go anywhere, the better part of your career is still ahead. So don't tell me you care as much as I do — you don't. Nobody does."

"You're wrong, Walker. Nothing is more important to me than the institute."

Barret glared at him cynically. "If that's true then why are you sleeping with the little slut who is trying to ruin us. Somehow, such actions make me doubt your loyalty."

"How did you know about that?"

"Oscar saw you."

"That's wonderful!" Ritter roared. "So now you and Mendel are spying on me, is that it?"

"Hear me good, Hank. If you want to let that bitch pussy-whip you, that's your business. When you let it interfere with your work here, it becomes my business . . . and Oscar's."

"Why Oscar's?"

"Because he's been here as long as I have," Barret said angrily. "He helped me build this place into what it is today. He loves this hospital as much as anyone."

Ritter looked dismayed. "I don't think you're being as objective about our problem as you should, Walker. Mendel's sick . . . very sick. That's pretty obvious. There's a fair chance he's been screwing up. If he has, then it's our job to find out about it and stop him now before he does any more damage."

Barret rubbed his face and looked away.

Hank went on. "All we want to do is double-check the slides. If he's clean, we'll all feel better and I'll apologize."

Barret shrugged hopelessly. "I doubt if we can ever be the same after this, but you've gone so far, I don't see how I can stop you. Get it over with quickly—and keep that bitch out of here."

Hank nodded and Barret glumly walked away.

Hank gathered together the slides of young, recent cancer patients and the bottles containing the whole breasts of these same patients. He left immediately to deliver the tissue to the medical school in Miami. It had a large transplant program, and was well equipped to do quick tissue typing.

Gordo left the hospital, intending to search for Carlsie. He was anxious to find her before she did anything desperate. He wished he'd had more faith in her from the beginning. In his heart he now knew they'd put her through an unnecessary hell.

Walker Barret went up to his office to call in the rest of his surgical staff and explain that he was allowing one more check to clear the situation up once and for all. Afterward, he talked to Val Ryan. She cried at the news.

"It's my fault," Barret confided, somewhat emotionally. "I should have paid more attention to what that girl was doing. She obviously was influenced by that boozer, Grossman." He sighed. "Who in hell would have imagined she could get so many intelligent people worked up like this?"

But Val was seeing the problem in a different way. "Think about all those poor women if it's true. My God, Walker. Mastectomies without a good reason? It's horrible! What are you going to do if it's all true?"

"It won't be. It couldn't be. I've never heard of such a thing."

"What if it is, though. Maybe Mendel's had seizures before and messed up."

He watched her cry for a moment before he answered. "Well, in that unlikely event I would have to think of something . . . some sort of story that could save the institute. I'd need a scapegoat, Val. It's callous to say it, but I couldn't let this hospital be destroyed, no matter what — it's more important than any of us."

Val stared at him in disgust. "I think you're pitiful."

His stony expression didn't change. "I don't give a damn what you think. You didn't slave for years to make this hospital what it is."

"And just what is so wonderful about this hospital?" she responded sarcastically. "At the present moment, the reason for its greatness seems to escape me."

He gazed impassively at her and did not respond.

Chapter Twenty-six

Carlsie, in hiding, spent the last few hours re-thinking her options. She wanted to consider every possibility before acting. She knew there was only one thing to do. She had to get proof. No one would listen to her now unless she had it. Her task was to get the tissue out of the lab and have it checked.

She bought supper at a burger joint, and was too frightened to eat it. If her plan went wrong tonight, she'd be in a lot more trouble than merely having the institute mad at her. This time she'd have to face the law. Breaking and entering. Judges didn't laugh such matters off and neither did state medical licensing boards. Jailbirds were not allowed to continue practicing medicine.

It won't matter anyway, she thought. I'll be better off in jail if I'm wrong. It will be the only safe place. Barret and Mendel will probably want to kill me for the trouble I've caused.

After dark she went to the hospital. Her firs
goal was to get through the front door by mingling
with a crowd of visitors. That done, she could find
someplace to hid out until the lab closed for the
night. Then, finally, she would be able to gather the
evidence she needed to prove what she so fervently
believed.

Chapter Twenty-seven

Oscar Mendel awoke in a hospital room. The smell of fresh flowers and antiseptic filled the air in a way that he found quite agreeable. For a short moment he was happy and secure. His ordeal was over at last. For the first time in as long as he could remember, things were good again. Life was sweet.

His euphoria faded as he realized where he was and why. The fear and anxiety returned. He immediately became furious at the surgeons — all of them, but particularly the woman who had brought this upon him. The headache began anew.

A nurse came into the room. Her presence irritated him, and he let her have it. "Get the hell out of here. When I need something, I'll press the goddamn buzzer. Got it?"

She was tolerant and conciliatory. Years of experience had taught her how inconsiderate sick people can be. Part of her job was to take abuse. "Calm down now, Doctor. I've medicine to give you. This will relax you." She displayed a syringe.

Mendel's pain was now exceeding his limit of tolerance.

He screamed at the nurse. "I said get out. I'm not taking any of your damned shots!"

"You don't have any choice!" she answered sternly. "You must take your medicine. Doctor's orders." She started toward him.

"Says who?" He pushed her away, violently. She stumbled back against the wall and collapsed to the floor calling for help.

His skull about to burst from pain, Mendel climbed from the bed and lumbered awkwardly toward her, clutching his exploding head. "I'm going to shut you up for good, you filth! You whore! You dirty cunt!"

A big orderly and several nurses quickly entered the room. Mendel brandished his food tray at them, and then shoved the bedside serving table toward them.

The orderly spoke to him slowly and evenly. "Take it easy now, fellow. We aren't going to hurt you. Just calm down."

With blurry eyes and a torture-wracked consciousness, Mendel appraised them carefully. They were the enemy. They deserved to be killed, chewed up, and spit out. They wanted to destroy him; it was obvious from their gestures. He emitted a low guttural sound and bared his teeth. His eyes were those of a trapped animal — wild, enraged, desperate.

"Easy now," soothed the orderly. "Just relax. Everything's gonna be all right." The whimpering nurse rose slowly from the floor.

Warily, Mendel studied them all, prepared to defend himself as he glanced around for a way out. There was none. He would be forced to mount a direct attack if he wished to escape. The big bastard, the orderly, kept trying to con him into letting down his guard. He would have none of it. Slowly he backed away from them, placing the bed between himself and his tormentors. Crouching down, hostile and frightened, he leered at them and waited for their next move.

Surprisingly the onslaught never came. They only talked and talked, lying to him about their intentions.

"Let us give you your shot now. It'll help you feel better," said the big man. "You're gonna be just fine."

Suddenly, Mendel realized that he was making a strategic error. Becoming irrational and being labeled as dangerous was not to his advantage, and he knew it. Although he still wanted to tear out the throats of these· assholes, he controlled himself, forcing his aggressiveness to dissipate.

As the headache faded and rationality returned, he felt calmer, less threatened. When he climbed back into bed, the orderly tried to restrain his arm so the nurse might inject it. But Mendel brought his elbow up quickly, clipping him solidly across the jaw. "Get off me!" he told the surprised man.

The nurse calmed the orderly, who was about to retaliate. "We'll call your doctor about this," she said threateningly to Mendel; then orderly and nurses retreated from the room. As he departed the orderly turned back and angrily pointed a finger at him. "You do that again and I'll break your neck!"

Mendel sneered. "I'll be ready."

Alone, he lay quietly considering his situation. He was in grave danger now. But he hardly had the spirit for a struggle. All he really wanted was rest and relief. He had done so much already. He didn't want any more pain.

The pain was a killer.

Worse than a killer. Death would be a pleasure by comparison. He couldn't go on living like this. He'd had enough of this torture.

Oscar Mendel lay unhappily in his hospital bed, and reminisced about the days before Belail, a time when he had still felt young and happy even though his youth had already escaped him. That had been a period of great success for him. His career and reputation had blossomed rapidly at the institute. He had enjoyed his work and his growing fame. Then this thing had come into his life. He decided it must be a long delayed punishment for the crime of his childhood — the fire at the orphanage — for which he had made no restitution.

How was it, he had often wondered in the last two years, that he had gone so long without worrying about the dozens of dead children and nuns, yet they had come back to haunt him at this late stage of his life? The blood on his hands had made him much more vulnerable to the offers and threats of one like Belail than he would have been if he'd had a clear conscience.

The remorse he felt about the fire, even though the nuns deserved it, had always fed his fear of exposure. Now the time had come to end it. He no longer cared what happened to himself, and by not caring he became less susceptible than he once was. The only thing he presently feared was the pain, and the only thing he wanted was freedom — freedom that he knew could only come in one way. It was the end for him, but he did not dread it.

Mendel rose from his hospital bed and crept quietly to the door. Cracking it open, he peered down the hallway. It was empty. Gently he closed the door, and went to his closet. He dressed in the clothes he had worn to work that morning, even put on his tie. Carefully he combed his hair and then brushed his teeth. He wanted to be clean and neat when they found him, just as he had always been in life. He couldn't stand the idea of allowing them to find anything about him disgusting, as he had found so many of the corpses he had autopsied.

He checked the hallway once again, then slipped out, unnoticed. Descending the rear stairs, he went down three flights, past the cafeteria which was closed at that time of night. He unlocked the lab and in the darkness crossed over to his private office.

He sat quietly for a while, thinking about everything, and was proud of himself for not feeling fear. He had dreaded this moment but had decided long ago that if exposed he would never be taken alive. The very thought of being dragged into courtrooms, facing questions from insolent prosecutors, the press; being humiliated, pitied — it was repugnant to him. He would rather die with honor, with glory, and with his manhood intact.

He had always known what might come, and had prepared for it. From his desk he withdrew the two small ampules of Sufentanil he had taken from the O.R. months ago. It was a narcotic anesthesiologists used. Like morphine. But he had been told it was one thousand times as potent. The amount he had could easily kill several people. He only needed it for one — himself. His death would be gentle and painless and very euphoric.

He had no feelings of weakness at going down this way. He felt like a soldier using a suicide pill to keep from being tortured into revealing all he knew. It was noble, in its own way, and honorable. He would give no one the satisfaction of interrogating him. There would be no reporters writing of his imprisonment. He would never have to explain why he had acted as he had. There would be no need to tell of the injustices committed against him and other men by women. He would not have to justify his hatred and disdain of them. There would be no attempt to psychoanalyze him, no pseudomedical diagnoses explaining away his abnormal behavior by blaming it on the early death of his mother and his mistreatment at the hands of the nuns.

No hotshot psychiatrist would tell the court and

the newspapers about his lifelong inability to come to terms with females. There would be no talk around the hospital about how "normal" he had seemed. No defense lawyer would be making up bullshit explanations in an attempt to get him acquitted.

And most of all there would be no verdict of insanity, no court-appointed psychiatrists, no panels trying to determine if he was "cured." No work therapy, no rehabilitation, no long-term institutionalization. There would be only glory. He had done what he had to do, and he had destroyed the surgeons he had always hated.

Only one task remained—punishing the woman that had brought him down. He was going to love hearing her scream. He doubted if others ever completed all their goals before life ended, but his final desire was attainable. It would be easy for him to stay out of sight until Carlsie showed up at her apartment as she inevitably would, since she seemed to have won this round of the battle. And when she did, he would be there. After he had savored her destruction, he would have the Sufentanil for himself. He would be in charge of his own destiny. He could choose when and where they would find him—and Carlsie, in her modified form, of course.

While preparing to leave the lab, he filled and lit his pipe for the last time in the office he had used for so many years. He drew the Sufentanil into a syringe and put it in his pocket. Then he took out his personal stationery and began to write. When

299

he'd finished what he had to say, he put the paper into an envelope, along with the small notebook within which he had recorded the names of the victims. That should keep the malpractice lawyers of South Florida driving Rolls Royces, he thought.

Finally, his preparations completed, he had nothing more to do than start his search for Carlsie. There was no rush. She would turn up sooner or later. He sat in the dark, smoking his pipe, waiting for the tobacco to burn out.

He noted with satisfaction that the other half of his personality had become strangely silent since he had made the decision to end it this way. Funny how things work out, he thought. He had never dreamed that he, Oscar, would survive as the dominant one. It was ironic that he had to kill himself to prove his superiority. But his essence would live on. He understood that now. His long-awaited ascension was at hand. He was getting closer to the nobility he coveted. Soon he would be a peer of those princes he had only served—the ones the foolish nuns had tried to teach him to fear.

How stupid they were to force-feed him such rubbish about that weakling Jesus. The man had not had enough power to keep himself from being nailed to a cross. Who could admire a being so impotent when there were so many more regal and noble? So many with strength, courage, and the intensity to make things happen the way they wanted. None of those he worshipped had ever been ridiculed or crucified in public. They exemplified what

300

he was to become. He awaited the rapidly approaching moment when he would join the ranks of the great ones, the ones he had always admired, the ones the foolish nuns had tried to teach him to hate:

Abaddon
Ahriman
Apollyon
Asmodeus
Azazel
Baal
Beelzebub
Hades
Diabolus
Lucifer
Mammon
Mephistopheles
Moloch
Samael
Set

He believed that soon he, too, would be independent and free, assured of eternal survival and consciousness. Immortality would be his, the need for embodiment forever finished.

Enjoying the unusual tranquillity and the dark loneliness of his normally bustling lab, Mendel decided to refill the pipe and light it again. He was in no hurry.

Chapter Twenty-eight

Gordon Keene dialed Ritter's number once more, hoping that he would be home. This time he was rewarded by Hank's tired, familiar voice.

"I can't find her," Gordo told him.

"Have you tried the beach?"

"Over and over. She's just not there. I'm beginning to wonder if she's left town."

"I hope she has. It would keep her from doing anything foolish."

Gordo agreed. "The thing is I know she's suffering because of all this. I wish I could at least tell her we're checking it out. The idea of her getting sick over this crap really bugs me."

"Yeah, I know what you mean. I can't think of anything else to do, though. I got the slides delivered. They'll have some results for us in the morning."

"I'm dreading that."

Ritter sighed. "Could be the end of everything,

Gordo."

Keene thought about his next move. "I think I'll go back over and check out the hospital again. She might be planning to break into the lab or something, hoping to convince us we should believe her."

"I guess I'll stay here and try to get some sleep," Hank said. "Tomorrow could be a rough day."

"Maybe she'll try to call you. I just don't know anyplace else to search, Hank. I'm so afraid she's going to get hurt."

"Well, wherever she is, she's probably all right. You know, Gordo, you're the best friend she ever had. She just doesn't know it. Whatever happens now, I intend to make her understand what a loyal friend you are."

Gordo didn't know how to respond to that. It seemed so ironic. How could Hank call him Carlsie's best friend. He hadn't become her lover; Hank had. It was all too painful to think about. Gordo decided it didn't make any difference. He just wanted to find Carlsie and make sure she was okay.

Chapter Twenty-nine

Getting inside the hospital was easier than Carlsie had anticipated. Slick as could be, she slipped past the reception desk with the visitors. The unfamiliar security guard in the front lobby paid her no attention. He was too busy chatting with the attractive volunteer working the patient-information desk.

Carlsie went directly to the second floor and sequestered herself in the back of the O.R. nurses' dressing room. She then passed several hours in the dark, listening for any approaching footsteps.

Around eleven, she took the back stairs down to the lab. The door was never locked since it linked two secure areas. She peeked through the small window. As she had expected, the room was dark and empty.

Quietly, she eased into the main laboratory. There was less light here than in the hall, so she waited for her eyes to accommodate. The large workroom was silent except for the low hum of the refrigeration units along a side wall.

She had decided that the individual gross specimens were going to be harder to locate than the slides, so she went after them first. The preserved breasts were stored in the old morgue; it had been used for temporary storage of bodies in the days when the institute had been a general hospital. It had a thick entryway opened by a pull rope which moved suspended weights that swung the quite heavy wooden door.

Inside was the horrifying collection of amputated breasts the institute had collected in recent years. Shelves from floor to ceiling were lined with half-gallon containers, each holding the preserved remains of what had once been an organ of beauty and function.

She turned on a light and was startled by the overwhelming impression of so many leathery nipples attached to a grayish tan skin and large fatty, greasy blobs of tissue. Each breast rested in its bottle in a different way. Some lay upright, posed as in life, while others were twisted, the nipples and areolae smashed against the bottles' sides. Others were inverted looking, not like breasts at all but more like mounds of fatty meat and preserved tissue.

Many still had the stitches which had closed the small incisions through which biopsies had been taken.

It was the first time Carlsie had been in such a place and the emotional impact was devastating. Surrounding her was evidence of hundreds of tragedies, of shattered lives, of beauty aborted. Even worse, she knew that some of these had been healthy organs.

Her anxiety about what she was doing did not prevent her from feeling profound compassion for the women whose fate had been determined here. She wished something could be done for the ones who had been mutilated unnecessarily — in the name of modern medicine. That was the part that hurt her the most.

Tears filled her eyes and rolled down her cheeks as she walked back and forth, searching for the names of recent cases. One by one she gathered up the bottles she wanted and stacked them by the door.

She couldn't keep from weeping when she found the breast of Melissa Bates, who had somehow seemed to know she had been cheated. It was almost too much for Carlsie to take. She resisted the urge to run away from it all and forced herself to go on. Her job was to get what she needed and then to retreat as quickly as she could.

Oscar Mendel stood in the shadows, beyond the light from the open door of the storage room. Fascinated, he watched her move the bottles from place to place, unaware that she was observed. Fortuitous circumstance had given him a glorious opportunity. He wondered why she was there and for what purpose she was stealing the specimens. Why this last insult to the integrity of his department?

From the moment he had heard the first noise she'd made on entering, he had known that fate was smiling upon him. His last wish was to be granted—and on his home turf. The bitch that had brought him down was now his, but curiosity held him back. What was she doing? Why this interest in these scraps of the surgeons' carvings? He waited, silently observing, looking for any hint as to her motive. It pleased him to consider the possibility that a streak of the bizarre existed in her. Perhaps she was collecting mementos for some personal private enjoyment.

He pondered how she was going to react when she learned that she, too, would soon contribute a part of herself to those bottles. He would leave her carcass to the world, as a ceremonial reminder of who he had been. It would be his last mortal pleasure.

Tiring of the wait, he turned off the lights when she made yet another trip to the back rows of shelves. He heard her gasp in surprise. After a noiseless pause, she slowly came forward. He lit a small Bunsen burner and waited for her to come out of the room.

Instinctively, Carlsie knew it was Mendel. Since there were no windows or exits, she prepared for the confrontation. Somehow she wasn't as frightened as she had thought she would be. Perhaps she could take her way through it. She found him just beyond the door, in the main lab, gazing into the faint light of blue hot flame. Flickering shadows exaggerated the movements of his arms and head. He looked up as she approached, allowing her a brief glimpse of the strange cast to his expression in the glow of the little fire.

He addressed her in a calm voice. "I always enjoy the dark. Don't you?"

Her immediate impression was that his voice was different. There was a new, somewhat strident, almost strained, quality to it.

"Not really," she answered quietly, coldly, while analyzing her routes of escape. There seemed to be none.

He switched on a small desk lamp that did little more to light up the room than had the burner. The effect was bizarre, creating strange disproportionate shadows of equipment and the two of them.

"This meeting has been a long time coming," he said.

She moved slowly toward him watching him carefully. There was much changed about Mendel since she had seen him last. For one thing, he appeared very tired, worn out. His face had lost its domineering harshness. It seemed sadder now. Maybe it was only her imagination, but she thought his eyes were different. They had the empty, dull appearance of the chronically ill.

And she noticed other differences in him. Even his mannerisms had changed. His gestures, the way he moved his arms . . . all somehow changed. He was slower, more tentative, like a very old person.

When he walked over to turn on an additional lamp, she was surprised by his gait. In place of Mendel's previous stride, which had been strong and proud, there was now a shuffling, almost sliding movement. He seemed broken.

Peering steadily at her, he seated himself on a tall stool. "So," he murmured. "Do you wish to talk about this first?"

She gladly bought time by agreeing to a discussion of their mutual dilemma, but decided it would not be wise to attempt to mislead him as to why she was there. He knew the truth; she was sure of it. Her one hope of escaping was to bargain with him . . . to attempt to work out some sort of deal.

As he sat rigidly, listening to her, she presented her analysis of the whole situation and outlined her understanding of what he had been doing and how it could be proven publicly if necessary. "I'm right, am I not?" she asked softly. She wanted to convey a nonjudgmental attitude to him. If she could keep him from perceiving her hostility, make him believe that she regarded the issue simply as a problem to be solved, she might have a chance of getting out of this. The problem was, she was dealing with a psychotic. "I know this is not all your fault. Who else was a part of it?" As she spoke, he stared at her in disbelief.

"If you think I needed help, then you really don't know how easy this was," he said. "It doesn't take much to fool surgeons."

"I'll make you a deal," she offered. "I'll call this

off if you will leave this hospital." Perhaps this bluff will gain me some time, she thought.

It didn't. The quiet, almost passive aura about Mendel vanished. In its place appeared an impassioned, vengeful maniac, dedicated to making her pay for her sins against him. His anger and bitterness erupted into full fury. "You insulting little whore!" he roared. Bellowing out the frustration caused by those who had defeated him, Mendel hurled uninterpretable obscenities at Carlsie.

She retreated along the only route open to her, back into the darkened storage room.

"I'll not be humiliated without revenge!" he shrieked and stepped into the doorway, blocking her attempt to close the door. "You have made a grave mistake, insulting me." He glared ferociously at her. "You thought I could be a game for you . . . well, this will be a very costly lesson, my dear." His voice grew even more vitriolic, more hostile. He was disgusted by her. She knew he wanted to tear her apart, wanted to enjoy her painful destruction.

"Why?" she asked, continuing to back farther into the room. "How could you do this to these people? What did they ever do to you? They were innocent."

"Never!" he screamed. "I never did it to an innocent one. Dancers, prostitutes, models, rich sluts who married older men for their money — they were all women who used their bodies to taunt men."

"Melissa Bates wasn't like that. Why her?"

"She was a bitch, all right. She was like you. She

311

chose to sully a male profession."

Carlsie saw a chance to make it to the door and took it. She pushed past a stack of boxes and leaped over a low table.

Reaching out as she dashed past him, Mendel rammed her in the chest and sent her sprawling across the floor. Her head slammed into a cabinet. A deep gash opened above her left eye. Blood ran across her face and dripped from her chin onto the front of her blouse. She was stunned and disoriented.

Before she could recover, he flipped her up onto a counter top and slid her rapidly down the length of it. She literally flew through the air to crash heavily into the wall, then collapse, an all but unconscious heap of limp humanity now bleeding from her nose as well. A tooth was broken, and she had bitten her tongue severely.

He gazed disdainfully at her, she was so easily defeated.

Carlsie moaned and struggled painfully to regain control of her brain. It wasn't functioning right. She was dizzy, her head hurt, and she couldn't get her body to stand or even to sit up. Slowly she realized where she was and what was happening. One knee was aching terribly from the wrenching twist it had undergone when she'd fallen.

Through bleary eyes she watched him pause, surveying her, his vanquished foe.

"You parasite," she muttered, glaring at him defiantly. "You can't beat me this easily. They will

312

make you pay for this. You are going to be exposed."

His eyes revealed his rage. He picked her up and heaved her over a chair. She was sent tumbling into a corner where shelves holding laboratory glassware collapsed and rained down upon her, sharp shards cutting into her like shrapnel. By now, she was bleeding from multiple injuries and her eyes weren't focusing.

Despite that, her defiance persisted. Defeat now was defeat forever, and she was not ready to give up. As Mendel watched, she spat blood toward him and cursed him again. Then she hurled broken glass in his direction and continued to insult him. "I will repay you a hundred times, you filth."

Amazed by her resilience, irritated by her stubborn unwillingness to capitulate to his superiority, and incensed by her curses, he stood above her. Slowly, spitefully, he opened his pants and urinated upon her.

Writhing awkwardly in vain attempts to evade his foul spray, Carlsie weakly threw more glass at him, and barely managed to project a wad of bloody spittle at him.

Enraged, he kicked her in the groin, and leaned down to grasp her left breast. With an excruciatingly painful twist, he yanked it so violently she screamed.

"You will die alone—now!" Mendel's body trembled with anger, a fierce leer spread over his face. He kicked her again. She had never known such hate, such need for vengeance; but it was equaled by her own revulsion for the horrible wicked thing he was. Again she spat. It was all, in her injured state, she could do.

"You fail, you suffer, and now you die," he screamed. Almost grinning, he leaned down, continuing to twist her injured breast, and slapped her across the face. Then he drove one gouging finger toward her right eye.

Frightened and facing imminent death, Carlsie struggled pitifully to get away. She was tired, she was bloodied, she was overwhelmed by his strength. His hideous glare burned unflinchingly into her until she was almost ready to accept defeat. She didn't want to suffer needless agony.

But spurred by a desperate desire to preserve her life, she marshaled her remaining energy and lunged upward, reaching for his face.

And found it.

This time he was the one who was unguarded.

Her grasp upon him became a death grip.

One finger dug deeply into his left eye, from which blood and a thick clear gelatinous substance flowed copiously. Her thumb had torn its way into a nostril. Her fingernail had penetrated to the bone just below his right eye. Carlsie wrapped her free arm around his head, consolidating her grip, and hung on with all the strength and will she had.

Mendel lurched backward, attempting to shake her loose.

She was like a bulldog.

He writhed and flailed, all the while screaming in pain, and attempted to get his hands on her own head. The more he struggled the more she could feel the tissue of his face being torn away. Her index finger now sank deeply into the socket that had been his left eye. It felt warm and slimy and she could feel the contents of the ruptured globe dripping down her hand in a sticky glob.

In a sudden burst, he pulled himself loose from her. Totally enraged, he heaved her into the air. She sailed into one of the cabinets of breasts. Its shelves collapsed upon her. Bottles crashed to the floor. Old breasts, formalin, and broken glass slithered in every direction.

As Carlsie lay barely conscious, he descended on her and ground one of the preserved specimens into her bruised face, forcing bits of it into her mouth and nostrils.

She was no longer able to respond. She didn't move, or even care what was occurring. She was lost.

Mendel, in profound pain, rose and patted his torn-up face with some paper towels. His left eye was gone, he knew that. It didn't matter, though. He could see fine with the other one. But the constant dripping of blood and intraocular matter was bothersome.

Carlsie was still, but she was breathing; he could see that. He grabbed her legs and dragged her across the breast-littered floor to the side room, where the old autopsy tables were.

After lifting her limp form onto the first table, he found some thick twine and securely restrained her legs. He then pulled her arms above her head and tied her wrists together, finally yanking them down over the upper end of the table and attaching them to it as tightly as he could. In response to the painful distortion of her shoulders, Carlsie moaned and struggled weakly, but there was no way she could get loose now even if she were fully awake.

Gingerly exploring his facial injuries with one finger, Mendel shuffled into his office and got a scalpel and some scissors. He also brought back a long intracardiac needle and a vial of potassium chloride, with which he could kill her instantly if she gave him any more trouble.

He wanted to punish her more than he had ever wanted to hurt anyone, and he was going to. No question about it.

Gordo pulled into the hospital parking lot and sat finishing his coffee, pondering the situation. He could think of nowhere else to search. He had been to her apartment repeatedly, to the beach and to every one of her hangouts he could think of — and had found nothing. No one had seen her. Still, he knew she was in town somewhere. She had too much tenacity to give up this easily. It made him nervous to contemplate what she might do. He had even gone over to Mendel's house just on the chance that she might be looking for him with some

316

wild plan in mind.

He went into the lobby and quizzed the guard there, but the man had not seen her. With nothing else to do, Gordo decided to hang around just in case. "I'm going down to check out the lab," he told the guard. "Page me if Dr. Camden happens to come in."

The guard gave Gordo the key to the door of the main lab, and promised to call him if the lady doctor showed up.

First, Mendel cut away Carlsie's bloody clothes, and poured water over her to clean her up. He wanted her to look good when they found her—a skillfully dissected specimen. The cold water roused her a little, which pleased him. He wanted her awake so she could appreciate his surgical talents. It was going to be rewarding to have a professionally knowledgeable patient.

He brought a specimen container into the room and placed it beside her. He was going to do this right. As he leaned over her, deciding where to make his incision, the bloody ooze from his face dripped onto her. Irritated, he wiped it off, then, reconsidering, scraped some of it from his face and smeared it onto hers. It seemed appropriate.

Roughly he handled her breasts. The left one was already swollen from the still-enlarging blood clot within it that he had caused. Perhaps it should be removed first, he thought. That would leave the best for last. He looked down at its pretty nipple and gentle feminine curves. Even with the pain he was in, he was going to enjoy what he was about to do, and he deserved this pleasure.

Mendel traced his incision lines once more before he started. He knew this work was going to get a lot of press coverage and he wanted it to look right. He turned on the overhead spotlight and picked up the scalpel. It gleamed brightly in his hand.

Gordo picked up another cup of coffee from the machine in the snack bar, and took the elevator downstairs. The hallways were dark, the area was quiet. Obviously no one was around. This was going to be another wild-goose chase. It made him sick to feel so impotent, so unable to help Carlsie. If only he could talk to her, explain what was going on.

He was surprised to find the lab door unlocked. Concerned, he stepped in. The room was dark except for a light at the back, in one of the rooms that had been used when the institute had been a regular hospital.

Mendel plunged the blade into the side of Carlsie's left breast just below her arm. The intense pain partially awakened her and she struggled pitifully. Moaning loudly, her face contorted into an expression of confused anguish, she recoiled from

318

the stabbing sensation, and even though restrained, she moved enough so that Mendel's blade came out of the incision. Bright red blood poured from her wound.

He reinserted the scalpel into her breast, began to extend the incision. This time she screamed and moved even more vigorously. Once again the blade slipped out after it had traveled only two inches down the side of her chest.

"Goddamn you! Hold still!" Mendel yelled. Frustrated by his inability to make the flawless cut he desired, he filled a syringe with potassium chloride and plunged the three-inch-long intracardiac needle through her anterior chest, just to the left of her sternum, and into her heart.

Bright red blood immediately erupted from the needle in strong pumping spurts. It splattered across her abdomen and ran down her side. He attached the potassium-filled syringe into the hub of the needle. "Let's see you move after this goes to work, bitch!"

At that moment he heard a noise in the main lab and looked up to see Gordo coming into the little room. Quickly, Mendel injected the potassium into Carlsie's heart. Then he picked up the scalpel, the only weapon he had.

"You bastard!" Keene shrieked and leaped toward him.

He slammed into Mendel with tremendous force, and the two men fell to the floor, locked in a death struggle. Mendel was more powerful, but Gordo had the benefit of youth and the edge Mendel's injuries gave him. In a vain effort to ward off his assailant, Mendel brought the scalpel down into Keene's back. The delicate blade hit a rib and broke off, inflicting only superficial damage.

As they fought, the potassium erupted in Carlsie's heart like fifty thousand volts. Pumped immediately into her coronary arteries and circulated to every muscle cell of her myocardium within a beat or two, the drug caused a sudden intense spasmodic systole and then cardiac arrest in ventricular fibrillation. The pulsatile flow from the needle within her heart slowed to a passive ooze.

Blood flow to her brain instantly ceased. A few seconds later, her faint consciousness dimmed. Her eyes remained open as their pupils dilated and became fixed in the early stage of death. She lay motionless as her color turned from pink to the ashen gray of the recently dead.

Gordo and Mendel were rolling over, kicking and struggling, knocking furniture about; each man doing everything he could to gain the advantage. Within moments, Gordo got his hands around Mendel's neck and his grasp became unbreakable. The pathologist flailed about, kicking at and beating upon Gordo but to no avail.

Gordo's grip was viselike. Fingers on one side of Mendel's trachea, thumb on the other, he squeezed until he could feel the cartilagenous rings just below the larynx begin to pop and break. He dug in deeper, compressing the carotoid arteries against the vertebral column and thus causing the blood flow to Mendel's tortured brain to slow to a trickle.

Then Mendel's trachea collapsed, crushed by the frenzied pressure of an enraged and frightened Gordo, desperate to get to Carlsie's side. His left hand was on the back of Mendel's neck reinforcing the security of his right hand's unbreakable grasp upon those vital structures.

The two twisted and turned. Mendel slapped at him, tried to hit him, kicked him, did everything he could to pry him loose from his neck. To no avail. Gordo was ferocious. Nothing loosened his grip. Despite Mendel's efforts, he prevailed.

Finally Gordo crushed Mendel's larynx, and the end result of the battle was foretold. Mendel had been delivered a mortal injury. The pathologist's face was contorted by the agony of suffocation. He had only a few minutes left. There was no fight left in him.

Gordo instantly released his defeated foe, and went to Carlsie. She looked dead, but her pupils were still reactive. He glanced at the empty vial of potassium, realized what Mendel had done, and knew she might be salvageable. He dialed the cardiac arrest number, told the operator where he was, and instituted CPR.

Mendel, still barely alive, his face cyanotic, its deep purple color indicative of the absence of oxygen in his blood, struggled, writhing weakly, sliding and twisting along the floor in constant motion as his injury smothered him. His legs and arms flailed

wildly. His body then started its terminal failure
He lapsed into unconsciousness and his muscle
grew flaccid as the cells of his brain began to die
Finally, he lay slumped upon the floor.

But his heart beat on, as hearts usually do, errati
cally while lack of oxygen takes its toll in the fina
stages of physiological death.

Gordo ignored Mendel's death throes, and did
everything he could do to keep Carlsie's brain
oxygenated while waiting for help to arrive. Me
thodically he did closed-chest cardiac massage, al
ternating with quick mouth-to-mouth respirations
Her color remained fairly good, and her pupils were
reactive, all excellent prognostic signs.

But her general appearance was terrible. Her face
was a mass of wounds inflicted by broken glass
teeth were broken, her knee was the size of a football, and she had bruises and blood blisters all over.
Blood and urine had matted her hair, her lips were
broken and bloodied, and one ear had been severely
bitten. Her face was smeared with some sort of jel-
lylike substance, and her brutalized left breast was
swollen grotesquely and had a deep cut along the
side.

The cardiac arrest team arrived and were stunned
by what they found. The lab was a wreck, Mendel
was dying in the corner.

"Ignore him," Gordo ordered. "He's dead. We
can save her." He continued the cardiac massage.
Tears were streaming down his face. He was struggling hard to remain calm, to think clearly and con-

rol the panic he was feeling. "Get the defibrillator, goddamn it! We can save her. Move it!"

A nurse started an intravenous while Gordo quickly intubated Carlsie's trachea. Within moments the resuscitation was well underway.

"Let's go! Let's go!" Gordo commanded as the defibrillator was placed beside her and the EKG electrodes were attached. A quick glance at the screen told him what he'd already suspected: coarse strong ventricular fibrillation. It was the most important moment of his entire medical career. More than anything he had ever desired, he wanted to save this woman. This human body, one out of the thousands he had cared for, meant more to him than his own. If he could breathe life back into the dead, he wanted to do it now. Please, he begged silently, please don't die. Part of him was thinking of Carlsie the person, the woman he knew and loved and was devoted to, while another part functioned as doctor, resuscitator, and technical expert.

"Stand back!" He placed the paddles across her chest and hit her with four hundred watt seconds. Her body heaved.

The inhalation therapist ventilating Carlsie's lungs with the ambu resuscitator bag continued to breath for her. Everyone else paused to watch her cardiogram as the machine recycled itself after the blast of electrical energy.

"Come on," mumbled Gordo. "Please, dear God, I want a sinus rhythm." With any luck we can get her back, he thought. And because she had been clinically dead for only a few minutes he felt she could recover normal brain function.

"Still fibrillating," one nurse called out.

"Don't die, girl. Don't!" Gordo murmured and restarted the cardiac massage. "More calcium, and let's hit her again." He was hoping desperately to reverse the immediate effects of the potassium and get her going.

Once more Carlsie was shocked, and once more everyone waited. Gordo's mind raced, reviewing everything he had ever learned about cardiac arrest and what could be done to restart the dying heart. Suddenly he remembered another point about the treatment of high blood levels of potassium. "Get some insulin and glucose ready," he said to one of the nurses. If there was anything more that he could do he didn't want to overlook it . . . not now, not with his own dear Carlsie. He glanced quickly at her face and curly hair. Even with her wounds, she was beautiful, more beautiful than anything he had ever seen. Oh God, how he wanted to save her!

"Please," he prayed.

He turned his eyes to the screen as someone called out what the others could see for themselves. "No change."

"Please!" Gordo groaned. "You can't die on me like this." Before he could regain his deteriorating composure, he barked angrily at the technician: "What the hell's wrong with this machine, goddamn it! Fix it! Turn it higher—do something, for Christ's sake!"

More calcium was administered and they prepared to shock her once more. Trembling and losing confidence, but not hope, Gordo placed the paddles across her bare chest. One was over her sternum, the other below it and lateral to her left breast. Before he squeezed the discharge button, there was an instant of motionless silence as everyone made sure to be out of contact with the body. Gordo gazed tenderly at Carlsie, at her closed eyes, her lips, her slender neck and delicate shoulders. Finally he looked at the soft roundness of her breasts and the prettiness of her nipples ... the flat smoothness of her exposed abdomen.

He loved her, totally and without reservation. He was willing to do anything, to pay any price to make her live. She was all he had ever wanted, would ever want from life.

He triggered the machine at the same instant he screamed her name in a long echoing plea. Her body heaved again, and he begged for success.

Slowly, hesitantly, her heart began a tortuous return toward viability.

"There's one beat," the tech called out.

"There's another."

"Slow sinus rhythm."

"Picking up speed!"

"She's going!"

The group cheered. Gordo covered his face with his hands and sobbed with relief, like a child rescued from a terrible fright.

As he watched, Carlsie stirred slightly, grimacing in pain from her wounds and from the trauma of resuscitation.

There was much still to be done to guarantee her survival. She could get recurrent arrhythmias from the elevated potassium, she might develop pericardial bleeding from the needle puncture of her heart, and she could have rib fractures or other complications from the resuscitation itself. She might even be brain damaged, but at least she had a chance.

Gordo fought back tears of joy and gazed down at the woman he loved so much—the woman he now understood more than anyone. If she lives she is going to need me, he thought. The months ahead would be tough ones, but he would be there to help her. Carlsie might never love him like she did Hank, he understood that and could live with it. If she would give him a chance to show her how happy he could make her, then everything would be all right. If she just wanted him and needed him, that would be enough. She didn't have to love him. Two out of three is not bad, he decided, considering everything.

Gordon Keene watched in delight as Carlsie grimaced and opened her eyes, obviously still completely disoriented but very much alive.

"Welcome back, angel," he said softly. "Welcome back."

Big splotches of blood along the walls and floor traced the path of Carlsie's struggle with Mendel.

The pathologist's twisted body lay amidst the breasts splattered about with the other debris. His face wore the terrified death mask of the strangulation victim. His head was bloated and swollen, its skin torn and gouged beyond recognition. The one remaining eye bulged out as if about to be extruded, while a clot of blood filled the socket of the other. A puffy tongue, enlarged to twice its normal size, protruded grotesquely from his bloodied lips; and his neck, twisted and misshapen, was severely bruised from the force of Gordo's grasp.

Mendel was an ugly sight. Gordo could hardly believe he had ever known this man he had killed.

Chapter Thirty

James T. Butler III, Palm Beach County state attorney, arrived at the institute a little after ten A.M. The coroner had already concluded an on-site evaluation, and the lab boys were hard at work. Shortly, the body was to be removed to the county morgue where an autopsy could be performed, but reports from the investigating officers indicated probable homicide, by strangulation. Still, this case seemed far from straightforward.

What wasn't so ordinary was the crime scene itself and the circumstances surrounding the deceased were downright odd. If the early reports were to be believed, and Butler wasn't ready to do that yet, a scandal of unprecedented proportions was unfolding. Criminal charges against some of the town's most prominent surgeons might follow, and God only knew how many malpractice suits. This case appeared destined to become the media event of the year in a town that dearly loved media events.

Already, scores of patients were being transferred from the hospital. Ambulances waited in a long line at the rear entrance to the building.

It was unusual for Butler to personally involve himself in the early investigatory stages of a homicide, but this was a tight election year, and those were genuine, authentic TV and newspaper reporters clustered around the entrance to the hospital. There was every indication that much would be made of this case in local, state, and even national news. Butler was not going to blow an opportunity like that. As a matter of fact, if this thing panned out, he planned to take charge of the whole situation himself, or at least as much of it as he could wrest away from the county sheriff, a publicity hound in his own right.

Butler was a short man and stocky, almost bulldogish. His physical image suited his personality perfectly. He was known for aggressive enthusiasm in pursuing convictions in controversial cases, as well as for winning the publicity-prone trials he frequently handled.

He passed through the press horde, saying repeating that he would comment as soon as he had gathered enough information. Impressed, as usual, by the ability of reporters to home in on the sensational so quickly, he crossed the crowded hospital lobby, and was shown to the laboratory by the officer awaiting for his arrival. Nothing in his professional experience prepared him for what he found there.

Butler had started off in criminal prosecution, with a stint in the felony division working out of Miami. He'd usually been assigned to prosecute homicides. He'd thought he had seen everything there. After that had come a period of heavy-duty white-collar crime work at the federal level, cracking price-fixing conspiracies. He had even worked on a few Medicare fraud cases. Homicidal psychotics and brilliant corporate-level criminals, he had studied them all and had taken them to trial. He had gone up against the best defense lawyers in the business and held his own. So, skeptical that this was anything other than a slightly unusual society-murder case, he stepped into the rampant confusion of the institute's pathology lab.

Photographers and swarms of forensic lab types were everywhere, while officers stood about in small groups, discussing their hypotheses and eyeballing the shattered breasts still scattered about the covered body of the victim. The room itself was a disaster zone. For Butler, it called to mind the Liberty City riots in Miami a few years back.

One of the younger detectives unzipped the vinyl bag to allow him a quick view of the grotesque corpse. "The things people do to have fun," Butler said sarcastically, shaking his head in disgust. Continuing to take in the full magnitude of the death scene, he gazed with interest at the multitude of breasts on the floor, in broken bottles, and at the few still preserved on shelves. "Are those what I think they are?"

He was told they were.

"Jesus," he muttered, "what a great shot for a movie."

"Mr. Butler?" A deputy sergeant approached him and pointed across the way. "Norris and the sheriff would like to see you in the victim's office."

Norris was chief of homicide, and excellent at his job. So was the sheriff when he wasn't performing for the camera. Butler greeted the two men and closed the door behind him.

"How do you figure it?" he asked, then added jokingly, "Attempted robbery?"

Neither man smiled.

"This is big, Jim," the sheriff answered. "Give him the lowdown, Norris."

Detective Norris was middle aged, a little too paunchy from the Italian food he loved so much, and too serious sometimes. Butler liked him a lot . . . mainly because it was easy to take his cases to court. The chief of homicide was experienced, quick, and compulsively thorough. If there was evidence to be found at a crime site, he made sure it was located and properly authenticated. He also took great pride in rapidly pulling together the loose details of a case so proper decisions could be made early on. This was a particularly valuable trait in a potentially politically sensitive situation such as this one.

"Here's what we have so far, and it's a mouthful," said Norris. "The victim was Dr. Oscar Mendel, chief of pathology here at the institute. He was well respected although not so well liked. A young lady doctor on the staff had recently accused him of misreading some surgical specimens. She claimed he was ordering unnecessary mastectomies on the patients here."

Butler whistled softly. "Wow."

Norris continued. "The chief of the hospital, a Dr. Walker Barret —"

"Yeah, I know him," Butler interjected. "Real big in social circles on the island."

"Fine. Well, this Barret says she was a psycho who had flipped out under the stress of doing a man's job. Her charges were groundless, he claims . . . says they did an audit of Mendel's work and it was perfect. So they fired this woman, Dr. Carlsie Camden."

Butler nodded knowingly. "The old story, eh? Revenge, woman scorned, that sort of thing?" He gazed out over the devastated room. "She must have been some kind of angry."

Norris and the sheriff exchanged glances. "You haven't heard the punch line yet," the detective said. "She didn't kill him. Apparently she was trying to, but Mendel got the best of her and tied her down

333

and started to slice her up. He was in the process of cutting off one of her tits when another doctor—a surgeon named Gordon Keene—came in and proceeded to finish Mendel off."

This even impressed Butler. "You're kidding."

Morris grinned. "It gets better. In the middle of all this, and I haven't figured it all out yet, somebody practically kills the girl with some sort of injection—right in the heart, no less."

Butler was appropriately awed.

Morris continued. "Now the good part. Mendel left this note on his desk. The handwriting is authentic according to Kaplan. He just finished going over it."

The state attorney took the letter offered to him and read it carefully. Dead men's notes were always interesting to him, even if only in a metaphysical sense, being messages from the grave. This one was particularly fascinating. In it Oscar Mendel, M.D., confessed to purposely misdiagnosing benign breast biopsy specimens as malignant and so causing scores of unnecessary breast removals.

The deceased's letter went on to explain that his motivation was to enhance the reputation of the institute by creating falsely high success rates in the surgical cure of a dreaded disease. He listed his conspirators in the scheme saying their motive was to enrich themselves: all the staff surgeons—Barret, Greer, Goldstein, and Ritter—and the chief resident, Dr. Gordon Keene.

A description of how the pathologist had perpetuated the deed, and a list of his victims preceded a final statement declaring that he was afraid he was in danger because he had threatened to expose the whole dirty conspiracy. He apologized for his deeds and asked forgiveness from his victims.

"Don't let me die in vain" was scribbled just above his signature.

"Wow . . . double wow," was all Butler could say. "Any of it verifiable?"

"Everything, so far. We found the bottle of cancers he was subbing in. The pathology lab at the medical school is doing some sort of tissue typing on a few specimens that could be matched up and, so far, two of the cancerous ones were definitely not from the patients whose names were on them. Another thing: we have independent verification that Dr. Barret did everything possible to protect Mendel from the woman doctor's accusations." Norris paused, and then added, "We've also learned that the surgeons here were among the richest and most famous in the country, partly because of this type of surgery."

Butler grimaced. "What do you know about Mendel himself? Any reason he would want to embarrass the others? Any vendettas or anything?"

"He's clean as a whistle. Patriotic, hardworking, plenty of money. Pretty religious man apparently. Served in Korea. Well respected medically. Published a lot of scientific papers."

335

Butler nodded. "Family?"

"Wife left him a number of years ago. No kids. No other family. Raised as an orphan."

"That's it?"

"That's it."

"What about this doctor, this Camden woman?"

"Dropped out of sight yesterday. She spent the night with one of the surgeons, a Dr. Ritter, and then took off. No one saw her until she turned up here."

Butler sighed, long and deeply. "What else do you have on her?"

"Not much. Supposedly real intelligent, good looking. Sleeps around a bit. Had a fling with the surgeon that rescued her. He's a pretty young guy, this Gordon Keene. A lady's man, they say."

"Was she screwing Mendel, too? Any chance there was some kind of kinky triangle going on here?"

"I considered that. Possible motive, I guess. I don't really buy it."

Butler nodded in agreement. "He was probably too old for her. Anything else of value?"

Norris glanced again at the sheriff. "Do you want to tell him or should I?

Sheriff Benson was a tall, graying man of quiet dignity. He was in uniform like his deputies, whereas the detective wore street clothes. He peered at Butler for a moment. "I know Walker Barrett, too, Jim. I've always respected him, but now . . .

336

well, I just don't know what to make of it. You know what he says about that young woman? He says this is all her doing, the letter and switching the tissue to make us believe it all. He says that's why she was in the hospital last night. She was trying to switch more tissue, make it look worse. He claims none of this is true and she's just trying to ruin the hospital. He thinks she's switched this stuff before, and that's why the tissue doesn't match."

Butler laughed. "So, it's all her fault, huh?"

The sheriff nodded. Norris grinned.

"Now I've heard it all!" snorted Butler, shaking his head in amazed disgust. He looked at the sheriff. "What do you think? Do we have a simple old-fashioned crime of passion . . . with the letter being a hoax or a subterfuge maybe? Or is this the criminal conspiracy of the century?"

The sheriff rose, went to the window, then again surveyed the incredible condition of the lab. Eventually he turned back to the man who would be in charge of the prosecution. "Big money does strange things to men . . . even doctors. These boys were making millions apiece off this operation." He thought for a moment more while Butler and Norris waited, in respect for his intuitive judgment. Then he said, "Mendel seemed to know he was in trouble. It looks like he was planning to commit suicide—there were some drugs stashed in his desk. It's hard to figure; dead men don't usually tell lies. I think the pieces of his story fit with what we

337

know." He nodded with conviction as he concluded. "I think we got ourselves one hell of a conspiracy!"

Butler rose to stand in front of his sheriff, somber agreement all over his face. "We have our work cut out for us, gentlemen." Again he shook his head in disgust. "What a bunch of turds these guys are. Unnecessary surgery for money. I tell you one thing: You book them . . . I'll put them away. I guarantee it."

The state attorney stared confidently out over the lab, watching as a man gathered up the scattered ugly breasts and dropped them into a big plastic garbage can. "One more thing, Sheriff. Close this goddam hellhole of a hospital before somebody burns it down."

"It's already done, counselor. Already done."

The meeting ended, and they went out to talk to the press. There was obviously going to be more than enough publicity to go around, Butler was thinking. What a case: murder, malpractice, fraud, conspiracy, assault and battery, and whatever. There was probably even a federal element to it since patients and insurance payments had come from all over the country.

And there were doctors—really big time doctors—to shoot down. It was the opportunity of a lifetime for a prosecutor. No way was he going to let these guys off the hook. No way!

Hopefully the Camden woman would be okay and could testify. With any luck at all, he could paint her as the brave little heroine in all this. A David against Goliaths, and all that. He hoped she hadn't slept with so many surgeons her effectiveness on the stand could be destroyed. Experience had taught him that even in this day and age, juries didn't like loose women.

Chapter Thirty-one

In her hospital room across the river at St. Mary's, where she had been transferred by ambulance since the institute did not have an intensive care unit, Carlsie slept, longer and more deeply than she ever had. Her struggles had exhausted her. She awakened late in the afternoon of the first day, sipped a little water, and then returned to somnolence . . . to peace and renewal. In sleep her energies were reborn. The emptiness that had overtaken her when she had been defeated by Mendel was being pushed away as her strength was being regained. On the morning of the second day she was whole again, despite being sore in every part of her body, and feeling and looking as if she had been brought back from the dead — which she had.

Her future had changed, of course. She didn't know what would happen now. She had been told that Mendel was dead, and one of the nurses had said that Dr. Keene had been the first to find her.

Dear Gordo, the man she had wounded, he still loved her. She hoped he would forgive her.

And there was Hank. She guessed he had been there too, to help rescue her. Surely he would now recognize that she had tried to do the right thing. She had wanted so badly to stop Mendel without causing a scandal. Obviously, she had failed at that, but perhaps Hank's career would not be too damaged. Surely the public would understand that the hospital had been sabotaged by a lunatic. In a way, maybe the fact that Mendel had tried to kill her would help mitigate the damage he had done to the institute. Everyone would understand that he was insane and the surgeons were not at fault.

Thinking about it made her tired again. She consoled herself with the knowledge that at least her primary goal had been accomplished. The terrorism at the hospital was over. Hank and the others would be affected, but not as badly as they would have been if it had gone on much longer.

At the very least, she and Hank still had each other and the time to savor the love they had found together. This thought kept her from total despair.

Drifting into sleep again, Carlsie wondered why no one had visited her. She assumed someone would be around soon.

In the late afternoon, she awoke again and cleaned up the tray of the food they brought her.

Only then did she read the newspaper which had accompanied her meal.

Headlines screamed out at her.

They had been tripped up once more by Mendel. The authorities had been fooled. Thinking they were reading the last words of a guilt-ridden, doomed man, they had believed the horrible lies he had written in a letter. The punishment that should have been his was now going to be imposed upon others.

The press and the citizens of Palm Beach had gone absolutely crazy over the discovery that tens, possibly hundreds, of women had undergone unjustifiable mastectomies at the hands of the corrupt surgeons of the Institute for the Breast. According to the article, this sadistic, inhuman plot had come to light only after the revenge murder of the chief of pathology, who had been planning to expose the whole sordid crime. Luckily for society and the law, the dead man had left an authenticated confession, telling all and implicating the wealthy surgeons who had coerced him into collaborating in the scheme. The paper said the police were still investigating the gruesome, strangulation slaying of the pathologist and the near murder of a female resident on the staff of the institute. She had apparently stumbled onto the horrible moneymaking conspiracy.

The write-up indicated that the sheriff's department and the state attorney had declared jointly that the guilty physicians would be prosecuted on a variety of charges, including fraud, assault and battery, homicide, and practically everything else in the book. The involved surgeons were in custody at their respective homes, and were expected to be formally arrested following a meeting, that afternoon, of the hospital board — made up primarily of the surgeons themselves — and the prosecutors from the state attorney's office.

Carlsie immediately tried to phone Hank and then Gordo but her calls went unanswered.

Stunned by the turnabout of what she had assumed would be an acceptable conclusion to the horror, Carlsie scanned the front pages of the larger national papers which an aid brought to her when she requested them. The story was the same everywhere. The wire services had picked up the news, and it was dominating headlines across the nation. From New York to Los Angeles the tragedy was decried, the hospital and its surgeons condemned. Editorials and articles lamented the absence of safeguards within modern medicine to prevent such disasters.

The A.M.A., The American College of Surgeons, and the American College of Pathologists had each issued bulletins blaming the institute for failing to follow proper quality assurance procedures and reassuring the public that such a thing could not possibly occur at other, properly run institutions.

The Joint Commission for Accreditation of Hospitals announced that a complete investigation would take place to consider revoking the accreditation of the institute — a threat which seemed ridiculous in light of the state's move to revoke the hospital's license and place the facility in receivership pending settlement of all claims against it.

Carlsie searched for any reference to comments by the accused surgeons and found none. She turned the TV to the cable news channel, where an interview with the president of the A.M.A. was underway. The doctor was defending the safety of hospitals and rebutting accusations the press and politicians were hurling at organized medicine for not having prevented the malpractice at the institute. There is no way to stop a well organized group of criminals from committing crimes if they are intent on doing so, he was saying. But it is the job of society to punish appropriately the individual involved, and thereby minimize the chance of a recurrence.

The local state attorney was then shown expressing his indignation that such a thing had been allowed to happen and guaranteeing the public that he would make sure such crimes were severely punished.

A U.S. Senator was televised announcing a senate investigation of the practice of medicine in this country. He promised to expose corruption in that profession and to make hospitals once again the safe places they used to be before doctors became so money hungry.

On and on it went, the major networks breaking in on their regularly scheduled programs to update the events in Palm Beach. Live-action cameras showed angry crowds milling about the hospital grounds, kept in check only by the scores of law enforcement officers on the scene to assist in the orderly evacuation of the few remaining patients. Already rocks and bottles had shattered most of the windows on the first two floors, and interviews with an outraged public brought forth innumerable denunciations of the institute and of the medical profession itself.

Since physicians wouldn't heal themselves, numerous politicians cried, the time had come for the government to do so. First, do no harm had always been the guiding motto of doctors; now they must be made to stand by it. It seemed a unanimous opinion. Enough was enough. Every politician agreed to lead the fight, and relished the opportunity to serve the electorate by doing so. It was going to be a new dawn, they said. From the ashes of this tragedy would rise a phoenix, a new form of organized medicine that would lead to a healthier and safer nation. Carlsie was disgusted by the grandstanding.

By late afternoon, interviews with the few mutilated patients who would talk were being broadcast. The women were understandably bitter. Carlsie recognized several of them.

One husband described the terrible depression his

wife had sunk into and how her new doctors, including a psychiatrist, had warned of potential suicide because she had reacted with such despair to being the last of the victims. "Just a couple of days," he said. "If we had just waited a few more days, she would have been safe." He candidly told the interviewer that if he could get his hands on the surgeons right then, he would kill them. "Someone ought to," he concluded, and broke down into sobs as the camera turned away.

And so it went.

Carlsie was immobilized for a while after comprehending the significance of what Mendel had done. He had turned his sadistic crimes into a national rout of medicine itself!

Equally important to her was his destruction of the careers of Hank and the others, who, while admittedly negligent in their watchdog duties, had not done the heinous things of which they were now accused.

She tried again to reach Hank or Gordo by phone. Unsuccessfully. The TV bulletins were becoming increasingly angry. Mendel's victory was complete. Why had this happened? Carlsie could think of no reason for everyone to believe Mendel and not the others. And why hadn't the police come to talk to her? She knew more about the whole mess than anybody. Why, why, why? The questions maddened her. How could this result be justified?

She desperately wished she had not been a part

of the madness. She wished that she and Hank could simply walk away from it and forget it. She tried to call him once more, and this time the phone was answered. He isn't here, she was told. He left with his attorney and the police for a meeting at the hospital.

She was desperate to talk to him. She wanted him to know how sorry she was that things had turned out as they had, how hard she had tried to prevent this from happening. Would he understand that she would do anything to reverse all this and bring life back to the way it was? Love of my life, she wanted to say, please don't leave me no matter what happens now. Frantic to reach him, she decided to meet him at the hospital and then contact the police.

Love of my life, she thought, sweet love of my life, please give me a chance to bring it all back. You just don't know what this really means to me.

Chapter Thirty-two

Debbie Hunter was emotionally numb. For two days she had skipped work at the Bloody Goose to stay home in front of the TV and watch the nightmare unfold. It was beyond her wildest imagination that doctors could do such things. All her life she had been taught to trust them. When she was a child, she had been convinced by her mother that people in the medical profession were good and loving, that the pain they inflicted was for good reason. As a young girl she had bravely accepted the shots they'd given, and as an adult she had believed in what physicians recommended. She knew they were not infallible — malpractice lawyers had proven that — but she had never considered the possibility that they could be as savage as she now knew them to be.

Never had she so unjustifiably put her faith in the integrity of others. She had been a complete fool to trust in doctors so completely, and the price she had paid for her naïveté was beyond measure. She had been raped and pillaged while the doctors got rich off the insurance money that paid their outrageous fees.

She had not believed the early reports. Then, when as the details became more clear and the crimes were proven, she had denied that she could have been operated on erroneously. Finally she had accepted what she had subconsciously known from the beginning: she had not needed a mastectomy. She had been unnecessarily maimed.

Her anger went beyond any emotion she had ever felt. A desire for vengeance consumed her, and as she continued to watch developments unfold, she knew that she could not let her desecration go unpunished. Those men had taken away her womanly pride, and she was not going to allow some fancy lawyer to get them off. As far as Debbie Hunter was concerned, money was not the issue. All the talk of financial compensation for the victims meant nothing to her. She had suffered, had had her life ruined, and if there was any way she could ruin the surgeons' lives, she would do it.

She dressed in sexy clothes she had worn before her surgery. The black halter top was tight and skimpy. It had once been worn over bountiful, well-shaped breasts. exposing her cleavage in an elegant way. Now it glaringly revealed the asymmetry of her chest and her ugly scar. I will look appropriate under the circumstances, she thought. She wanted these butchers to know what they had done to her when she made them pay for it.

Debbie removed the .38 caliber handgun from the bedside table where she kept it, and made sure it was loaded. She emptied her purse and put in the weapon. Just to be sure she could finish what she was going to start, she dropped in a handful of extra bullets.

Self-assured and exhilarated over what was to come, she left for the hospital. The TV had said the doctors were going to be meeting there with legal authorities. She believed this was going to be the most important night of her life.

Chapter Thirty-three

The change in the institute since Carlsie had last seen it was appalling. The upper floors were dark, windows were broken, and its impressive façade and grounds had been desecrated with splotches of paint and garbage.

A raucous crowd had gathered on the front lawn in the hope of glimpsing the newly notorious surgeons. TV trucks, police cars, and other vehicles jammed the street, forcing her to circle around to the back of the now sad-looking old structure.

The doctors' entrance was closed, so Carlsie was compelled to fight her way through to the front doors and into the crowded lobby.

Finally, she caught a glimpse of Gordo exiting the elevator and forced her way to him. Overjoyed and relieved to see her, he put his arms around her and hugged her almost desperately, telling her he had been worried about her. He inspected her wounds, gently touching her swollen face and asking how she was. "They just released me," he said. "I was coming over to see you."

It felt so good to be near someone she trusted, Carlsie became teary-eyed with relief. She had found him . . . had found someone who still cared for her, understood her. She thanked Gordo for what he had done.

He continued to examine the marks of her battle. "It must have been rough," he whispered quietly, and hugged her again. "I'm just glad you're alive."

She pumped him for information about the legal situation.

"They let me off," he said. "I guess they figured I was too poor to be in on this so-called conspiracy."

"How is Hank?"

Gordo grimaced. "In trouble, depressed . . . beaten. He's not taking this well at all. Barret's okay, though. He's letting off steam at everyone and everything. He plans to sue everybody, except you, that is. You, he wants to kill. I'm sure you guessed that."

"Does Hank blame me?" Carlsie tried hard to keep from appearing to be interested only in Hank, though in truth she was, now that she knew Gordo was okay. Gordo seemed to understand, even though his feelings were hurt.

"Hank doesn't know who to blame . . . or what to do, for that matter. He's having a hard time just figuring out what's happened. I don't think he even realizes how serious this is. He keeps talking about getting things straightened out so we can get back to work. He's acting a bit inappropriately, if you ask me."

She nodded in understanding. It was breaking her heart. More than anything she wanted to see Hank, to tell him how sorry she was that it had turned out so badly and to let him know she wanted them to go somewhere else and start all over. Just the two of them.

Gordo was watching her intently. "You're in love with him, aren't you?"

Carlsie didn't answer, but her expression revealed the sadness within her.

Gordo eventually glanced away, his pain evident. "You sure have bad timing, girl."

"I'm sorry, Gordo. About what Mendel did. About the way it all exploded." There was a long pause, then, "I'm sorry about us too."

He looked at her with understanding and affection. "None of this is your fault. I know that and so does Hank."

She wanted that to be true, more than he could ever know. "Are you sure, Gordo? Are you really sure?"

"Hank's just like me. He couldn't blame you any more than I can. We both love you."

Suddenly a sheriff's deputy was telling everyone to stand back, to clear a path. The authorities and the suspects were coming through. The crowd was pushed aside, and a police line formed, opening up the sidewalk from the doorway to the police vans on the street. TV floodlights came on, and photographers jostled for positions along with the morbidly curious who lined up to get their long-awaited view of the sadistic surgeons now under official arrest.

It was a disgusting sight. Hundreds of people shoving and pushing in order to get as close as possible to the path Hank and the others would take, and not one sympathetic face in the lot. Carlsie heard curses, accusations, and incredible exaggerations of the crimes the surgeons were supposed to have committed — things that made her sick, charges that made her angry.

She clutched Gordo's arm to keep from being trampled by the mob; then the elevator opened and there was Hank.

He looked beautiful — exhausted, whipped, beaten, but still so very beautiful.

Their eyes met immediately. The corners of his mouth turned up into the faintest of all possible smiles. But she could see it clearly. She raised one hand in a silent gesture of greeting and tried to speak. The noise drowned her words.

Strobes were flashing all around them, and everyone seemed to be yelling questions at the doctors, the lawyers, and the sheriff who accompanied them. Carlsie's eyes never left Hank while he was led slowly past her. The crowd closed in on them overcoming every effort by the police to prevent that from happening.

Despite his fatigue, there was a spark in Hank's

gaze, an electricity that told her he still loved her. His warm brown eyes lingered upon her, even as he was guided farther and farther away.

She shrugged valiantly to move closer to him, to touch him, but failed. At her urgent request, she was lifted up by Gordo, and had one final long moment of unspoken communication with Hank when he was delayed at the doorway while the mob was forced back. Then she moved along with the crowd and was carried outside into the cacophony created by the aroused spectators.

Eventually he and the others were led out. A deputy shoved him forward and into the glare of the TV lights.

Tears filled Carlsie's eyes, and her mood sank even lower. She loved him, she needed him; yet there was nothing she could do to ease his humiliation or mitigate his pain. The throng was shouting taunts and insults at the four surgeons who were gradually making their way to the street, single file, Barret in the lead.

Carlsie started to cry, but stopped when she suddenly saw a woman along the path of the surgeons, holding a gun partially hidden by her purse.

Panicked, Carlsie clawed her way forward. As two deputies tried to block her progress, she screamed a warning. "There's a gun! Someone has a gun!"

"Shut up, lady!" an officer said, and grabbed her arm.

"A gun! Someone wants to shoot them!" she

shrieked, near hysteria now. Why wouldn't he listen?

She was now in the grasp of two policemen, who were struggling to wrestle her down. But the people near her understood what she was saying and hurriedly began to back away from her. Someone else misunderstood her warning, and soon several voices were accusing her of having a gun.

People began to run, panic was building. Shouts about guns seemed to be coming from every side.

"I said shut up, lady!" one of her captors bellowed again, and he tried to twist her to the ground. Unexpectedly she slipped loose.

By this time the disturbance around Carlsie had grown loud enough to attract the attention of the spectators and officers farther down the sidewalk. The forward progress of the four prisoners had halted. She stared in horror down the length of the walkway. The deputies had turned and were now rushing toward her, abandoning Hank and the others.

Carlsie stood alone for an instant in the glare of the lights and cameras which quickly turned upon her, as were the puzzled eyes of almost everyone, including Hank.

Just as the police closed in on her, she had one agonizing glimpse of the assassin. It was the bartender from the strip joint, Debbie Hunter. The pretty one who had been a stripper before Hank had done a mastectomy on her.

She looked so different from when Carlsie had

first seen her. No longer unkempt but made up, coiffed, and dressed as if for the stage. She wore black-sequinned skin-tight pants and a tiny halter top that barely covered her one remaining breast and clearly revealed the absence of the other.

An expression of calm purpose on her face, Debbie stepped confidently into the path of the surgeons, who were still staring, in confusion, back at Carlsie. She held the big pistol with two hands.

Aimed carefully.

Fired.

A penetrating blast filled the air. It sounded, to Carlsie, more like an explosion than a gunshot.

Barret went down.

The weapon discharged again.

Hank was turning back to the source of the shot when he collapsed, heavily, limply.

The crowd was starting to react now.

The girl calmly pulled the trigger once more.

Fulton Greer went down.

Then Goldstein.

The panicked mob ran, tumbling and trampling over one another. There were screams and cries. A woman was shouting "Oh my God" over and over. It was a horrifying scene. A nightmare. No one was standing. Even the officers had reflexively hit the ground.

For a solemn haunting instant the girl from the strip joint stood above her victims . . . and then she dropped her gun. Her tortured eyes met Carlsie's just before she was submerged in a wave of deputies. In that instant Carlsie sensed Debbie's misery and hopelessness . . . and more. An aura of completeness had come over Debbie now that her justice had been done. Revenge had been hers.

Bedlam took over.

Police ran up and down the sidewalk, people were screaming and crying, camera strobes were coming back to life.

On the ground lay the four surgeons. Only three of them were moving. In the confusion Carlsie could not determine which three. She moved quickly toward them.

Goldstein was trying to stand up.

Fulton Greer was on his back, screaming in agony and writhing about, his shirt and coat becoming increasingly bloody.

Walker Barret was lying face-down, unmoving. Blood flowed freely from the hole in the back of his head, onto the pavement, into an expanding pool of bright red liquid. As Carlsie approached, someone turned Barret over. His face, which had been the exit point of the bullet, no longer existed having become a distorted mass of shattered bone, teeth, and tissue.

Hank was crumpled on his side, his arms and legs flopping pitifully. Carlsie knelt beside him, gently turned him onto his back, and cradled his head in her lap. Across his abdomen and lower chest, his clothing was drenched with blood. His face was contorted into a grimace of extreme agony.

She bent down to him and called his name, and

360

his eyes opened slowly and focused on her. He recognized her, she knew he did. She kissed him gently, and squeezed his hand . . . and a very faint squeeze came back. "I didn't know about it," he whispered weakly. "I swear I didn't know."

She shushed him. "Don't talk, darling. Rest now."

He was lying still now as she spoke to him, comforting him, telling him that help was coming and that his injuries didn't look too bad, which was a lie.

His blood was everywhere, his color was pale and pasty, and his respiration was becoming more shallow and rapid. But the fear and doom in his eyes seemed to recede at the sound of her voice.

She spoke unceasingly, and he listened, his eyes locked on hers. She told him she loved him, and that everything was going to be fine. She was getting things all worked out, and, Jesus, she loved him and wasn't it good that they had found each other.

On and on she went. Even when he closed his eyes and didn't seem to be listening anymore, she whispered tender things to him and told him how she was going to help him get well, how they were going to take walks together and go fishing. Oh yes, they were going to do lots and lots of fishing, and boating and traveling. She was looking forward to being taken to the Bahamas.

He no longer squeezed her hand when she squeezed his. That was only because he was resting; she knew it, and told him it was all right. He needed to get some rest and she would be there when he awoke. It was okay. He should just lie still for a while . . . that was good for him.

And it was okay for him not to open his eyes because she knew he understood that she was there and she was going to make everything all right. And he was not to worry about all the blood and the bullets and things because people got shot every day and did just fine. So would he, because she loved him so much. It was important for him not to give up. He couldn't quit on her. Not now, not after everything they had been through. Not after they had finally found each other.

It wouldn't be fair, she told him, if he died now.

No, he couldn't do that. She loved him too much.

Didn't he hear her?

She loved him! She loved him more than life itself.

She had sacrificed everything for him.

"Hank!" she screamed over his motionless body. "Hank! Hank! Don't go! I love you Hank, I love you!"

He lay silently in her arms. Eyes shut. Muscles limp. As still as death. She cradled him, hugged him, and refused to release him.

When they came to take him away she screamed and fought and struggled and wouldn't let him go. She kissed him, caressed him, and whispered in his ear, begging him not to leave her. Finally she collapsed in Gordo's arms and waited for the pain to ease.

And after a while it did.

After a while she could breathe again.

Slowly her agony abated enough for her to live.

With Gordo's assistance she wiped Hank's blood from her and stood up to face the rest of her life.

Red lights were blinking, sirens were wailing. Policemen and paramedics moved here and there, gathering up the shattered remains of the infamous surgeons. Dried and clotted blood, huge pools of it, marred the smooth grayness of the walk. People crowded in for a closer view as the bodies were removed.

Of the four, Goldstein alone still lived.

Carlsie walked passively alongside the stretcher that carried Hank, covered by a soiled brown blanket, to the ambulance he no longer needed. She stood in despair as the doors were secured and the cumbersome vehicle moved slowly, painstakingly down the crowded street, its twirling light flashing rhythmically across her and the other onlookers.

The titillated crowd was becoming more noisy as people recounted what they had seen, but the police were beginning to rope off the area and scatter the uninvolved. She fell in with the others, along with Gordo who had stayed at her side through it all.

"Do you want to go to the hospital with him?" he asked, his grief unhidden.

She indicated that she did not. Hank was gone and she knew it. What use would it be now? she thought. Hank didn't need to go where they were taking him. He didn't need anything . . . or anyone. He needed nothing at all.

She turned for a long painful look at the institute. How different it was from when she had first seen it, on that fateful day so many months ago. Then she had been filled with confidence and enthusiasm about the phenomenal surgery practiced within. How life changes, she thought. How disappointing it can be.

"Let me take you home," Gordo was saying. He really wanted to help, she knew it. There was nothing he could do, though. It was over now. All over.

Time and eternity were running down for her. Sweetness was gone, the desire to go on was missing, and her inner self was empty. She felt more dead than alive, and that was just fine because life was nothing . . . a hollow meaningless void once filled with spirit that had now been consumed.

"I loved him, too," Gordo said quietly.

She understood his sadness. He had studied Hank, almost worshipped him for years. She remembered the pride that had emanated from Gordo when he'd introduced her to the greatest plastic surgeon of their time, his mentor.

"He was the best," Gordo added. "The very best."

She nodded. "In every way . . . every possible way."

They stood quietly together amidst the chaos, not really knowing where to go or what to do. A light misty rain had begun to fall, and as they watched, it began to wash away the dark stains of blood.

Several large clots remained intact, however, glistening in the glare of the lights.

Carlsie wondered how it was that everything had ended so badly.

Chapter Thirty-four

Ritter's body was shipped west in the company of his father and his longtime girlfriend, Maria. Carlsie and Gordo helped them make the final arrangements, and then rode with the hearse that delivered the casket to the airport. The funeral was to be held in Texas. For several reasons Carlsie decided not to make the trip. Instead, she kept a lonely vigil beside Hank's open casket the night before they took him away.

The weeks that followed were difficult ones, but she survived them and along the way grew steadily stronger. The spectacle created by the revelations of the social and physical tragedies of the many bitter women who'd been operated on unnecessarily, along with the resulting dismantling of everything the institute had been, distracted her from the deep depression to which she had initially succumbed.

Eventually the worst seemed over.

About a month after Hank was gone, she ambled

along the beach one morning an hour or so before sunrise. She was heading toward her favorite spot — the overgrown banyan near the inlet. She stood for a while at the water's edge, the calm surf rolling in gently and swirling about her feet as sand gathered around her toes. In the faint light of the approaching dawn, small waves sparkled and glittered, the phosphorescence of the night plankton not quite gone. She watched as the sand grew deep enough to submerge her ankles, then stepped away to continue her final journey along the path that had been so calming for her in the last few months.

Her mood was introspective as she contemplated her recent experience. When finally played out to the full, life had given her quite a surprise. She wondered how different it would have been had she traveled a different road. She wasn't angry. Not really. Not anymore. She wished things had worked out better for the others as well as for herself, but she had come to accept all that had happened. She believed it had been out of her control from the beginning. She had been merely an instrument that had precipitated the final result. If she hadn't, someone else would have sounded the alarm, the truth would have emerged, and chaos would have resulted.

The tranquillity she had achieved was comforting, considering how she had suffered during the last few weeks. Her sense of guilt had been, at first, oppressive. But she had overcome it, and was ready once more to go on with her life. All pain eventually ends.

Her possessions were packed and ready for the truck coming later that morning. Her flight for New Orleans was departing in the afternoon. By nightfall she would be home.

Carlsie watched the sun peek up over the horizon, filling the eastern sky for a brief interval with a brilliant array of pinks and oranges before finally lifting herself into the full glory of a Florida morning. She glanced at her watch, and headed back down the beach at a brisk pace. She had promised to meet Gordo for breakfast on this her last day in Palm Beach. First, she had wanted to spend an hour alone absorbing the majesty of this special spot.

Just being able to be by herself was a welcome relief from the hectic demands put on her by the press in the last few weeks. Although the media had not grown tired of the story, they had, at last, become convinced that she was unwilling to discuss it with them anymore.

The national news continued to be dominated by the scandal, evidence that nothing as easily sensationalized was happening. Enterprising reporters had dug up every detail of Mendel's life. She had read a recent story about a psychiatrist in Boston who'd identified the pathologist, from a picture in a news magazine, as a former patient of his. He claimed that Mendel had consulted him under an

369

assumed name for evaluation of a seizure disorder and headaches. The psychiatric workup had revealed severely disordered thought processes associated with the seizures. The psychiatrist had diagnosed Mendel as schizophrenic. It sounded like Mendel had believed he was losing control of his mind to a secondary, inner identity that was giving him instructions—detailed instructions on the negative nature of women and on what he should do about it.

An autopsy had discovered a small glioma, a tumor, at the base of Mendel's temporal lobe which perhaps explained his bizarre behavior. Carlsie wondered about that, but she didn't really care too much what had been functionally wrong with the man. She was just glad Mendel was dead. She awakened sometimes, frightened by dreams of the night he had nearly killed her.

The wound along her left breast had become infected and formed an ugly scar that would eventually have to be surgically revised. It was still tender and swollen, and it reminded her constantly of what Mendel had tried to do. It also served to make her recall what Gordo had done for her.

She still wondered how close she had come to being dead. Her distorted, partial memories of the episode resembled the descriptions of others who had experienced near death, among them the sensation of having been an observer of her own resuscitation. She read everything she could find that might increase her understanding of what had happened to her—books on philosophy, metaphysics, religion, out-of-body experiences, oriental concepts of life, and theology. By plowing through volumes of dusty old tomes as well as new publications, she hoped to glean some answers from others who had been through what she had. But she found little she could believe in.

After Carlsie had exhausted the public library, she roamed the aisles of a bookstore devoted to mysticism and psychic teachings, and came away unsatisfied. Out of all of it, only one book had interested her. In it, people who had been clinically dead for a period of time and who had been brought back to life by vigorous resuscitative techniques had described what they recalled. The dreamy experience of being above it all, being aware of one's death and then being called back at the last instant, was distinctly familiar to Carlsie. For the first time in her life she was able to relate to these stories even though she had previously scoffed at them. The uncanny similarity of the tales was impressive.

Over and over again, she had made Gordo describe how close she had come to being dead. He was convinced that she had not been hypoxic for more than a minute or two before he had started CPR.

She owed him a lot, she knew that. He had been the one who'd never given up on her. It was Gordo who had started the ball rolling on getting the specimens checked out, and in the end he had never stopped searching for her. His loyalty—his heroism—had saved her life. And it had helped her realize how very much he loved her and wanted to make sure she was all right. He was the best friend she had ever had.

Arriving early at the little café where they had agreed to meet, Carlsie ordered coffee and sat thinking about the two men recently in her life. In hindsight, she now realized how and why she had underestimated Gordo. She had been blinded by the glamour and glory that Hank represented. His fame and talent had dazzled her. These, combined with his masculine attractiveness and his sensitivity, had proved overpowering.

Carlsie thought that no woman could have resisted Hank. In reflecting upon her emotions, though, she was coming to the conclusion that what she had felt might have been more of an infatuation than the profound love she had believed it to be. Perhaps she had been in love with the image of what she had thought he was—like being in love with love. It was hard to tell.

Now that he was gone and could never be more than a sweet memory for her, it seemed important to overcome her grief and put their relationship into proper perspective. Very likely, the passion that had engulfed them would have receded with time. No fire could remain as hot as theirs was burning for very long. And with a man like Hank, a man married to his profession and one who never did anything halfway, when the passion died it was likely that the relationship died too.

A bittersweet thought. Some things are too beautiful, too spectacular to exist for more than a brief burst of life. A rose blooms and soon afterward wilts.

Carlsie finished her coffee, ordered another cup, and then Gordo arrived. She was happy to see him smiling again. He had been so depressed the first weeks after the tragedy that she had felt he was not coping well. In the last few days, however, he had seemed to be coming around. His outlook on life was improving, and he was even beginning to make plans for the continuation of his career.

She was glad about that. There was more reason than ever for Gordo to go on with his work. He was the only living surgeon that had worked with Hank closely enough to really understand his advanced techniques. The scientific articles Hank had written and the lectures he had given could not prepare anyone to actually do the operations, but the experience Gordo had gained could. Gordo had already been contacted by other institutions and by medical schools. Several of them had made very good offers.

Carlsie was happy for him, and she encouraged him to consider his opportunities carefully.

Gordo gave her a little peck of a kiss, then sat down beside her. Before he spoke, he took a sip of her coffee. "You look beautiful as usual," he said. He gazed fondly at her, and suddenly he was softly singing the words of an old song: "Jeepers, creepers, where'd you get those peepers?"

She grinned.

He sighed melodramatically. "Some morning I'd love to wake up looking into those mysterious green eyes of yours."

The old Gordo was coming out again. This was the first time in weeks and weeks that he had teased about going to bed with him. It was a good sign. She put her hand into his blond hair and roughed it up affectionately. "So, you're getting interested in women again, huh?"

He nodded. "Not women, though . . . woman." He emphasized the singularity of the noun.

"Well, there're plenty around," she said. "It shouldn't be too hard to get one isolated."

"There's a particular one I'm interested in. And she's a hard case."

She smiled. When he was on keel, Gordo invariably made her feel happy. It made her feel good to know that they were still close friends . . . that they still had a chance. The thing about Gordo was that he was such a buddy. He was real and lovable. Hank had been more of a symbol, an unattainable perfection. Gordo was someone a girl could be comfortable with—a source of contentment and comfort.

It was too soon yet, but given a little time, a

period for both of them to recover from the trauma of the disaster at the institute, Carlsie felt they just might make it. It was certainly worth trying, anyway. Gordo was a man any woman could love.

"So when are you coming to New Orleans for a visit?" she asked. "My father wants to meet the man that saved my life."

He gazed at her seriously. "Do you really want me to come? That's what counts the most. I only want to do it if you care enough for me to keep on trying. Otherwise, it would be better for me to stay away. We could write and stay in touch, of course . . . but I could start putting you out of my mind."

She stirred her coffee and thought about it. "Give me a few months, Gordo. Why don't you come for Mardi gras in February? I'll be feeling better by then . . . if you're still interested."

He reached out to hold her hand. He was smiling, satisfied with her proposal. A few months wasn't too long to wait. He had been after her for a long time already. He could hold on a little longer. Maybe a fresh beginning was just what they needed. By the new year they might both be ready to forget the past and move into their future.

His gaze alternated between her expressive eyes and her lips. He loved Carlsie and he knew he always would. He was confident that given the chance he would win her affection and loyalty. And if she did love him, he would make it wonderful for her. There would be nothing he wouldn't do to assure her happiness.

For the first time in many weeks, he was feeling great again, optimistic about the future.

She could sense it, and was pleased that she could still do that to him.

Epilogue

Drs. Gordon and Carlsie Keene now live in Slidell, Louisana, where they both have successful careers in medicine. Most days they commute together across the lake into New Orleans where she serves as assistant professor of surgery at the medical school and Gordo is chief of the Reconstructive Breast Surgery Service. However, once a week Carlsie travels deep into the bayou to staff a free clinic for those back-country people who cannot afford modern medical care. She is revered by the patients she voluntarily serves.

And she rarely thinks of Hank, anymore, or of the events in Palm Beach. She is happy now, contented with her new life, and she thrives on her growing relationship with Gordo, needing and wanting his companionship more and more as time goes by. She loves him, and has come to realize how perfect a mate he is for her.

Gordo remains dedicated to her happiness, and

devoted to building an ideal life for the two of them. Well on his way to achieving an international reputation in his specialty, he is a sought-after speaker at medical conferences and seminars. Rumors are rife in the medical school that within the next year he will be promoted to the rank of full professor of surgery and will be the youngest physician to have reached that level in the history of the institution. No woman has ever been more proud of her husband than Carlsie is.

Together, they work to improve fail-safe procedures in the care of surgical patients. They have been disappointed by the endemic resistance to change within organized medicine, but they are confident that improvements are being made.

Their first children were born recently. The little girl is blond with dark green eyes: her fraternal twin is darker, like his mother, and he, too, has those Camden eyes. The love of Carlsie and Gordo has deepened from sharing the joy of offspring, and their friendly family, a familiar sight around the community, is known for its weekend bicycle outings. There are few intrusions on the quiet, small-town life they enjoy. Yet every now and then, though, reporters come around to see what happened to Dr. Carlsie Camden.

She is not often willing to talk much about the past, but occasionally she will describe with great emotion how her husband did not give up on her on that awful night. She tells how he continued to search for her when it seemed hopeless, and how he risked his own life to rescue her from certain death. Gordo usually smiles when she finishes the story, and she always gives him a kiss.

Then Carlsie explains that there comes a time in every lady's life when she really needs a hero, and she adds that she is glad Gordo became hers.

THE BESTSELLING NOVELS
BEHIND THE BLOCKBUSTER MOVIES —
ZEBRA'S MOVIE MYSTERY GREATS!

HIGH SIERRA (2059, $3.50)
by W.R. Burnett
A dangerous criminal on the lam is trapped in a terrifying web of circumstance. The tension-packed novel that inspired the 1955 film classic starring Humphrey Bogart and directed by John Houston.

MR. ARKADIN (2145, $3.50)
by Orson Welles
A playboy's search to uncover the secrets of financier Gregory Arkadin's hidden past exposes a worldwide intrigue of big money, corruption — and murder. Orson Welles's only novel, and the basis for the acclaimed film written by, directed by, and starring himself.

NOBODY LIVES FOREVER (2217, $3.50)
by W.R. Burnett
Jim Farrar's con game backfires when his beautiful victim lures him into a dangerous deception that could only end in death. A 1946 cinema classic starring John Garfield and Geraldine Fitzgerald. (AVAILABLE IN FEBRUARY 1988)

BUILD MY GALLOWS HIGH (2341, $3.50)
by Geoffrey Homes
When Red Bailey's former lover Mumsie McGonigle lured him from the Nevada hills back to the deadly hustle of New York City, the last thing the ex-detective expected was to be set up as a patsy and framed for a murder he didn't commit. The novel that inspired the screen gem OUT OF THE PAST, starring Robert Mitchum and Kirk Douglas. (AVAILABLE IN APRIL 1988)

Available wherever paperbacks are sold, or order direct from the Publisher. Send cover price plus 50¢ per copy for mailing and handling to Zebra Books, Dept. 2351, 475 Park Avenue South, New York, N.Y. 10016. Residents of New York, New Jersey and Pennsylvania must include sales tax. DO NOT SEND CASH.